Slowly, he pulled her arm away and, still holding her, took the .38 Special out of the nightstand. "Nice piece. Dumb move."

She stood still, her back to his chest. She turned her head to look at him, those ice blue eyes boring into hers, his fingers wrapped around her forearm. "I don't know if anything you're saying is true."

"I don't think there are too many people out there who know who your father really is. That's going to have to suffice." He held up the weapon. "Any more where this came from?"

"No."

"And I'm supposed to trust you?"

"The same way I'm supposed to trust you," she said sweetly, her heart still pounding as he brought his face closer to hers, his voice a rough growl that shot through her like fire.

"Touché. But know this, Sky—you'll gain nothing by killing me. If I were here to kill you, you'd have been dead when you opened the front door. I was sent by your father— he's a man of few words. I have my orders and I plan on following them." He turned to leave the bedroom, calling, "I want to see the letter," over his shoulder.

Sky. No one had called her that in a long time—she'd insisted on her full name since she left college and entered the world of illness and hospitals. But something about the way Cam said it made her not correct him.

LIE with ME

STEPHANIE TYLER

A SHADOW FORCE NOVEL

A DELL BOOK

NEW YORK

A Dell Mass Market Original

Copyright © 2010 by Stephanie Tyler

Published in the United States by Dell, an imprint of
The Random House Publishing Group, a division of Random House, Inc.,
New York.

DELL is a registered trademark of Random House, Inc., and
the colophon is a trademark of Random House, Inc.

ISBN 978-0-440-24596-4
eBook ISBN 978-0-440-33970-0

Cover design: Lynn Andreozzi
Cover illustration: Blake Morrow

Printed in the United States of America

www.bantamdell.com

2 4 6 8 9 7 5 3 1

As always, for Zoo, Lily, and Gus,

for always being there, and for always believing

ACKNOWLEDGMENTS

As always, I have many people to thank.

My editor, Shauna Summers, for her unwavering support, and everyone at Bantam Dell who helped during the making of this book, which includes Jessica Sebor, Evan Camfield, Pam Feinstein, and the art department, who rock my world with their covers.

My agent, Irene Goodman—for believing and for listening.

Larissa Ione, because I could not do this writing thing without you.

My amazing support system of Lara Adrian, Maya Banks, Jaci Burton, and Amy Knupp—you guys help keep me (semi)sane. (I know, who am I kidding...)

All my amazing, wonderful readers, who make my day with their emails and letters and blog posts and shout-outs on Twitter and Facebook. And a special shout out to LIST and the Writeminded Loop!

LIE WITH ME

CHAPTER
1

Parting is all we know of heaven,
And all we need of hell.
Emily Dickinson

The sleek, dark bitch tailing him over the crest of the mountain was definitely not standard Army issue.

Cameron Moore ignored both the snow swirling furiously around his Harley and the classified stealth helo on his six as he began his ascent up the thin, curved ridge ringed by stone that would lead him to his destination.

Half a mile earlier, when he'd heard the familiar thump of the quiet bird over the roar of his bike, the hairs on the back of his neck had risen. Now his gut tightened in tandem with the heavy whir of the rotors, and *fuck,* he'd thought this was over and done with.

He'd had nearly five months of freedom, having been assured that his debt was paid in full, which meant there would be no more black ops jobs involving the CIA and this fucking helo from hell following him. But he'd been down this road before—after five years, eight years, ten years. The promise of release had never been kept, eleven years and counting.

It'll never be fully paid. You knew that... you just didn't want to believe it.

And still, he pushed on, trying to ignore the past that wouldn't let him forget.

He'd only been back from a mission with Delta Force for forty-eight hours, on leave for the past twenty and headed to visit Dylan Scott—a man he'd met through Delta, and his best friend—in the Catskills when he'd been tracked.

One of these days, Gabriel Creighton—CIA chameleon extraordinaire—wouldn't be able to find Cam anymore. The chip that had once been implanted in Cam's right forearm was only as big as a postage stamp, and as slim as one too... and was long gone. He'd convinced himself that Gabriel couldn't track him without it.

Obviously, Cam had been way fucking wrong.

He didn't have to wonder what his life would be like if he'd never met the man—he'd still be in jail, serving two consecutive life sentences. And he despised Gabriel more than his father, which was really damned hard to do, considering his father had framed him for the murders and left him to rot in a maximum security cell.

For eleven years, Gabriel had been both mentor and taskmaster. Cam had never asked Gabriel for anything, not a single goddamned favor.

The favors Gabriel insisted Cam provide for him were

always dangerous and usually above the law. Jobs that necessitated a non-CIA operator with insider information, which Cam indeed was, hiding in the job of a Delta Force operator.

If Cam's immediate sups knew what the jobs he did for Creighton really entailed, they'd never let on. And so Cam lived and worked, waiting for the magic number—the time limit Gabriel had imposed on him when Cam had been nineteen and willing to do anything to get out of that cell. An expiration date that only Gabriel knew.

Now he stared down at the mark on the inside of his left forearm—the result of a tattoo that had been lasered off. It wasn't completely erased, was still a reminder.

That was the thing about pasts, you could never fully eradicate them, and fuck it all, he'd tried to more than once.

Finally, he stopped the bike on the edge of one of the small cliffs, pulled as close to it as he possibly could. The wind whipped him, making it hard to hold on to his footing, never mind the heavy metal between his legs.

The stealth hovered, unable to land, but more than willing to block him. As he stared down at the dark, cavernous chasm ahead of him, he knew his choices were limited. Going down would be the coward's way out—and he was anything but.

He'd never let go of the idea of vengeance, tasted it like a fine wine on his tongue—it ran heated through his blood, slamming his veins with a barely concealed fury.

In all his years of military service, he'd saved a lot of people, killed more and prayed for salvation daily.

In so many ways, he'd never left the ten-by-ten cell where he'd lived for twenty-three months, four days and ten hours. At the time, he'd been wary of his rescuer, but he'd assumed things couldn't have gotten worse.

He'd been so fucking young—fear and bravado mixing together in a heady combination. He'd been a punk, a fighter, willing to do anything to stay alive. Had kept his pride during those years, refusing to let prison take it from him, the way his freedom had been ripped away.

Pride had been all he had.

He finally turned around on the mountain, the way he had eleven years earlier when the police chased him between a rock and a hard place. That night, the police had impounded his bike.

Now Cam knew that a good operative never left anything behind. He revved his bike and let it ride over the edge without him, listened as it screeched and crashed against the mountain walls below.

And then he walked to the helo and used the rope ladder they'd lowered to climb aboard.

Two years of max security had taught him many things—that life wasn't fair; that typically the bigger you were, the more shit you talked and the harder you went down; that this life wasn't for the weak. His time in the Rangers and Delta Force had refined those teachings until his mind functioned like the elite warrior he was; but make no mistake, he was still that same damned punk—and he wouldn't take Gabriel Creighton's shit anymore.

This time, he would shoot the messenger Gabriel always sent, no matter what the job entailed, and then he would walk away and deal with the consequences—any and all, because the yoke around his neck had finally tightened to where he could no longer breathe.

As it turned out, the messenger wanted to shoot him as well.

Cam noted the gun in the suit's hands as he hauled his ass into the helo, and then his gaze moved quickly to the ankle cuffs on the bench and he snapped to attention. Instead of waiting for the man to aim the Glock directly at him, Cam lunged, using the shaky motion of the struggling helo to propel him into the man's chest even as the man barked at him to sit down.

He was too far into fight-or-flight mode to do anything else, could smell the setup as surely as helo fuel. He'd done this dance too many times, and it had never, ever looked like this before.

They went down hard, sliding into the co-pilot's seat. The gun clattered from the suit's hands and Cam stared into his eyes—it was the same man, always the same man, although he never spoke to Cam, had always pointed to the phone or the laptop where Cam would get his orders.

Cam wondered what this guy had done in his life to become Gabriel's minion.

"We...talk..." the suit croaked as Cam kept his forearm across his throat. Cam wondered what the man's story would be, if he'd gain anything by letting him speak his peace.

But the ache in his gut was swift and sudden as he remembered that he didn't trust most people, especially strangers.

"I don't talk to people who want to kill me." As quickly and cleanly as possible, Cam shifted and put his hands on either side of the man's head. A sharp twist to the right and the suit was gone, his eyes open, his stare as dead as he was.

But the fight wasn't over yet.

Cam wouldn't let the pilots take off with him inside, would rather free-fall out than be carried off, and they knew that—Cam saw it in the brace of the co-pilot's back the second he'd climbed on board—and as the man lunged, Cam was ready, even as the obviously well-trained man threw a nice left hook, which caught Cam square on the jaw. The helo banked a hard left and Cam lost his footing for a second, hitting his head on a sharp piece of metal used to hold the hooks for the parachutes. The co-pilot also fell, and Cam was the quicker one up and at the ready, slamming his boot into the guy's chest.

He struggled, his hands around Cam's ankle—but Cam's footing was too strong. The co-pilot knew Cam fully intended to leave alive and didn't care who he took out in his wake, and he stopped fighting.

"Who the hell sent you?" Cam asked, but neither man answered. "Where are you supposed to bring me?"

Again, nothing.

Cam didn't know friends from enemies anymore in this game, the wilderness of mirrors that spooks and spies dealt with on a daily—and lifetime—basis. As he stared between the man under his boot and the pilot, who held the gun in a shaky hand while he tried to wrestle the helo with the other, Cam told them, "My fight's not with you."

The pilot's eyes held his for a second—Cam wondered if he'd been pressed into service as well or if he was flying this bastard bird of his own free will.

It didn't matter; Cam didn't have time to play savior

now, not when he'd just committed suicide himself. "I'm out of here."

He took his foot off the man's chest, turned and didn't look back, wondered for a fleeting second if he'd get shot in the back, and then dropped out of the helo and onto the hard ground, with a vicious slam. He curled in a ball as it rose, the wind buffeting him with a harsh hand as the stealth left him behind and headed back to report the incident to Gabriel.

As he stared after the bird, well after its lights disappeared, he wondered why the hell they hadn't simply killed him when they'd had the chance—while he was climbing up into the helo. When he was vulnerable.

What the hell did he know that made him worth something? What did Gabriel want from him?

After he'd cleaned the blood off his hands and his bearded face with snow, Cam hitched a ride with a trucker, got dropped off halfway up the mountain to Dylan's house and then ran the rest of the way, his bag slapping against his back, wind whipping his face—his heart beating so fast from stress and fear, he was pretty damned sure it would rip from his chest.

Dylan opened the door as Cam pounded on it. He didn't ask any questions, not even when Cam shoved him aside and slammed the door behind him to peer out the window.

He hadn't been followed. He wouldn't be—not tonight. Probably not tomorrow. But when he reported back into work, there could be consequences.

You've lived with the consequences for years—how much fucking worse could it be?

He felt empowered and freaked all at once.

"Did you crash?" Dylan asked finally.

Cam turned, still needing to catch his breath. His hands were shaking. He'd never been like this on a mission before—but this . . . this was personal. His life.

The words spilled out. "Gabriel sent a stealth—same kind, same suit waiting for me. He had a gun. There were restraints. I killed him, and the helo took off with the dead guy and the pilots."

"Breathe, man, breathe." Dylan handed him a brandy—Cam gulped it down and then poured another before noticing that Dylan also had a towel waiting for him.

He rubbed the towel over his face and hair, then stared at his friend. "They wanted intel from me—or else they could've killed me a thousand times over before I got on board. I'm done, Dylan. No way out."

His friend didn't say anything for a long moment and then he walked over to a bookshelf that lined a far wall of the room. He pulled out a hardcover book and handed it to Cam. "Open to the back . . . the author."

Cam did as Dylan asked, staring at the picture of a beautiful young woman named Skylar Slavin at the back of the novel. "Are you setting me up with her? Because I don't think I'm really dating material right now."

"She's Gabriel Creighton's daughter, Cam. His only child. The only thing he cares about in this fucking world. Skylar Slavin's the key to your future."

Cam didn't say anything, continued to stare at the picture as the woman with the clear green eyes stared back at him. She wasn't smiling—in fact, he'd say she looked slightly haunted.

But still, the woman must have had a better life than him—been loved and protected by her father. She was probably just like Gabriel—cold and cunning, with a heart of steel.

"How long have you known about her?" Cam demanded. Dylan simply shrugged, that noncommittal kind he typically reserved for authority figures. Which was why he didn't last long in the military at all, yet somehow managed to get out with an honorable discharge and several medals of honor.

Fucking bastard.

"How long?" he asked again, with enough of an edge to his voice for Dylan to know this wasn't the time to fuck around.

"Five months."

"Five months? Five motherfucking months?" Nearly blind from rage, Cam leaped at his best friend in the world, ready to kill him as soon as he could wrap his hands around his neck.

Dylan readied for him, but Cam was like a charging bull and knocked him to the ground, hard. Dylan grunted as he attempted to roll Cam off him—when he couldn't, he swung and punched Cam in the face a couple of times, reopening the gash above his eye.

"Fucking asshole," Cam said through clenched teeth, the blood dripping into his eye and onto Dylan's shirt. "You had something on Gabriel and you didn't tell me?"

"Because you weren't ready to hear it, to use it," Dylan

growled, his breath coming in quick gasps because Cam was sitting on his chest, punching him anywhere he could.

He and Dylan were evenly matched, but not when Cam's temper was riled by anything involving Gabriel Creighton. Then he ran on pure adrenaline, an anger machine.

"I found out...*after* your last mission. It wouldn't have...changed the outcome. You always said...it was your fight. That I needed to...stay out of it. And...I did. For the most part. Jesus Christ, Cam, Gabriel was...leaving you alone, and I didn't want you to...bring trouble on yourself you didn't need." Dylan took a stuttered breath while holding his rib cage. "I'm going to kill you if you broke my ribs."

Cam leaned back on his elbows and tried to ignore the blood running from Dylan's nose. Blood was running from Cam's mouth and forehead as well.

"Look, tonight you made the move. There's no turning back. If I'd told you about Gabriel's daughter earlier...I didn't want you to do anything else that could weigh on your conscience. Didn't want to give you a choice like that, didn't want you to run off half-cocked and do something that really would land your ass in jail, for good this time." Dylan fell back on the carpet heavily. "You weren't ready until tonight. I know you, Cam. Now you've got no choice but to move forward out of hell."

Cam let his head fall back and stared up at the high-beamed ceiling. Of course, Dylan was right—not that Cam would admit that to the man's face...or in writing. Ever. Dylan liked to say that Cam had been born with an extra dose of conscience while Dylan himself had skipped that line entirely when they were handing them out. *Probably off getting laid somewhere,* Dylan would say.

Dylan, the man who would never betray him, the one who knew him better than anyone.

"I'm sorry, man," Cam breathed, his gaze still on the ceiling, until he heard a crack and a small whimper—Dylan setting his own nose back in place. His friend would have two black eyes by morning. "So you want me to fuck with his family?"

"He fucked with yours, didn't he?" Dylan's eyes blazed. He was a fierce warrior and just as fiercely loyal when it came to Cam.

"I don't have proof." Cam's jaw hurt from keeping it clenched, and both men knew that he had no way of getting any.

Gabriel Creighton had a lot of ways to kill a man. Cam's father, just as many. But Gabriel killing Howie didn't make sense. Pretending to help in the search for what happened to Howie kept Cam on the line just as effectively.

And still, the questions always lingered. He stared down at the photo on the book and Skylar stared back at him. "What the hell do I do, man, hold her hostage?"

"Yeah, for starters. Gabriel's obviously kept her existence a secret for a reason, so tell him you'll expose her as his daughter. Kidnap her. Seduce her—and make her fall in love with you. Tell him you'll kill her. And then be prepared to do that if it's necessary."

Cam stared at his friend. "Why the hell would I need to kill her?"

"If it comes down to you or her, it needs to be you. You

have to be prepared to make any and every choice to take this all the way."

Jesus, that made the already splitting pain in his head worsen. "What's to stop him from throwing my ass in jail, or killing me?"

"He can't, if he realizes you and another person know about his daughter. Tell Gabriel that someone else knows who Skylar is. I'm your backup, your safety. Gabriel doesn't know about me . . . he'll only know that if you die, Skylar will never be safe. The two of you will come to a mutual agreement to live and let live."

Dylan had been straddling the line for far too long, and yet Cam knew his friend was absolutely right. "I need a better plan, I need time."

"You don't have that. Once you threaten to expose her, it's over. Besides, she's kind of famous."

Kind of, yes. He stared at her picture at the back of the book again and his stomach turned.

Like father, like daughter.

It was finally time. "How did you find out about this?"

Dylan sighed before he answered, "I slept with someone. Broke into her files. And then she shot me, so I figured it was pretty damned important information she had about Gabriel and his family."

Jesus. Dylan had cut it closer to the edge than ever. Cam had met Dylan five years earlier—they'd served together in Delta for mere months before Dylan retired. Dylan had been a risk taker then, but went well beyond that these days.

Now, his friend rattled off Skylar's current address.

"She's on vacation for a week." He paused. "Why don't you let me take care of all this?"

It would be too easy to let Dylan do it, to let himself off the hook. He'd been passive in this situation for far too long, though, fighting to keep the street kid inside of him dead and buried. His friend knew that better than anyone.

Dylan was a good enough friend to make that offer.

"Thanks. But this is my fight. Always has been."

He despised Gabriel, would have no problem putting his hands around the man's neck and squeezing, tight, but slowly, so he could watch him struggle, the way Gabriel had been watching Cam struggle for years.

Payback would be fucking fantastic, to crush that bastard under his shoe, to watch everything he'd worked for crumble, like the soul-sucking little bastard he really was.

It was easy for Gabriel to sit back and fire orders, to have the ultimate power over Cam. Cam knew the man was nothing more than an empty, pathetic shell who took out his misery on others—the world was full of sad little people like that, who reveled in whatever power they had to make others feel as shitty as they did.

Most people could only dream of getting revenge on those who'd wronged them. Cam's would soon be a reality, and she was staring at him from the photograph.

Gabriel had always told him, *You don't get something for nothing.* The man would finally feel the truth of those words, at Cam's hands.

And if Gabriel didn't comply, didn't care about his flesh and blood enough to free Cam from his service, Cam would have to decide what he'd do next.

You don't get something for nothing.

"You do this and then you let it go," Dylan said quietly, and Cam realized he was holding the book so tightly he'd bent the hard cover.

Did he even know how to let it go? He'd lived with it for so long, it was like a well-worn fabric. An excuse. Something to fall back on when things were shitty. Woven into the texture of his life.

Could he really do this?

You have no fucking choice, unless you want to spend the rest of your life hiding.

He finally had collateral. Leverage. He'd use it to his full advantage ... had to be prepared to do anything it took to grab hold of his freedom.

K ill her."

Elijah gave the order without even looking at the man in front of him. Instead, he slid the picture and the address toward his associate. "Call her when you land. Tell her to meet you. She'll be expecting the call, but not what comes after that."

When he looked up, the man he'd given the instructions to had exited his office wordlessly, and silently. Perfect.

He didn't give a shit about most of the people who worked for him—just the core group of six who ran his operations, and even then he wasn't ever sure they wouldn't stab him in the back, literally, given the opportunity.

Which was why he never turned his back. And why he changed his appearance so often.

He'd been nameless and faceless for so long, and yet

DMH's reputation proceeded him. Men and women followed him. Listened to him. Killed for him.

He was thirty-five, looked younger and easily passed for someone who wasn't a cold-blooded killer.

It's what helped his group stay so successful—he recruited men and women who were like him, who could pass for normal.

Who could kill on command.

DMH was one of the most respected and feared groups overseas and had a growing reputation as a potentially major terror organization in the United States because of that. It was exactly the way Elijah saw the operation growing. First, the funded terror camps, then branch out to black market weapons and organ trafficking.

However, they'd just discovered a traitor in their midst. That wasn't shocking, of course. In his line of work, pure loyalty was hard to come by, and they were all stepping on one another's backs in order to survive, to get to the top.

It was nearly impossible to stay on top, but Elijah planned on doing so. And he had the magic formula, right in the cell below him...the husband of a CIA operative who'd been killed because of her association with DMH, and apparently a CIA operative in his own right. To be infiltrated once was bad enough; to have it happen again was unforgiveable. How had he allowed this?

Because you're getting old. Paranoid. To him, everyone and anyone was the enemy, which meant he cast equal suspicion over all of them.

According to his source, the guy was the real deal—a high-ranking CIA agent with enough knowledge inside his brain to push DMH to the head of the class.

If that were true, Mr. CIA already had enough evidence to take DMH down brick by brick. The risk they always took with a new initiate.

But now he had leverage.

He stared at the pretty blond woman on the back of the thick, hardbound book, and he smiled.

The man he'd known only as Gabe would bring so many plans to fruition once he started talking. And he would talk.

Any man who nearly gave his life for his child would no doubt do so again. All Elijah had to do was get Skylar Slavin in his grasp, and he'd have a nice chunk of the world for his taking.

CHAPTER
2

Skylar Slavin cursed her BlackBerry's spotty service and realized she was way too addicted to the little machine.

Way too addicted to avoiding work as well, and she threw the device across the room to the couch, watched it land with a soft bounce on the cushion. Then she shoved her sleeves up and bent over the open notebook in front of her, because she couldn't bear to think about actually opening the laptop just yet.

Her brain felt dusty from neglect, like if she shook her head, the cobwebs might actually clear. Maybe then she could let her pen fly across the pages, merely a scribe to her story.

God, she'd loved those days, the early ones, when the

writing was simply a part of her and she'd never had to question its loyalty.

But now, as she'd feared, the words wouldn't come. Constant worry and a long-assed recovery from surgery did not make for a happy writer.

She'd thought coming back from the dead would be the hardest thing she'd ever done in her life, but she'd been dead wrong.

Disgusted, she threw down the pen and stared out the window.

She'd purposely chosen to vacation-slash-work in the mountains of the Adirondacks, rather than Florida, to avoid the distraction of beautiful, warm weather outside her door. Here was only cold and snow and inside was cozy and warm—perfect writing weather.

She rubbed her arms and then threw on a cardigan. She continued to have a hard time regulating her body temperature, but the doctors assured her that would improve.

Her lower back still ached, but the meds had finally stopped making her sick. Five months and counting and life was pretty well back to normal for her. Better than normal, since she'd survived the transplant and her body hadn't rejected the kidney.

She was still in the danger zone, had to get past the first year to dramatically improve her chances of survival, but she refused to think of the alternative. Been there, done that for the better part of the six months leading up to her surgery, while they'd exhausted a donor list and she was pretty sure it was the end for her. Until her father had saved the day by donating one of his kidneys.

Her father, who could be anywhere in the world right

now. Together, they'd recovered for two months. She didn't know how or why he'd gotten that much time off—that had never happened before. Ever.

It had been really nice, even though she'd spent most of the first month on pain meds, weak as a newborn kitten.

She'd been so close to the edge, so close to death, and her father had risked his own life for hers.

She could only hope karma would be as kind to him. Couldn't check on it, because who the heck had heard from the man?

Three months, and nothing.

If he'd been sick, she would've known—he'd be home and would have no reason not to contact her. But his secretary refused to give her any information, which screamed mission, and MIA, always a possibility. Still, it had been ingrained into her not to panic easily during stretches of non-contact like this one.

Growing up, there had been times that saw her father gone for the better part of a year, only to have him stroll in one evening as though he hadn't missed a day of her life, sit down to supper and, for that moment, life would be normal.

Bitterness swelled in her throat and she choked it down. Tried to forget about the odd fan mail that had come to her P.O. box.

I know who you really are.

That same message, received daily for a week. No return address on the envelope, no way to trace it, all with the same words inside.

Her publicist, Pam, who'd discovered them, had wanted to call the police—her agent and editor had agreed, but

Sky told them they were overreacting. The letters hadn't come to her home address, she reasoned, but they weren't buying it.

And so she'd sat in her apartment with two detectives who were nice and hadn't heard of her or her books and she'd lied to them about her father—told them he was long since deceased. No other family. No known enemies.

They suggested she change her P.O. box and make sure her address and numbers were unlisted. Easily done.

But still, Sky had to admit she was relieved to be able to get out of town and away from the city. She'd refused Pam's offer to go with her, or to hire someone to watch her.

With any luck, she'd hear from her father soon.

I know who you really are.

Her father had accrued many enemies over the years—powerful ones. Men, and women, who'd like nothing more than to take out their vengeance on his family.

They'd already done so to her mother, who'd also been a CIA agent. After her murder, Skylar's last name had been officially changed, along with her Social Security number. Her past was reconstructed and life went on.

After years of tight security, things loosened. Her life was divergent from her father's and he stayed away so much that tying the two of them together as family would be nearly impossible.

Receiving odd fan mail had happened before—usually, it was nothing, a fan who'd gone into creepy mode or someone who thought she looked good on the back of the book and decided they loved her. Those were random, few and far between, and each time, her father would investigate, and the problem would go away. But those were different, never anything that was a true threat based on who she was.

She'd feel better if she could simply talk with him, tell him. Get his reassurance that he'd take care of everything. She'd been calling about that daily, sometimes twice a day, for the past week—and nothing. *Nothing.*

With that worry hanging over her head, she padded to the kitchen in her thick socks and began to prepare dinner—a nice, big, complicated meal, because procrastination was an art form and these days she'd become a damned master.

Twenty minutes later, the knock on the door was sharp and sure. She heard it over the music she played loud as she stirred the sauce.

Hurriedly, she went to answer. The staff of the resort where she'd rented the townhouse told her they typically checked in on their guests staying alone, especially right before a storm. So she threw open the door expecting to see... anyone but the mountain man with the thick beard in front of her.

Every impulse told her to shut the door in his face, to scream, except... those eyes. Ice blue. Intense. Kind. And really, really sexy—enough to make heat flood her body and the cardigan she wore unnecessary even with the freezing air.

She really needed to get a life. "Can I help you?"

"My name is Cameron Moore. I'm here on Gabriel Creighton's orders," he said, and at the sound of her father's name, her world spun.

She wanted to ask if her dad was all right, but stopped herself.

The man looked over her shoulder. "Can I please come in, ma'am?"

Ma'am. She must look worse than she thought. "I need to see some ID."

Even as she spoke, he was handing her a military issue ID card as light snow blew in from behind him. Cameron Moore. Sergeant First Class. Army.

"Your father sent me. You are Skylar Slavin, his daughter, correct?"

She nodded, relieved that he knew that information, and still she shifted her weight from foot to foot, as if preparing for flight. Except there was nowhere to run.

This man probably thought his military background would be a comfort to her, but Skylar didn't trust military. Didn't trust FBI or CIA agents either; that had been drummed into her early, thanks to her parents. Always start with suspicion, they would say.

They had always tried to ensure that she could take care of herself in any situation. She was fully firearm trained and knew a variety of self-defense moves. She could handle explosives, pick locks, hotwire cars and generally get into places she wasn't supposed to be. She knew how to get information from people who weren't supposed to—and didn't want to—talk.

As a writer of thrillers, that last skill was priceless. Her work held an authenticity noted by reviewers and she was often jokingly asked in interviews if she was indeed a spy herself.

It wasn't true at all, but if it helped her to sell more books, Skylar would neither confirm nor deny.

Having kidney failure—and nearly dying—had been

something she hadn't been prepared for. And now, firmly on the road to recovery, she hadn't expected to find herself facing life or death again. But when her father sent someone to her like this, it was that serious.

If he'd sent Cameron.

But if Cameron wanted her dead, he could've killed her already. The area was secluded enough. And so she moved aside to let him pass while self-consciously pulling the sweater more tightly around her. Underneath, she wore a tank top and her pajama bottoms, which had tiny hearts all over them. Like she was twelve or something.

God, she was babbling inside her head—she knew that—but it was better than thinking about what the hell was wrong with her father and why he hadn't come for her himself.

Cam dropped his heavy bag in the middle of the living room—it looked like standard military issue.

But he spoke quickly and calmly once she shut the door behind him. "I've worked with your father and the CIA on and off for eleven years now. Only for him."

She handed him back his identification. "You said my father sent you to me."

"Yes." He was walking through the house, closing blinds and curtains tight. "There's been a threat."

No mention of the many calls she'd put in to her father. "When did you talk to him?"

Cam didn't answer her, was still walking around the rental house as if danger was imminent.

And suddenly, she was tired of being ignored—by her father and his assistant, and by this big man stomping through her working vacation and her life.

She was next to him in seconds, tapping him hard on the shoulder. "Hey, I asked you a question."

He turned to stare at her, unblinking. "About five hours ago."

She searched his face for any indications of a lie. Of course, if he wasn't telling the truth, she wouldn't be able to tell—these men were trained in the art of the lie until they didn't even know what end was up any longer. "I need to speak with him."

"That's not possible tonight."

She was already going for her phone, before remembering the no-signal thing. She stared at the useless piece of equipment, spoke to Cam without looking at him. "I haven't heard from my father in three months—he never answered my calls. I need to know he's really okay, I want to hear his voice. You have to understand that."

"I'll give you more information when I can," he told her in a tone that said, *Deal with it.* "I know this must be hard on you."

She wanted to tell him to shut up, that he didn't know anything—but there was something in his voice akin to a secret pain that stopped her. "You've got to tell me the truth about what kind of danger I'm in and from whom."

He rubbed his forehead with a palm, then held it there as if trying to ease a massive headache. "It's deep and it's real. It's a kidnapping threat from an enemy of your father. And if they can't take you ..."

"They'll kill me instead," she heard herself say, and fiercely forced that thought from her mind. "My dad doesn't know about the letters I've been getting." She hadn't mentioned them when she'd called her father—couldn't, just in case. Just left messages and asked for him to call her.

But at the mention of the letters, Cam snapped to attention. "Do you have them?"

She had one she'd kept back—it had been waiting for her in the old P.O. box the very afternoon she'd met with the detectives. She'd decided to take it with her in case she'd heard from her father. "I have one in my suitcase."

"And they're threats?"

"Very much so." To her anyway. To her publicist, agent, and editor, who had no idea who her father was and what those words might mean, it seemed more like a stalker— bad enough, she reasoned, although that was nothing compared to the type of people her father knew.

"Why didn't you do anything about this sooner?" he demanded. So either her father wasn't getting her messages . . . or Cam was full of shit.

"I tried to get in touch with my dad. He's the only one I contact. I can't just call the CIA. My father hasn't been around much, but he's always made sure I was safe, especially since—"

She stopped abruptly, because she'd said too much, revealed something she'd sworn never to do. And, as her near admission hung between them, she wondered if he'd push her to say more.

"I'll go get the letter," she offered casually. The letter, and her gun.

He nodded, seemed distracted as his gaze continued to sweep the townhouse and she hightailed it to the bedroom. Her suitcase was on the chest at the end of the bed—she'd only been here for one night, and although she'd promised herself she'd unpack today, thus far she'd avoided the task.

Last night, she'd been so tired after the long drive, the only thing she'd done after taking her medicine was retrieve the gun from her bag and put it in the bedside table drawer. Now she opened the drawer, relief washing over her at the sight of the familiar black-and-chrome piece, and reached inside to grab it.

Cam's hand curled around her arm, his breath warm against her ear . . . and he was so close. Too close. And yet, for some reason, she wanted him closer, even when his words came out harshly. "Drop the fucking gun."

She hadn't heard him come into the room, never mind ending up nearly on top of her.

She swallowed hard and did as he asked. It had been a stupid move anyway.

Slowly, he pulled her arm away and, still holding her, took the .38 Special out of the nightstand. "Nice piece. Dumb move."

She stood still, her back to his chest. She turned her head to look at him, those ice blue eyes boring into hers, his fingers wrapped around her forearm. "I don't know if anything you're saying is true."

"I don't think there are too many people out there who know who your father really is. That's going to have to suffice." He held up the weapon. "Any more where this came from?"

"No."

"And I'm supposed to trust you?"

"The same way I'm supposed to trust you," she said sweetly, her heart still pounding as he brought his face closer to hers, his voice a rough growl that shot through her like fire.

"Touché. But know this, Sky—you'll gain nothing by killing me. If I were here to kill you, you'd have been dead when you opened the front door. I was sent by your father—he's a man of few words. I have my orders and I plan on following them." He turned to leave the bedroom, calling, "I want to see the letter," over his shoulder.

Sky. No one had called her that in a long time—she'd insisted on her full name since she left college and entered the world of illness and hospitals. But something about the way Cam said it made her not correct him.

Skylar didn't trust him worth a damn, didn't seem to like him much, and still Cam was pretty sure that if he kissed her she'd kiss him back.

He hadn't expected to be blown away by her in person, figured that, if anything, the photo on the book jacket had been airbrushed.

But she was perfect, even in a pair of pajamas and an old sweater—tall and slim, with blond hair skimming straight down her back and soft green eyes that sucked him in the second she'd opened the door.

The haunted look, though . . . that was still there.

While she remained inside the bedroom, getting him the letter and deciding whether or not to believe what he'd told her, he took the opportunity to flip through the notebook on the table—lots of crossed-out paragraphs, nothing of substance. A closed laptop sat nearby. And her cell phone, which he noted had no signal.

Perfect, since he'd already cut the landline, ensuring the only way for Gabriel to make contact would be through Cam's phone. If Gabriel was even around to make contact with.

Because *three months*. That wasn't a good sign at all, not when Cam took into account what happened on the helo the night before. If Gabriel had been given a burn notice, or even killed, the powers-that-be might look into killing anyone remotely associated with him. So it might not have been Gabriel's orders to grab him after all.

You're getting ahead of yourself. Just because he's not in touch with his daughter doesn't mean anything.

Didn't mean the plan he and Dylan had concocted, telling Skylar there was a threat in order to get Cam in the door, wasn't a total and complete goatfuck. Didn't mean he hadn't almost blown everything by not knowing how hard she'd been trying to reach her father.

It was only then he noticed the pills, set up like a row of soldiers on a side table across from the fireplace. He noted the names—recognized some as immunosuppressants and quickly made a note to check out what they were for.

If she was sick . . .

Fuck, if she was sick, his plan might work better than he'd anticipated, assuming he could get in touch with Gabriel. Now he had to figure out how long of a supply of meds she had.

"Here it is," she said, walking out of the bedroom holding a single white envelope. And looking decidedly healthy, with the high flush from getting caught with the gun still marking her cheeks. "The police have the rest of them. I kept one to show my father."

She cut her gaze to the medications and then back to his face, her eyes defiant.

"What are they for?" he demanded.

She looked pained and then annoyed. "What does it matter?"

"What are they for?"

"I had a kidney transplant, okay? I have to take the medications so I don't reject it and die. Is that explanation satisfactory?"

Her eyes blazed, and yeah, that was a pretty damned good reason. Somehow, that major piece of news had escaped Dylan's background checks. "You need to keep them packed at all times."

"Why?"

"In case we have to leave suddenly."

"In the middle of a blizzard?"

Yes, another complication—the storm had picked up steam far more quickly than the weather services had anticipated. "Stop arguing and do it."

"Your personality blows," she muttered.

Yeah, it did. Always had, and it wasn't changing anytime soon. She continued to mumble as she left the room, came back with a bag to dump the bottles into, and he swore he heard a curse or two with his name attached. Strangely enough, that made him hard.

To distract himself, he looked at the letter. It was dated last week. No return address. Plain, white business envelope available in ten million stores worldwide.

There was one line of computer-generated text across the center of the page.

I know who you really are.

"They all say the same thing," she offered. "Type's identical too."

"They've scared you."

"Coupled with your arrival, most definitely. Like you said, my connection to my father's not common knowledge."

She was scared of the situation, probably even of him somewhat. The fact that she'd been so sick, that she needed all those medications, nearly made him walk out of the house, straight into the storm, and forget his entire plan.

The letter he held in his hand stopped him. He definitely wasn't the only dangerous person after Skylar Slavin, but he was the safest of the two threats, and fuck, he didn't want to be. He wanted to hate her. Wanted her to be as cold and calculating as Gabriel—who the hell knew, maybe she was.

Cam had looked up to Gabriel at first, had thought he'd been saved and would go on to great things. And he had, both thanks to and in spite of the CIA agent who took the skills Cam had learned in the military and twisted them for his own purposes, be they legal or not.

It's for the good of your country, Gabriel would say. And as much as Cam wanted to believe that, the fact was, if caught on one of the black ops missions, he'd be hung out to dry— left for dead.

"How did you meet my father?" Sky asked him after a long silence. She stood there, holding the bag with her bottles of medicine, asking for something, anything, from him.

He would give it to her. "He helped me out of a rough situation."

The truth seemed the way to go. Partial truth anyway,

but still she narrowed her eyes. "He's not the type to mentor anyone."

"No, he's not. He always says, you can't get something for nothing."

Her eyes widened and he knew she recognized the statement. It meant that she might actually start to trust him.

Of course, trusting him would be the worst thing she could do, especially since he wasn't sure how far he would take this—how far he'd have to. "Look, I know this is a lot to take in."

But suddenly, Skylar wasn't in the living room with him any longer—at least not that particular living room. No, she was somewhere far away, reliving something that made her eyes wet.

"Skylar, what's wrong?" He kept his voice low and calm and she broke from her silent reverie and shook her head.

"Nothing."

Yeah, that wasn't nothing, but he'd leave it for now. There was a lot more he needed to learn about Skylar—and from the looks of things, plenty of time to do so.

First, get her to trust you, Dylan's voice echoed in his head, and yeah, Cam knew how to do that. It was one of the first things he'd learned in the Rangers, the most important skill, whether the person could really afford to trust you or not.

"I'm having dinner now. You can do whatever the hell you want," she told him, and walked away haughtily, holding the bag of pills and muttering, "I'm ready to run at any moment, Army guy."

And then get her to like you.

That part might take a little longer. She was slamming plates around and muttering about him again.

Finally, she pointed to the stove without turning around to look at him. "I've got dinner here—way too much for me. And since it looks like we're not going anywhere fast..."

She set out an extra plate without waiting for him to answer. Truth was, he was starving, and so he sat at the island stool and let her dish him out a big plate of fettuccini alfredo. He waited until she made her own plate and cut bread and got them both something to drink—water for him and some kind of juice for her—and then they ate silently for a few moments.

He'd turned on the radio and together they listened to the local weather reports, warning people to stay indoors until the worst of the storm was over. By tomorrow, mid-morning, Cam would be able to get her out of here, as planned.

There were so many ways this could go down. What would happen when and if Gabriel made contact with Sky and heard Cam's name come out of his daughter's mouth was anyone's guess. Whether Gabriel would let on that Cam wasn't there on orders at all, or if Gabriel would simply play along. Cam guessed the latter. Hoped for it anyway. Prayed that Gabriel wouldn't try anything stupid or put his daughter in the position to do the same.

Of course, that's if Gabriel wasn't MIA. Because, fuck, that seemed like a real possibility.

If there were problems, he could bring Skylar to Dylan. Dylan would be able to take care of it without the gut-churning guilt Cam was experiencing.

Dylan would sleep with her.

That thought made his teeth clench so hard his jaw ached.

"Was your father an agent too?" she asked.

"ATF," Cam said shortly because, fuck it, why shouldn't she know? Her future hung in the balance because of what went down between their fathers. Whether he'd ever tell her that much of the story remained to be seen.

"So you grew up without your dad too."

He didn't answer that, continued to eat the pasta she'd cooked. "This is great," he said finally.

"Thanks. It's about all I can make."

She smiled then, accentuating a deep dimple on her left cheek, close to her lips. Her face was slightly flushed, her body relaxed enough that the sweater she wore had fallen open to reveal her tank top and the fact that she wasn't wearing a bra. She didn't need one—her breasts were of the most perfect variety, on the smaller side but still round and soft, ones he could imagine himself palming . . . tasting.

He needed to call Dylan ASAP, to remind himself why the hell he was here, risking everything.

He was doing it because he'd already risked it all when he'd killed that suit on the helo. Gabriel or no Gabriel, he was in deep shit.

Skylar was his only way out of the pit.

"My dad was never around," he agreed finally, realizing that she was ferreting information out of him and she was dangerously good at it. Easy to talk to.

She wouldn't get anything he didn't want her to know.

"He went on an extended deep undercover op when I

was fourteen and he never came out of his role," he continued. "He successfully infiltrated one of the more well-known motorcycle gangs on the East Coast."

But in doing so, Howie Moore lost his entire identity and fucked up any chance he'd ever had of getting into the CIA.

"Once he patched in, which took two years, it was all over." His father had watched as another agent was killed in the line of duty trying to earn his rocker to become a full-fledged member of a rival gang. It hadn't stopped Howie. He'd lived as a motorcycle gang member for so long, had absorbed the culture and the mindset, there was no getting him back in the end. His parents had divorced and Cam and his mom had lived in a tiny house in the same neighborhood where his father's gang reigned supreme.

"So you weren't hidden, then?" she asked.

"After my mom died, I went to live with my dad. He had to keep up the cover and he didn't want me going into foster care."

She leaned forward, elbow on the counter and chin in hand, listening intently, and yeah, a sixteen-year-old boy living among one of the most notorious motorcycle gangs was a pretty fascinating story. Even more so, considering his dad's ATF contacts hadn't tried to keep Cam out of the situation. "Dad threatened to pull out of the op if I wasn't allowed to live with him—he'd been a month away from getting patched in after years of work and the ATF didn't want to risk blowing an entire operation that was supposed to bring down a huge portion of the gang on firearms and drug charges."

"Was the investigation a success?"

Was it? The evidence garnered a lot of convictions, but it also got Cam his two years in jail. Howie Moore vanished into thin air, and here Cam was, sitting across from the daughter of the man responsible for it all. "Yeah, you could call it that."

He stared down at the spot where his gang tattoo had been, remembered sitting with his old man at midnight in one of his buddies' houses, *Getting my boy's first ink*.

The only good thing was that because of his association with the gang no one fucked with Cam, at least not before his incarceration. Cam was always big and broad and tough—his father hadn't been the type to coddle anyone and his son had learned early how to defend himself, to handle weapons. To kill, if necessary.

He'd come close to having to do that in prison.

"Where's your dad now?" Sky asked.

He looked into her light green eyes and said, "I lost track of him when I was seventeen. I don't even know if he's still alive."

Cam hadn't realized he'd been clutching his glass as if it was someone's throat as he spoke, but Skylar had noticed. He let it go, but it was too late. She now watched him, eyes wide with revelation, the way they had been earlier.

"You're angry at your father, aren't you?"

He didn't deny it. Couldn't.

"I'm angry at mine too—more often than I'd like to admit," she whispered, more to herself than to him as she stared down at her half-eaten dinner. "Sometimes I hate my father because of his job."

He heard her soft confession—it made him want to

comfort her, and he hated that he knew how she really felt, wanting to love her father, thinking he was the greatest.

Cam wanted her to be just like Gabriel, so he could hate her too.

Sky pushed her plate away and felt the tears well. She wiped her cheeks hastily with the palm of her hand, embarrassed and angry.

"I didn't mean to dredge up things about your family," Cam said quietly.

"It's not that. I've come to terms with it—as much as I can anyway. It's just . . . At first I thought maybe it was simply worry about my dad, that I haven't heard from him. But I don't think that's it. I was hoping I could get away from it all." She put her head in her hands for a second to collect herself. When she looked back up, Cam's gaze nearly leveled her. "Obviously, it's not working."

"Coming here all alone might not have been the smartest thing," he said, but there wasn't any judgment in his tone.

"I know that, but I had to. You don't understand, I needed to try." She sighed. "It's about work."

"You're an author."

"I guess. I don't feel like one. Authors are supposed to write. And I'm not writing."

Cam was looking at her, waiting patiently.

"Sorry—you're not here to be my shrink, just my bodyguard."

Still, nothing.

Don't trust, Skylar. She pictured her father's face, his eyes hard, his words harsh whenever he told her that. Since the death of her mother, he spoke that phrase often.

And still, Cam had told her something about his life she was pretty sure he didn't share often. And what she had to get off her chest had nothing to do with life or death—not the way he thought of it anyway. "I've lost it. When I was sick, the words came so fast, like I knew I was on some sort of twisted race against time. It wasn't hard at all. I loved what I was doing. And now . . . now I fight for every single goddamned word."

"You'll get it back," he told her.

But she shook her head. "I don't know, maybe it was only meant to get me through a tough time, and now I don't need it anymore."

But she did need it, so much, wanted to put words to paper to the depths of her soul. Roughly, she pushed tears away and stared at Cam's ice blue eyes. "This must sound so ridiculous to you, based on what you do for a living. You deal with life and death."

"This is important to you. It means something." His voice was tight—she'd obviously hit on a sore subject for him. She knew that most military men didn't like talking about their service, good or bad, never mind life or death. For them, like with her father, it just *was.*

As though attaching itself to her quiet fury, the storm picked up then, and the radio had a severe storm warning even as the power flickered around them.

There were portable lamps in the closet, and flashlights and candles, and gathering those cut the conversation short as both Skylar and Cam abandoned their dinners to get the supplies ready, her confession echoing inside her mind.

She was rummaging in the closet when the lights blinked and then went out. She'd had her hand on one of the lamps but started at the sudden darkness. Started more when Cam's hand touched her shoulder and he said, "Let me," and his touch went through her as hotly as it had earlier. Maybe even more so.

It was only then she understood why she was having such trouble writing her current book. Her publisher had wanted a thriller with a prominent love story—the twists and turns of the murders in the book would be easy enough, but wrapping her mind around the romance seemed an insurmountable task.

Cam's hand remained on her shoulder, probably because she hadn't moved. She shifted to let him search the closet himself with the flashlight he'd found.

How could she write about love, about a man's touch on a woman's body when she couldn't remember it, couldn't imagine it even when she closed her eyes or touched herself?

It had been over a year since she'd gotten really sick. Before that, she counted less than a handful of times spent with men, men who, as it turned out, she didn't want to— or couldn't—get close to.

But when she looked at Cam, everything warmed. Instant spring thaw.

She stood abruptly and waited near him, nibbling her bottom lip.

The fact that he'd known her father's favorite saying had given her some small comfort—it had been the tipping point. But she felt most comforted by the fact that Cam was as bothered by his father's work as she was by hers. That was certainly something that bonded them together—until you'd lived the life of the child of an undercover agent, you couldn't understand.

Cam got it.

He also knew more about the threats against her that had gotten him sent to her than he'd told her, but he wasn't budging. And her choices were truly limited.

So yes, Cameron Moore was already here, in her house, with his big hands and, no doubt, bigger weapons, and she wanted to hate how he made her body come alive when he brushed past her, but she couldn't.

"We've got everything—go finish your dinner while I start a fire." He emerged from the closet with three portable lamps and another flashlight, which he handed to her.

"I'm not really hungry."

"If you're recovering from surgery, you need to keep your strength up."

She sighed, because yes, that had been a constant complaint from the doctors—that she needed to eat, to put on weight or her immune system could get compromised more easily. And so she sat at the island and Cam joined her once he got a big fire crackling in the stone fireplace. She finished her food in silence with the soft light of the lamps shining between them and the warmth from the fire at her back.

He spoke first, after he'd eaten two plates of pasta. "Are you feeling okay?"

"I'm fine."

"Do you have enough medication to get you through the next couple of days with the storm?"

"I've got a ten-day supply left—I was planning on refilling them up here," she said, and the realization of having to refill them hit her hard. Because when she did so, she could be tracked.

As if he read her mind, Cam said, "We'll take care of it. I'll make sure you've got whatever it is you need. That's my job."

"What exactly is our plan? I mean, you're here with me, so I'm assuming my father is looking for whoever's threatening me, right?"

"How far out from surgery are you?" Cam asked instead of answering her question, and she sighed.

"Five months."

"Do you want to talk about it?"

She didn't, hated discussing it, but found herself telling him the story. Maybe he'd have some sympathy toward her and tell her his plan.

Doubtful, of course.

She didn't sense danger from him but he was surely as dangerous as whoever was after her—as dangerous as he needed to be.

And yet she ignored the niggle in the pit of her stomach, wondered if her instincts were skewed—for the past ten years, she'd stayed inside her own world, her own head, and ignored everything else. "I was seventeen when I got sick. It happened right before I went away to college."

She'd been diagnosed with adult polycystic kidney disease that subsequently turned chronic. "I lost my first kidney when I was eighteen."

"That's tough, Sky...you were just a kid. The whole world ahead of you," he murmured.

For the next six years, she remained closely monitored in hopes her remaining kidney would not fail. And for a while, it looked very promising. But when she was twenty-four, things took a turn for the worse and she found herself in end-stage renal disease within a month's period of time and totally dependant on dialysis.

When she'd lost the first kidney, she'd only been in the third month of her freshman year, and after the operation, she never went back. That was when the writing started in earnest.

Looking back, she knew she was incredibly lucky. She had talent, yes, but in the publishing business, that didn't always equate with success. She'd had both, in short order, had been nineteen and pretty and the media liked her.

In interviews, she'd said she was an orphan. Most of the time, she felt like one.

She wasn't being fair to her father, or to the memory of her mother; she knew that. Spoiled-brat moments were few and far between, but with this hulking man here, ready to turn her life upside down just when she'd gotten it right side up, they were breaking through.

"I'm a tough blood type to match," she said. "For a while, I didn't think I was going to make it. Neither did anyone else."

"But a donor came through."

"Yes, a donor came through," she echoed, thought about telling him who the donor actually was but held back.

He was a good listener. Typically that meant he wasn't much of a talker. Normally, she wasn't either, but nerves and lust mixed to make a combination far more potent than alcohol.

She wanted to know what he looked like without the

beard. He'd already pulled his heavy sweatshirt off, revealing a T-shirt that stretched across a broad chest and well-muscled arms.

She shrugged her sweater off, didn't care that it fell to the floor.

He was watching her with an odd look on his face, and no, he wasn't the typical bodyguard. She pulled her gaze away and stood.

"There's more pasta here if you want," she offered, picked up the bowl from near the stove and began to walk toward him.

Army. Ranger maybe, but she'd bet on Delta. He'd seen things, done things that would haunt him for the rest of his life, if he had a conscience.

If he didn't...

"I don't," he said and the bowl slid out of her hands to crash on the floor.

"Shit."

He was up in a second, stopping her from moving. "You'll cut your feet. Let me." He lifted her by her hips and set her down on the other side of the island.

And as she turned to watch, he bent to clean up the shards of broken ceramic dish off the hard tile floor with his own hands, obviously not worried about cutting himself.

Maybe this guy's for real.

CHAPTER
3

Five months earlier

He'd broken into her floor safe, the unbreakable, unbeatable secure piece of crap created to keep Riley's secure files out of the way of prying eyes.

Those eyes included some of the best spies and thieves, although in this business, the two could be interchangeable. And Dylan Scott, of course, who seemed to be on both no one's and everyone's side at the same time, depending on which way the bankroll rolled.

It had to be him. He'd made no attempt to hide what he'd done, arrogantly left the safe door wide open and the files he'd been looking through askew and out of order. At the top of the messy pile was the folder on Gabriel Creighton.

What did Dylan want with Gabriel Creighton? And what else had he seen?

She refused to let her plan be compromised now. Even if it meant she'd have to eliminate a man she could possibly love.

But there was no room for emotion in the spy game, where nothing was fair in love and everything was done in the name of war.

There was so much at stake here—she'd put everything into this plan, her job and her life on the line, in order to clear her father.

She remembered the day so clearly—her mother being told her husband, Riley's father, was never coming home. That he'd been a CIA agent who'd turned traitor to his country. And just like that, everything changed. No more checks, no insurance; it was as if her father hadn't existed.

They'd never even been given a grave site to visit.

Up until that point, Riley had thought her father was an executive at a major corporation. She'd been fifteen when he'd died, too young to know the truth about such a sensitive situation, and yet her mom told her who her father really was.

Riley wanted her innocence—and her ignorance—back.

She'd been sitting at the kitchen table with her mother, going over the details for her sweet sixteen party that was to happen in three months. Truth be told, she'd been planning that party since she'd turned thirteen. Because it was the thing to do, because her family had plenty of money and clout, and beyond getting grades that could see her into an

Ivy League school, there wasn't really anything at all Riley had to worry about.

Until that day. Men in suits. Her mother screaming *No!* A doctor coming, telling Riley he'd given her mother something for the pain.

At the time, Riley had misunderstood, thought there was a shot that could actually ease heartache.

God, she wished that were true. Wished she could go back to those moments when she was so innocent, until she reminded herself she'd been horribly vulnerable. Easy prey for the CIA to fake her father's suicide—a fact she only discovered later, thanks to information her mother had withheld and a coroner's report that had been tampered with.

Even now the pain of that loss hit her hard, made her chest ache and her eyes water. She and her mom hadn't been given any time to mourn. His death and subsequent disgrace made the papers the next day.

"It wasn't a suicide," her mother kept repeating in her haze. "He would never."

Years later, Riley would unravel the complicated mission that had been her father's last for the CIA—and the fact that he had been killed by another agent for being a traitor, a double agent. Which prompted the loss of all family assets.

Everything was taken from them within forty-eight hours. They'd each packed a couple of suitcases and whatever else they could fit into the car, which they owned outright in her mother's name.

So she'd gone from planning a sweet sixteen party to sleeping in the backseat of the car and then a homeless shelter, on a lumpy cot with a threadbare blanket. Riley would've cried herself to sleep every night, except her mom cried in her sleep enough for both of them.

But slowly, her mom had come out of her stupor of pain... and then she was angry. And she was resourceful, did the best she could.

By the time Riley was done with high school, they'd graduated from a shitty motel to an equally shitty but slightly larger and more private apartment.

Riley remembered being scared all the time.

She remembered learning how to fight. And then her mom's illness couldn't be overlooked any longer. It happened so fast, when Riley was deployed overseas. By the time she got back on family leave, Mom had died alone in a state-funded nursing home, and all Riley could do was identify the body, clean out the apartment and head back to the Navy.

After that she'd tried to gain entrance into either the CIA or the FBI, but was turned away from both, despite a sterling military record and recommendations from her sups.

She remained in the Navy for five years, worked her way through the ranks, did things by the book and tried to find out any and all intel on her father and the CIA.

Finally, she left the Navy and began to work black and gray ops while investigating her father's case.

After years and years, she'd found a way to get the intel she'd been looking for. Finally, she had a real chance of finding out what happened to her father.... She was so close to Gabriel Creighton, the man rumored to have killed her father, and couldn't afford anyone getting in her way.

But then Dylan Scott emerged from the shadows of the storage space she'd rented under an assumed name and he was definitely in her way. Tears blurred her eyes as he held up his hands and she forced her thoughts back to her mother, dying in that horrible nursing home because Riley couldn't afford anything better.

She didn't say anything, couldn't, and couldn't let him talk, because then she'd cave. She leveled the gun at his side and shot twice, careful to wound but not kill. Because she wanted Dylan Scott out of her life for good, didn't want him coming around her any longer, but didn't want him dead . . . and didn't want to need him.

She noted the surprise in his eyes before he put a hand to his side. The blood seeped between his fingers and he fell to his knees on the floor.

She waited until he'd pulled out a cell phone to call for help. Only then did she grab the files and run from him, afraid she'd kneel and cradle him in her arms. And when she reached the car, she sobbed, the first time she'd cried since her mother's funeral.

Present day

Dylan would've found the look on Riley Sacadano's face priceless if he could get over the fact that she'd actually shot him five months ago to get out of their relationship.

Granted, he knew he was partially to blame for what happened—he'd pushed her and she'd pushed back. Hard. His side ached just thinking about it. Scar tissue that yanked at him at the most inopportune times.

He'd known when he'd broken into the safe that he was on to something big, but he hadn't known just how big until she'd shot him and walked away. He still didn't know the entire deal, but it was time to find out more, especially since Cam was involved.

Now Riley just stared and shook her head and finally managed, "You."

He gave a small wave from where he sat on her couch, feet up on her expensive coffee table, the way he'd been waiting for her for the better part of two hours. "Me. Back like a bad penny, Riley."

"I thought my message was loud and clear, Dylan. Seriously, what else do I need to do to convince you to stay the hell away from me?"

Why did it bother him that, once her initial shock wore off, she seemed more annoyed than contrite?

Ah, well, that's what he got for falling for an operative with a penchant for double-agenting and God knew what else on the side.

It was why he liked her so damned much—the first woman in forever to actually remind him he had a heart as well as a dick.

He dropped his booted feet to the ground hard and she winced as sand sprayed her deep-pile white shag carpeting.

God, she looked really good—long bare legs, tanned against the short sundress that went to a deep V between her breasts. Breasts he'd buried his face in when he came so he didn't shout out anything stupid, like *I love you.*

She moved and he tensed, but she didn't pull her gun, or even a knife. Instead, she reached up and loosened her long,

dark hair, letting it fall over her shoulders before attempting
to walk past him and head for her bedroom.

He was up, his palm encircling a slim, muscular biceps,
pinning her to the wall. She raised her chin as she allowed
that. She could throw him off but she wouldn't win this
one, not unless he allowed her to.

He'd given her a chance once. That proved to be one
chance too many.

As soon as Cam had left his place early that morning,
Dylan knew what he'd have to do. Within the hour, he'd
been at the airport, flying to sunny South Beach and breaking into the house of the woman who'd shot him and hadn't
looked back.

He'd planned on confronting Riley long before this, and
yet found himself avoiding her. Keeping tabs on her
through the loose network of spies and operatives and such,
just enough to know where she was and that she was okay.

Not that he should give a fuck. But he did. And in his
business, caring like that was a huge liability.

It was one of the main reasons he worked alone. The
reason he'd pulled away from Delta and the concept of
team. This way, he only had himself to count on—and
himself to blame.

Of course, somewhere along the way, he'd started counting on Cam. It happened on one of Dylan's last missions
with Delta, when he'd been hit. For twenty-four hours, he'd
waited in the darkness until the backup came. Listened to
the heavy fire that crossed the rapidly evacuating downtown area of the Chadian capital of N'djamena.

He'd gotten a radio signal that help had arrived. Would

be waiting in the building across the street from where Dylan was, would make contact and then come get him.

He'd never met Cam before. But he saw him now, across the road, motioning to him in the dark with a penlight.

I'm coming to you.

Dylan remembered his pride rearing up. *Fuck that. I'm coming to you.* Forced himself to his feet.

In the heat of that kill zone, he'd instinctively put into action everything he'd learned. He filtered out chaos, put up a mental curtain between himself and the confusion, and went into survival mode. Made the dash to the waiting Delta.

Dylan had to be half dragged from that point. Would've been easier for Cam to carry him, but Dylan had to continue to prove he wasn't out of the game completely.

Until he'd passed out, and then Cam had slung him over his shoulder and trotted them both to the LZ.

Later, when Dylan had been released from the hospital, he'd sought out Cam. Shook his hand. Thanked him.

"Don't worry about it."

"Someone saves your life, you're indebted to them," Dylan had told him.

Cam punched him then, blood spattering from Dylan's nose. "Fuck you. I don't want you in my debt."

It took months before Cam told Dylan everything, until Dylan finally understood why his words had freaked his friend out so much.

He guessed Riley flipped out because she felt the same kind of debt to him.

He'd been so close to death, so many times, she'd been sure the bullet she fired had done nothing more than kill their relationship. And that was the shot she hadn't wanted to misfire.

She'd severed a line straight through anything they'd ever had together—or so she'd thought.

With the crap raining down on Cam's head, Dylan's focus was pulled tighter. And if helping Cam was in direct opposition to keeping Riley alive, he'd have to find a way to reconcile that.

Jesus, just thinking about it made him ache.

"What do you want?" she asked him, but beyond wanting *her,* he had no clue.

He'd left Delta Force five years earlier, having lacked the discipline not to tell any and all authority figures to go fuck themselves, and these days spent his time working for anyone who paid him enough money. Half mercenary, part spook, and altogether wild man, he came across as calm, cool, and collected—yet felt anything but inside, since the death of his parents when he'd been twenty and in Ranger School.

They'd been adventure-seekers with a hell of a lot of money, had been killed in Egypt on some kind of archeological expedition in a freak cave collapse. Dylan had finished raising his two younger brothers—Cael was nearly seventeen and Zane fifteen. Dylan went to court, was granted custody with the stipulation that Cael and Zane would live with an aunt at first, while Dylan was required to live on post, and then only when he was out on manuevers.

Caleb had followed in his footsteps, going first to Ranger School and now was in Delta Force as part of Cam's team. Zane went Navy—had been with the SEALs for a few years now, and caused more trouble than Dylan ever had, which was saying something.

These days, Dylan didn't get to spend nearly enough time with his brothers, who were usually in far-flung, dangerous places, enjoying the hell out of their lives. And he was thirty-three years old with a past that would make anyone fucking blush.

Except Riley Sacadano.

Dylan's touch had always made her weak, but this time, it was for an entirely different reason.

As Riley looked into his cool green eyes, she prayed her knees would hold out. She was barely keeping it together—only years of training and a will of steel had kept her from losing her shit completely at the sight of him sitting on her couch.

He leaned in close to her. "You never stopped to check for a pulse," he reminded her. "By the way, I lived."

When she'd shot him, she'd known she wasn't killing him, had hit him so she'd have time to get away. So he'd stop trying to be her moral compass. So he'd be so angry and hurt he'd never want anything to do with her again.

She figured shooting him on purpose would take care of that, but obviously she'd been wrong.

He pressed his body to hers; she felt his arousal brush her belly. She tilted her face up, their mouths mere inches from each other. "I'm usually a much better shot."

Obviously, the man really was always one step ahead of her, and she wasn't sure why that made her feel all warm and fuzzy inside; she was not a warm and fuzzy kind of girl.

He hadn't answered her question yet, seemed almost suspended in time, and for a fleeting moment she was sure he'd kiss her.

She couldn't let that happen, pushed against him with her free hand and forced him to give her some space. "Why are you here?"

His eyes turned hard. "I need to know more about Gabriel Creighton."

She'd always known Dylan to have a one-track mind when he wanted something, although it typically didn't have anything to do with another man. "No. Now please leave."

"You ask so nicely, and without the bullets this time, but I like it here. I might go for a swim." He smiled and her heart sank because, even though he'd released her, he began to strip. Shirt first, revealing an impossibly hard chest and ripped abs—she attempted to tear her gaze away, but couldn't. Not when his shorts dropped and he stood completely, unabashedly, naked. "Want to join me?"

"No thanks."

He walked past her, out the double doors to the pool, his ass firmly muscled as he strode along the deck and then dove into the pool.

She followed and stood at the edge, watching as he swam laps back and forth. She had few options. One involved shooting him, again—which hadn't worked so well the last time.

The other was to bring in backup, but she didn't want to deal with the questions.

She didn't think there was anyone else in the world who

wanted to know more about Gabriel Creighton than she did, and so she'd wait Dylan out.

Cam had left Skylar at her opened laptop. There was no Internet access tonight, but she'd said she planned on writing until her battery wore out, and he figured she was safe enough locked in the house in the middle of a blizzard, with no comms, to give him a few minutes of peace.

Peace. What a fucking joke; he hadn't had that in years. Sitting with Skylar, watching her breasts through the thin tank top, wasn't doing anything to help that either, and so he excused himself.

She seemed happy enough to be rid of him, had actually waved one hand distractedly as if dismissing him.

He needed a shower anyway. A cold one maybe, and a nice shave. It had been too long since he'd seen his own face. As he cut away the growth he thought about the months he'd spent reconning in Afghanistan, about how he'd almost managed to forget everything about his early life. About how, with the Delta team, he was simply one of the guys.

When he looked in the mirror, he realized he looked much younger than he felt.

He stripped down in the soft light the portable lamp provided and noted the small scar on his arm—white against his tanned skin.

He'd almost forgotten about it.

After his last mission, the first thing he'd done was cut out the chip Gabriel had implanted into his arm so long ago. Now he stared at the line that Dylan had stitched up for him after digging the chip out, and thought about it sitting in Dylan's steel-encased safe. Thanks to the steel, not only couldn't Gabriel track him any longer, but Dylan's house couldn't be tracked either.

Yet Gabriel had found him. The man always could.

Stick with the plan, Cameron. Get close to Sky.

Yeah, no problem staying close. But there were other problems that could prove to be more complicated than he and Dylan had planned. Dylan, who he'd called three times over the past hour, to no avail. But finally, Dylan buzzed him back.

Cam turned on the water before he spoke. "Gabriel's missing."

"Spooks are never missing, Cam, you know that." Dylan's voice remained easy, but Cam knew his friend was anything but. Dylan was always coiled to strike when and if necessary, and this job would prove no exception.

"He hasn't contacted Skylar—she's left messages. Someone's threatening her." He told Dylan about the letters and his friend let out a small whistle.

"When you step in it, you really step in it."

"Yeah, thanks." He paused. "I found a picture of Gabriel." It had been in Sky's things, her wallet, which Cam had searched on his way to the bathroom. Gabriel had been younger, but it was him. Cam had taken a picture of the photo with his cell phone and he emailed it to Dylan even as they spoke. "I thought maybe, with the new information about the Outlaw Angel in jail . . ."

Another man who'd known Howie. It would probably yield nothing, just like all the others, but Cam would keep trying, even though he actually already had the leverage he needed in the next room. He was always big on backup plans.

"Good, that's good. Look, I'll get more information—about Gabriel and the OA lead," his friend promised.

"I'm staying put tonight. Storm's too bad to risk it. I'll move out with her tomorrow, head to the first location," Cam said. He and Dylan had carefully mapped a zigzag route that would keep Skylar off balance and everyone else off his tail. "What the hell's going on here?"

"Could be anything. Watch your back as carefully as you watch hers," Dylan advised before clicking off.

Cam could've sworn he'd heard salsa music in the background and wondered what the hell his friend was up to now. He left the phone on the counter and looked out the window. The snow was piling up already—fat flakes that came down hard enough that visibility was fucked.

It had been a night like this when he'd been arrested—driving his hog through the snow because he'd been young and stupid and distraught—something he'd stopped himself from telling Skylar. He'd been damned close, though. She was far too easy to talk to.

She understood.

Earlier, he'd watched her hands fist on the table in front of her, her voice holding a bleak despair that had cut him to his soul. That told him what she was feeling when she spoke about her work, and her father.

The night of the murders and Cam's subsequent arrest was still vague—a shake at three A.M., his father whispering, "Cover for me. I won't let anything happen to you."

He'd done what his father had asked, headed two doors

down with the key his father had given him and grabbed the mail off the dining room table.

And saw the two dead bodies lying side by side on the floor, the blood pooling around their heads still fresh. And then he'd backed out of the house, unable to tear his eyes away from the gory scene in front of him—and finally left. Ran, actually.

He had no idea when doing so that he'd be indicted for the death of the two FBI agents found murdered at that house. When the police pulled him over on his Harley, lights flashing and sirens blazing, Cam hadn't argued. And something inside of him had died when he'd realized just how easily his father had set him up.

A war hero, a former Special Operations specialist, Howie Moore'd had a brilliant future...and no honor. That's what Gabriel had told Cam in that small interrogation room at the prison.

No honor, not like you have, Gabriel said.

In the beginning, Cam had been so grateful. Even though he'd realized that Gabriel would own him for a while, Cam had agreed, and was given a clean record, an admission to the Army, and placed on the fast track, first to Ranger School and then onto Delta Force.

After prison, it had taken him a little while to get used to the team motto. Didn't think he could—didn't want to—trust anyone beyond himself, but he'd learned. Struggled. Worked his ass off. And in those dark spaces he tried so hard to block from his memory, he followed Gabriel Creighton's off-the-record orders.

The first years, the missions were similar to his Delta

ones. Cam got the feeling he was being groomed, as if prepping to become part of Gabriel's private army, his personal arsenal of tricks.

He wasn't innocent. Not by a long shot. But as a member of Delta Force, he knew what side of the law he was on, however thin the line was sometimes. He was proud as hell of the work he'd done with his team.

With Delta Force, he knew the *why* of the missions. And even if some of them turned his stomach, he recognized ultimately, that they were for the greater good—of his country, of any country they were attempting to help.

With Gabriel's missions, he was never privy to the reasons behind the task, never knew if he was truly helping anyone. Being at the end of someone's fucking puppet strings like that twisted his horns, made his normally calm demeanor trigger to instant anger.

And then the jobs for Gabriel increased in quantity and grew exponentially trickier. When Cam balked, that's when he learned the truth, that he would always be under the threat of being sent back to jail and having the life he'd built for himself taken from him.

Gabriel made sure to emphasize that noncompliance would get him thrown back into his life sentences in the blink of an eye.

And so Cam lived in the prison of Gabriel's making, year after year, praying that his time in hell would soon be done.

They were black ops missions, which meant they didn't officially exist. If Cam was captured or jailed, no one would come to get him. And in that precarious and frightening world, he learned that he'd never really left prison.

With Delta, he had his team. Led his team. They reported to him, admired him, counted on him—and he was damned good at keeping his men alive and well. Even when the op required him to work alone, his team was always close, surveilling. They would never leave him behind as long as there was breath in their bodies. And still, apart from missions, Cam couldn't allow himself to get close to any of them on a personal level.

Dylan Scott had gotten in under the wire with his friendship, before Cam realized just how insidious Gabriel's reach would be. Until he began to suspect that Gabriel had been the reason he'd been framed for murder in the first place.

And now Dylan had proven his loyalty once again by giving Cam the information about Skylar. If he'd met Dylan later than he had, Cam never would've trusted the man enough to give him a chance to prove that loyalty. But fate had intervened, and now Cam wasn't sure what he would've done all these years without his friend.

Cam had never spoken about his dad to anyone but Dylan—and even then, he'd glossed over a lot of it, hadn't let his emotions show through. Had pretended it didn't matter, when it had, when every choice he made in life was colored by that moment in time he'd been betrayed.

He would never let it happen again—not by Gabriel, or by his daughter.

The words came. She'd felt the familiar urge hit, a strange sensation Skylar nearly didn't recognize, and she couldn't get to the computer fast enough.

With the only light the battery power of her monitor, she typed furiously as the storm turned from snow to sleet, and hail battered the townhouse, the tap-tap of the keys keeping time with the howl of the wind as she raced the storm, as if needing to harness its power.

Her fingers ached when she was done—nearly twenty pages in a short span of time—and her body sagged from mental exhaustion.

Spent, she sat back and took a breath, well aware she'd been holding it on and off as she wrote, the words tumbling out of her. She saved her work on the memory stick as the last of her battery power wore away. *Mental note: Charge the damned thing every once in a while, Sky, okay?*

She was more than satisfied. So was Violet McCabe, the futuristic bounty hunter and all around kick-ass lead character of Skylar's latest series.

Violet, who had all the physical strength that Sky herself didn't. *Yet,* she told herself fiercely. Soon she'd be back running and lifting weights, the way she had before.

Violet's words at the end of the scene she'd just written echoed in her head. *Don't count me out. Ever.*

But even as her heroine threw out those last, cocky words, Sky doubted herself. Could it really be this easy again? Would the words come back tomorrow?

The monitor flickered in warning and she shut the laptop down and closed the lid. Suddenly, with the light gone, the storm turned from her ally to her enemy, as every sound became someone scratching at the door to get in.

She almost called for Cam, then heard the running water and realized he was showering.

Instead, she reached for her BlackBerry and noted that

she had a few bars of service. Spotty, but enough, and so she quickly dialed her father's number, and got his voice mail message. Again. "Hey, it's me. I just wanted to let you know that Cameron Moore is here—he told me you sent him. Can you please call me, though? I need to speak to—"

Dead air. Well, at least hopefully the message had gotten through.

Cameron Moore is here. And he seems to get me.

Holding a lantern, she walked along the hallway in the suddenly too dark townhouse until she reached the bathroom.

He'd left the door open. With his own lantern on the countertop, she could look at the half-steamed mirror and see him through the clear-glass shower door.

She wanted to look away but couldn't. Soap slid between his shoulder blades, over the ridge of his lower back, coursing down thighs, which were solid ridges of muscles, as were his calves, and his feet . . . yes, they were large.

Stupid wives' tale, she told herself, even as he turned around—and no, this was definitely not an old wives' tale.

It was only then she realized he could see her watching him if he turned his face toward the mirror. And still she didn't move, running her gaze up his body toward his face when he turned the water off.

She moved to leave the doorway and her ankle caught on the doorjamb and twisted—she cried out and went down hard.

Cam was by her side in seconds, still dripping wet, towel around his waist. "You okay?"

He'd shaved his face clean, making his blue eyes stand out in stark relief, his chiseled cheekbones striking. His hair was wet, slicked back, and he was seriously, devastatingly handsome.

Her face flushed hot. If he knew she'd been spying, he didn't say... but something about the look in his eyes told her he guessed.

"I'm fine," she insisted, and then, in the next breath, she corrected herself. "No, I'm not fine. I haven't been fine for a long time."

He remained on his knees, next to her, listening.

"But here with you, I feel like I can be fine. I want to be fine." She reached up tentatively, slid her hands over his shoulders, feeling the slick, damp skin that was hot under her fingers.

"Sky..." His tone held a warning, letting her know she was about to push things too far with her soft touch, but she couldn't stop now. Wanted to play with fire.

She trailed her hands down his chest, stopping midway, tracing the cuts on his abs with a finger.

When she looked up at him, he nearly lost it. He'd been hard from the second he'd caught her looking at him, but now, watching her studying his body... wanting him, his blood surged.

"We can't do this," he heard himself say—the voice of reason.

"I want you, Cam. Please, don't turn me down."

Jesus H. Christ. He didn't say anything, and her hand moved down farther, until it rested where the ends of his towel tucked into each other.

Her next words were halting. "I haven't... not for a long time. A couple of years."

"Years?"

"I know—hard for a man to understand, I'm sure." She shrugged to hide her embarrassment, but her cheeks betrayed her by flushing hot. "It's not that I haven't thought about it, wanted it..."

She swallowed hard and moved her hand. "I can't believe I asked you. I'm sorry."

She made a move to rise, but he stopped her. "It's okay that you asked," he said, because sleeping with her was all part of the plan.

Sleeping with her would be the worst thing he could possibly do. But right now, it was the only thing he wanted.

With that, he lifted her from the floor in one swift, sure movement and carried her into the bedroom.

CHAPTER
4

The bed was soft, inviting—like Sky. When Cam placed her on the mattress, a part of him said, *Leave her.*

The other, more demanding part had been fully engaged from the time he'd sensed her watching him in the shower.

He hadn't kissed her yet, simply lowered his body to hers in a way that was far too familiar for the strangers they were.

Except they weren't strangers any longer, hadn't been since he'd told her about his life growing up. Willingly.

Dammit.

He realized he'd been tracing a finger along the side of her neck while she stared at him. Her hands were still fisted around his biceps, and when he shifted, his towel slipped off, remained between them, along with her clothing.

The cool air played on his still-damp back and he fought a shiver. "Has it really been that long for you?"

Her cheeks flushed. "Why would I lie about that?"

In his experience, women—everyone—lied about nearly everything, in order to get what they wanted. Sky had grown up with a professional liar. Had she known that, been able to see right through it?

Would she be able to see through him? "I don't think you'd make that up, no."

Two fingers, pressed to the pulse point on the side of her neck. Her pulse was fast, practically jumping against his skin.

Could he kill her? Dylan could, would if necessity reared its head; he was ruthless in all things, love and war.

Cam could be so as well, had emotion trained out of him for situations like this. And he flashed back to a different time and place with a much different woman underneath him, one as ruthless and hardened as Cam had once thought he was. One who'd planned on killing him before he killed her.

He'd thought she was innocent. Even so, he'd let his guard down too far. She'd tried to slice his throat and his balls all at once.

It had taken him a long time after that mission to bed a woman. The few times he had, he'd ended up tying their hands just so he could come and get it over with faster.

The women he'd picked hadn't seemed to mind. And so far, the images of violence still mingled in his thoughts during sex.

Even though he should be more than used to the violence, if anything, his tenure under Gabriel made his stomach turn more often than not. Instead of becoming numb and violent, he'd stopped sleeping, because the nightmares got too bad, and he'd started praying.

Sometimes, there will be collateral damage, his CO had told him, years earlier, when he'd first been admitted to Delta training. *You'll feel like shit, which should reassure you that you are, indeed, human. And usually it's just when you start to believe you're super-fucking-man. It's a good thing, because you* are *human, blood and bone, and you can break.*

He forced himself back to the present, to the beautiful, unarmed woman lying beneath him. Helpless and still, her gaze locked to his with a mix of power and challenge that made his dick throb.

He was most definitely human. And this was nothing like his last mission.

Why this time would be different, he didn't know, but it was. Maybe because her touches were both hesitant and knowing. The way her tongue darted out quickly to the corner of her mouth when her hands ran along his shoulders.

She swallowed, her throat moving against his palm, her hips pushing toward his in an almost unconscious movement.

"Are you sure you're physically okay?" he murmured, and she nodded.

He ran his hand along her throat as he lowered his mouth to hers. The kiss shot through him with an unexpected jolt as her tongue hungrily found his, and he shifted his weight and tried to ground himself.

As he kissed her, his fingers splayed along her collarbone, his palm resting at the base of her throat. Close enough to do the job easily—he wouldn't need to use much pressure . . . she wouldn't fight until it was too late.

Speaking of too late, his own breath caught as her hand reached between them and circled his cock. The touch was tentative, but somehow, all the more sexy because she was unsure . . . because she wanted to prove to him that she could please him.

She had, she was—and he was in more trouble than he ever fucking thought possible.

"Harder," he urged, and she smiled, and fuck, it was beautiful. She stroked and he kissed and his hand remained just above her clavicle.

You could do it, if you had to, he tried to tell himself.

But tonight, he didn't have to and so he let his hand trail down to her breast instead.

"This isn't all that fair—me naked and you fully clothed," he told her.

She bit her bottom lip, and then, "Maybe you should do something about that."

"I plan to." As much as he didn't want her hands to leave him, he wanted her naked more, and so he caught her wrist and she blushed and moved her hand. He got to his knees for a second, used his teeth to pull her tank top over her breasts. They were perfect—small, with rose-colored nipples that were already taut. He suckled one, hard, felt her jump against him and then sigh with pleasure.

It spurred him onward, his fingers tugging at the free nipple, pulling it to a stiff peak as his mouth worked the other. Her hands moved along his shoulders, wound through his damp hair as the storm intensified. The room was nearly dark, save for the portable lantern on the dresser across the room, and the sharp sounds of hail let him know they were safe, for tonight, from the outside world.

He eased her low-slung pajama bottoms down, his hands running along her hips as he pushed the fabric far enough for her to kick it off, making sure to take off her bikini underwear as well, and then he gazed at her naked body.

Mine.

It was the only word that came to mind, a sharp, biting sensation following in the pit of his stomach as his eyes caught on the scar—thin, reddish-pink and raised, maybe ten inches running on a diagonal across her abdomen toward her left side. He sucked in a breath, because he'd forgotten, because he hated to see the remnants of how much pain she'd had to endure.

This woman was as much of a survivor as he was.

He traced the scar with his finger and she froze in his arms. When he glanced back up, she looked so raw and vulnerable, like she was ready to shield her body from his with her arms, to crawl under the sheets.

He murmured, "It's okay. You're beautiful."

"I'm already naked—you don't have to give me compliments."

"I don't say anything I don't mean, Sky—that's one thing you need to learn about me," he told her before he dragged his finger lower, to dip between her legs. Her sex was wet and hot, and her eyes closed at the contact, even as she held her breath for a few seconds.

She was so serious in her pleasure, as if she hadn't felt any in a long time and wasn't sure how to react anymore.

But when he entered her with first one finger and then two, her eyes widened, her breath quickened. He used the pad of his thumb to caress the swollen bundle of nerves at the same time, forcing her hips to rock to his rhythm. "Beautiful."

She shook her head, as if refusing to listen to his words. She bit her bottom lip as he stroked and caressed the delicate flesh, and she was so close to orgasm. Looked so hot getting there that he knew he would make her come a second time ... and a third.

How it would feel once he was fully inside of her.

There was no turning back—his way out from Gabriel's grasp was just outside his grasp. Or in it. Under it ...

How had this gotten so fucking far in so short a period of time?

"Cam!" Her sharp cry broke his reverie, unfettered by hate or the mission.

"This is mine," he heard himself mutter thickly before he could help himself, the blood pounding behind his eyes as if he was the one ready to orgasm. He suckled a nipple and felt the first shudder of release break through her. Her legs stiffened, she pressed herself against his hands as a hard-won moan escaped from the back of her throat.

It was the first show of surrender to him, and it made him want to throw his head back and roar.

The frost was over. First, the words and now the orgasm, rolling through her with an intensity Sky swore she'd never experienced.

She was well aware she'd cried out Cam's name—even

more aware that she'd attempted to muffle it by yanking his body close and burying her face against his shoulder.

She might've even bitten him, but he hadn't complained. Had muttered something under his breath, but remained focused on her. Even as she still shuddered, he was sliding down her body, his mouth kissing its way down, farther and farther until . . .

"Oh!"

She heard him laugh before his tongue found her core again, licked another long stroke down her sex while his fingers tugged a nipple. Her hands wound in his hair, not sure if she was attempting to stop him, or to keep him from stopping. Her sex felt tender, overly sensitive, but his tongue probed gently, persistently.

Her back arched as pleasure speared her—she couldn't remember being this wet before. She spread her legs and forgot about being scared or worrying about anything beyond the flick of a tongue on the bundled pillow of nerves that had remained dormant for too long. Under her own touch, it had felt numb.

Under Cam's probing, though, she was alive. Flourishing.

She brought her hand to rest on his, the one that was playing with her nipple, heard him murmur, "Oh, yeah," as she caressed herself at the same time he caressed her.

A hot rush of pure heat flooded her as he took her core like a starving man. She tried to gain footing on the sheets, ended up with her feet on his shoulders as her release overtook her body. She arched off the bed, grabbing for any kind of quarter, hoped he was holding on tightly, because she was losing track of everything except the slow throb through her womb.

And then she shattered, climaxed against his mouth, her cries incoherent. She lay, an arm over her eyes, her breathing fast, Cam's warm breath still on her thigh. Her nerves strummed to the point of overstimulation.

Cam seemed to know, let her come down from her high for a bit. And then his kisses rode up her stomach, her breasts, her neck, until they were thigh to thigh. He shifted slightly when her hand strayed between his legs, wanting to feel that power again. And he froze a little, then started as she began to explore further, almost as if the move was unexpected.

But he didn't stop her, and she continued to stroke him—he was so hard, the skin so soft. So much power in one place.

He traced the shell of her ear with his tongue, nipped the lobe, licked the sensitive patch along her neck until she realized she'd been raising her hips in a slow grind, pressing his shaft against her sex. Ready again, pushing for more.

Her skin was damp from nerves and exertion, his body hot against hers, making her hot and bothered.

He took her by the wrists and held them both together in one hand over her head as he bent to suckle a nipple and it was exciting, being held down—and open to him.

The man was big. Everywhere. Big hands, big feet, big shoulders ... and the arousal that pressed against her sex was impressively so. His eyes were heavy-lidded. Lazy, even though there was nothing else about this man that could be called so.

"Hang on, I'll be right back," he told her, left the room and indeed returned quickly, condoms in hand.

Yes, protection. She was glad one of them was thinking, as she wasn't permitted to use birth control beyond condoms because of her condition.

He got back on the bed with her—back onto her. "You okay?"

"Yes." She touched his face. Without the beard, the sharp cheekbones, the line of the strong jaw, everything was clearer.

God, he was handsome. And even though his eyes held a kindness, she knew that it must serve to hide the rough and ready soldier she shared this bed with. He was experienced, knew how to give her pleasure—made it his mission to do so, even as he prepared to take his own. He ripped the package open and rolled the condom on, and within seconds, his body covered hers, his hand once again imprisoning her wrists over her head.

With his thigh spreading her legs, he shifted to his knees and used his free hand to guide himself inside of her. She moaned as he penetrated—slow and steady at first, and then finally he drove home into her, stretching her in a mix of slight pain and pleasure, which soon turned to all pleasure.

She tried to tug her hands loose, but he wasn't having it, kept a steady pressure there as he rocked with her. Her legs instinctively went around his waist to lock her ankles behind his back—her own version of tying him down.

The sex was rougher than she was used to—almost as if he was fighting something within himself, fighting her at the same time. And still, it was exhilarating, and her responses showed that this was something she'd obviously craved.

He bucked against her, the loss of control evident in his features—and she was the one doing that to him. She was responsible for it.

He never took his eyes off of her, not even when he came, a moment after her orgasm. Hers pulled him over the edge, his pupils darkening, his mouth opened with a long groan escaping. And then her name was on his lips, and she liked that. So much. Wanted to hear him say it again and again.

She hadn't felt like herself for a long time. She was always sick Skylar and then dying Skylar, and finally recovering Skylar. The one whose life was in danger, even now.

She was still too thin, her breasts smaller than they were before the surgery, despite the fact that she was eating right—and still Cam stared at her like he'd never wanted anyone more.

It's okay. You're beautiful.

Right now she didn't care if that was actually the truth or not.

She'd wanted to cry when he said that earlier, had kissed him instead, since that was far more satisfying. And now the hardness pressing her sex had nothing at all to do with pity. Cam wanted her—really, truly wanted her. She could see it in his eyes, feel it with his every touch.

Before this, she'd felt empty, almost brittle, and even when Cam first touched her, she'd expected to hear the subtle snap.

But she hadn't broken, not even with the heavy weight of his body on hers.

Finally, he let go of her wrists as he rolled off her. He rubbed her arms, which felt like jelly, as did her legs, and basically every other part of her body.

"I think I forgot how good this was. No, I take that back, it was never this good."

He gave her a small smile. "We're not done, Sky. Not nearly done."

She swallowed hard and readied herself as he took her again, wrapped her legs around him, and this time, this time, he didn't hold her wrists, let her clutch his shoulders and touch his hair, even scrape her nails along his back when she climaxed, hard.

W hen Dylan had come up for air after swimming laps in the cold water, in the hope of tamping down his needs, he noted Riley had gone inside, but kept the shades across the sliding glass pulled back so he could see her sitting at the dining table.

He'd laid out on a lounge chair, alternately reading a magazine and watching Riley sort through her mail, talk on the phone and watch him at various random intervals.

She'd also turned on salsa music letting it blast through the patio speakers. She knew he hated salsa music.

It was like a big game of chicken, except this was much more pleasant, especially with the beer he'd grabbed from the fully stocked outdoor bar.

Riley was living well. She used to be on the right side of

the law. For all he knew, she still might be—but in the spy-for-hire game, all bets were usually off.

There were so many rumors floating around about her that Dylan could barely keep track. The only solid fact was that she'd lived in Maryland until she was fifteen and joined the Navy at eighteen, serving five years. After that, things were muddied. Some intel had her being courted by the FBI before deciding to go and play the spy game on her own.

He knew for sure was that there was no trace of Riley Sacadano in the military, CIA, or FBI systems, which was odd. If she was a rogue, both agencies would've been watching her carefully. And she'd been regular Navy—not Special Forces, which would have necessitated the secrecy surrounding her files.

Unless she was working with someone on the inside who covered for her. Unless she actually worked with Gabriel Creighton, which was always a possibility. One he hated to consider, and something he would find out ASAP.

Dylan had known about her long before he'd met her, but when he'd finally laid eyes on her, it had been explosive. Literally.

She'd blown up his car.

Luckily he'd had Autostart and had remembered to use it that day.

That had simply been a job for her. She hadn't known him from Adam and had been following her orders. But the night three years later she'd shot him . . . He'd been furious, because it had been so fucking personal.

And it had hurt him so unexpectedly, left him spiraling

for months. Dylan stayed up many a night wondering if he'd miscalculated, if the heat between them was only that—heat. Lust. If he'd been crazy to think he loved Riley.

She wouldn't have been the first woman to betray him, but she was the first to get the better of him. No, most of the women he'd been with were in the same line of work as he, where love and loyalty were two commodities no one could keep their hands on.

Cut the maudlin shit and connect the dots, Dylan.

Okay, yeah, he never really knew exactly what Riley's job was. Whether she was a double—or triple—agent, or a private contractor, as he'd suspected later, was something that didn't bother him. He'd seen too much to question anyone's motives or morals, including his own.

Under orders, spies, spooks and Special Forces did things that the general public never knew about, and wouldn't want to.

But when human emotions broke through, agents got turned around. When they started to question, to hesitate, it was time to back away. Because a constant stream of black ops . . . well, that could fry a man's—or a woman's—soul. If they had one in the first place.

Cam was more sensitive than most. It just happened to be couched in steel precision. But everyone had his breaking point.

His friend had reached his when Gabriel's men tried to kill him on the helo. But Cam most definitely had a soul— Dylan knew that for sure.

Whether Riley still had one that could be saved remained up to him to find out.

She'd had one three years earlier, when she had only known his alias and not his real name. The two days and nights in that hotel in Bogotá, they'd pretended the world didn't exist. Room service, time in the Jacuzzi. Lots of time in bed, on the floor, anyplace they landed.

Yes, he remembered those nights well.

"Who are you, Riley?"

She turned her face on the pillow, stared at him with those dark eyes that made him hunger for her again. "I'm just like you."

Frustrated, he turned away, onto his back.

"Riley is my real name," she said finally, her words drifting lazily between them, as if this was a first date and there weren't matching his-and-hers automatic weapons on the floor of the closet, hidden from room service's prying eyes.

He moved his hand to find hers, still without looking at her. "Deacon's not mine." Again, silence, albeit a more comfortable one as she squeezed his hand lightly. "Riley sounds like a boy's name."

"That's what my dad wanted."

He snorted. "I'm glad he didn't get what he wanted." And then, "My real name is Dylan Scott."

It felt odd saying it, like he was talking about a stranger. He'd been Deacon Sanders for so long, and a variety of other last names when they suited his purpose to protect his brothers. He had sworn he'd never go back to his old name.

He'd also sworn not to fall in love, but that promise was shot to shit.

When he'd woken up on the third morning, she'd been gone. He hadn't seen her again for six months, on a job in Ibiza. They'd been after the same man, but for different reasons. He'd gotten to the guy first, and Riley hadn't been happy.

He'd made up for it—put a smile on her face that he knew lasted for weeks. He still grinned when he thought about it.

There were three other meetings after that, all unplanned, in three different countries, with absolutely no promises made between them.

He'd wanted them, but his pride—and his inherent distrust—had stopped him from pursuing more at that time.

The one promise he'd never break would be to Cam. He would get his friend free, or die trying.

He almost had.

Why'd you do it, Riley? What's so bad you had to shoot me, and not look back?

His ringing phone stopped him from mulling over that question further. He glanced at the call screen, saw it was Zane.

Dylan didn't have too many people he trusted beyond Cam and his brothers. And so, in times like these, when he needed intel from many different sources—and quickly— he turned to his brother Zane for help.

His two younger brothers were as different as night and day.

Caleb—or Cael—the middle one, was serious. Military. *Law-abiding,* as Zane would say with a roll of his eyes, like Caleb had some sort of disease.

He needs a personality transplant, Zane would often comment, although he'd do it out of reach of Cael's hearing.

Caleb had recently been assigned to Cam's Delta Force

team, and Dylan didn't want to get him involved in Cam's life like that.

Getting Zane involved, though, wasn't an issue. His youngest brother was always up for anything, especially a party. Dylan knew that facade let Zane keep his past tamped down—so far, it had worked for his brother. A Navy SEAL with a penchant for black ops, gray ops and any other color in between, Zane always approached Dylan for work when he was on leave. Mainly because Zane tended to get into trouble when he didn't keep busy.

Dylan figured that if Zane was going to get into trouble, at least it would be trouble Dylan would be able to help him out of.

And Zane had gotten damned good at getting places Dylan couldn't, which annoyed the shit out of Dylan and made Zane pretty damned pleased with himself.

Fucking and fighting were all part of the same game for Dylan's youngest brother, and Zane seemed to always have the fucking part outweighing the fighting by a mile.

It was why Zane was able to get more intel on Riley in twenty-four hours than Dylan had been able to get in three years between his CIA contacts and others.

"You weren't looking in the right place," Zane told him now over the phone. "I've got the scratches down my back to prove it."

Dylan put a hand on his head. "Don't want to hear it."

"Why? Rumor has it that you're not getting any of your own."

"Do you have any intel for me?"

"Creighton's gone."

"So I've heard—spies always disappear."

"Not like this. The CIA denies sending him on a mission—they claim he was kidnapped and killed after he resigned. And they never admit shit like that."

Dylan ran his hands through his hair, pushing it off his face. "They never admit it unless that's the story they want us to buy. There's a hell of a lot more to this than that. When the hell did he leave the CIA?"

"Near as I can tell, sometime in the last six months. And I got some early intel on your Riley too," Zane continued. "I hooked up with a girl she went to high school with. You didn't go back far enough."

"And?"

"It's about Riley's family. Apparently, until her dad died, the family was loaded—like, really fucking wealthy. Riley went to private schools, lived in a mansion, the whole deal. And then her dad died and they lost everything. Immediately. Bank accounts were stripped, the house went into foreclosure and Riley's mom took jobs cleaning houses."

"That's odd."

"Yeah. I've got the official death cert on her dad, which claims suicide. Would explain why they didn't get life insurance, but not why their bank accounts were stripped. But there's barely anything on the guy, just that he was a CEO for a major corporation. Except that the company has no record of him ever working there. I checked Riley's birth certificate. Her dad's name was listed, but there were no other records for him past the age of twenty-two, beyond the death cert."

Bells went off in Dylan's head, as he was sure they had in Zane's. "Agent."

"Smells like it to me, but I can't get any further. A few years after Riley's dad died, her mom got really sick. Cancer. She died in a state hospital—a major dump that the state closed down three times for all different reasons, from patient abuse to uncleanliness. It's a place to die, a convalescent home for people who don't have insurance, or money to pay hospital treatment bills. They don't even give pain meds at this place." Zane sounded disgusted. "Riley was eighteen when her mom died."

Dylan leaned his head back against the lounge chair and stared in the direction of the sliding glass doors again. "Are you thinking what I'm thinking?"

"Creighton's got a big reach, brother. You need to be careful," Zane warned before hanging up the phone.

Aʟʟ Cam wanted to do was sleep, with Sky wrapped around him—wanted to feel normal again. But that wouldn't happen . . . at least not tonight.

Before he'd even entered the house, before he'd met Sky, he'd set a perimeter. He'd know if danger was approaching from any angle. Before he'd called Dylan, he'd wired the windows.

If someone was coming, he'd have enough warning to do some damage.

I know who you really are.

He stared out the window and calculated. Planned. Because he couldn't sleep with a woman next to him, couldn't risk waking up in some kind of PTSD-induced dream, holding her down and flashing back to that night five months earlier, on his last mission for Gabriel, when he'd blown everything.

God, that mission had fucked him up—and he hadn't even been the cause of the collateral damage that time. Dylan had forced the truth out of him, and then Cam had buried it deep down. Until tonight—no, until last night, when his freedom flashed before his eyes and threatened to disappear.

When he closed his eyes, he saw the woman who'd tried to kill him, and he saw that cell he'd spent two years in that could become his permanent home again—and both those images made staying awake imperative.

The last mission for Gabriel had been different from the start. A man he knew only by the nickname of Bullet was his target. Bullet was rumored to have affiliations with various terrorist groups, but Cam's initial research didn't turn up much intel. Unfortunately, he couldn't risk a more intense search, because that could trigger attention and put Bullet himself on high alert. He'd known going in that it would be a major risk.

He'd also known that handling this assignment alone was along the lines of a suicide mission.

But there had been an angel on his shoulder, and the intel Gabriel had given him was spot-on about how to get close to his mark.

In order to get close to Bullet, it was necessary for him to get close to Bullet's girlfriend, Mariana.

And he had. He'd been able to meet her easily enough when Bullet was away, going on the knowledge that the woman liked clandestine affairs with American men.

Mariana was predatory. Sexually restless. Ruthless. She

liked to both receive and inflict pain during intercourse, and otherwise.

There was nothing behind her eyes, and that's what worried Cam the most. Behind the charisma, the beauty, there was nothing there. An empty shell, with no conscience, no soul.

He'd almost been afraid it would rub off on him, as if evil could be transferred by touch.

But he knew if that was true, he'd have turned a hell of a long time before.

The bed in her house in Morocco was opulent. Ornate. And in it, he performed a chore that turned his stomach.

Whoever said there was no such thing as bad sex had never been forced to have it under a guillotine.

He fast became an expert at faking orgasms—it had been the only thing that saved him. He'd never have been able to protect himself when he was coming. It was a rare man who could.

"You are so handsome... fuck me harder, my American stud," she'd whisper as her long red nails raked his back.

She liked pain, and for a week he'd given her what she wanted.

At the end of that time, Bullet was due home. And Cam would be ready.

Except... Mariana called him that evening, said that Bullet had been delayed. That they had more time together.

But there had been an anger in her tone, one he'd misjudged.

Bullet had changed his itinerary, probably did so on a regular basis, and normally, waiting him out wouldn't have been a problem. Until Mariana went insane.

Cam had been on the receiving end of a woman wanting vengeance. A woman scorned who'd wanted to screw him while she was screwing him. Because during that last sex session, Mariana had tried to jam a knife into his carotid, and when that hadn't worked, she'd gone for his balls.

He'd bucked her off of him, grabbed the knife. Pushed her away. Suddenly they both pulled a gun.

The slamming open of the bedroom door had surprised them equally. Cam knew Mariana had a son, but he'd never seen any signs that the boy was home, had no way of knowing he'd arrived from boarding school hours earlier.

Until he'd seen the boy holding the machine gun—pointed directly at Mariana. Heard him scream, "You're screwing around on my father, disrespecting him," in Spanish.

Cam had waited for the bullets to hit him, unwilling—hell, maybe even unable—to shoot the boy, or kill his mother in front of him.

When the shot rang out from Mariana's gun—now purposefully aimed at her son—the boy's eyes went wide with surprise and shock, his mouth moving but no sounds coming out.

Cam was pretty sure the boy was trying to say *Momma*.

Cam's only recourse at that point was to save himself from the gun now aimed in his direction.

Two shots—one from him, one from Mariana. Cam wiped his fingerprints down, stepped over the bodies and didn't look back when he'd boarded the flight home. He'd left Morocco with enough blood on his hands to ensure sleeping through the night would most likely never happen again.

He realized now that he'd broken out in a cold sweat, cursed himself for letting himself drift into that space, suspended between wake and sleep, where he could see the entire incident playing out clearly in his mind.

Killing that woman saved people, he told himself, even if the main objective, killing Bullet, had not been accomplished. He had to, or else he'd go crazy. And there were plenty of other things in his mind that could drive him over the edge anyway, like wondering if his father was really still alive.

For years, he'd told himself that Howie had been killed the night Cam was arrested—that was the only way he lived with it all. He'd done what Gabriel had wanted, to stay free of jail... and because Gabriel had promised he'd find out what happened to Howie Moore.

But that intel never surfaced. No leads, no body.

He owed it to himself to find out exactly what happened the night of his arrest.

Gabriel never gave him any information about his father. And after the Morocco mission, hadn't contacted him at all. Cam waited for the retaliation for not staying on and completing his job—the phone call, the circling harbinger of doom in the form of a helo.

For five months, nothing happened. The chip remained in Dylan's safe, even though his friend urged him to destroy it for good. But it was a symbol of his survival. Cam didn't destroy symbols like that.

Sky was a symbol too, of just how far he might need to

go to truly break his connection with Gabriel, to save his own life, all wrapped up in one sleek, scarred package.

Collateral damage. Dead or alive, she was nothing but collateral damage, he tried to tell himself, but he was long past believing it. He'd always known that, if he wasn't careful, he'd be an empty shell when all was said and done. No better than Gabriel himself. And Cam refused to end up that way.

Sky shifted. Murmured his name in her sleep, her naked thigh rubbing his. Her skin was warm, and her leg felt like silk against his.

His hand rested on her hip as his gaze lowered to her scar. He thought about the medicines she had to take—the pain she'd endured.

He'd bonded with her, all right—more effectively than he'd wanted to. He pictured Skylar, tied for his pleasure, not for the mission, and his blood quickened.

She might not be an innocent, but Cam doubted she had anything to do with his own particular brand of hell, delivered by Gabriel. She'd been hurt by her father's career too. In another world, she'd be Cam's kindred spirit.

His hand fisted in his own hair and he almost pulled away from her completely, ready to leave the bed and this place, snowstorm be damned.

He'd traveled in worse.

But he wouldn't run anymore, not from Gabriel and not from anyone.

He was still on the mission, sticking with the plan to leverage Sky—Gabriel wouldn't get off easily.

He thought about Dylan's mantra—one he'd gleaned

from Delta Force—lie, cheat, steal, seduce. Or kill. Whatever it took to get the job done.

He was three for five right now, in less than twelve hours, and he still didn't know his own boundaries, how far he would go.

Just then, Sky reached out sleepily and stroked him, and he relented, stayed, because she needed him.

He needed redemption, whatever path that took. But he needed freedom more.

Sky could possibly be the key to both.

The door opened and Gabriel squinted when the light from the hallway hit his face.

The man at the door was big, and after Gabriel's eyes adjusted, he noted it was the same man who'd waited outside the door when he'd been shoved down in the basement. A man he'd never seen before—the others called him Ben.

Ben was holding something in his hand—a cell phone. He pushed a few buttons and played a message on speaker, one from Gabriel's own phone.

Gabriel didn't flinch when he heard Skylar's voice, low, as if she didn't want to be overheard.

"I'm here with Cameron Moore—he said he knows you, that you sent him here to me. I'm just checking to make sure."

She didn't call him Dad—she never did when she left him messages, and it left an ache in his chest every single time.

Ben asked, "Want us to give your daughter a message?"

Gabriel's voice was rough from underuse, and he forced himself not to jump at the fact that they'd made the connection. *Your daughter.* "Here's a message for you: Go to hell."

The man chuckled. "You're more than halfway there already—save me a spot."

CHAPTER
5

Sky woke in an empty bed, the cold gray light of the morning a most unwelcome intrusion.

Cam's missing presence made the chill worse, despite the fact that she was still burrowed under the covers. Her face burned when she thought about last night, about the way Cam had touched her. The way she'd cried out—over and over.

It had been the kind of sex that stayed with you for days. She still felt him, as though he'd just been inside her. And he had. She recalled him waking her a couple of hours earlier by burying himself in her—she'd encouraged him like she'd been on some kind of wild ride, her orgasm as intense as the ones she'd had earlier.

She hadn't been able to get enough. Then again, neither had he. He'd been relentless, constantly seeking more. Of her. He'd been insatiable last night. More so that morning.

She'd woken because she'd been shivering—even under the covers, with Cam's body nearby. The lack of power and her own core body temperature had proved too much, and her body felt battered by the cold—it had almost been painful.

Cam had been awake, reached out to touch her shoulder.

"Cold," she'd told him.

"Warm," he'd murmured back, pulled her close with ease. In the warm nook of his body, the chill had faded and heat flooded her quickly.

Even now she flushed remembering how his hands had roamed her naked body under the heavy quilt. With her eyes still shut, she'd had little defense. Not that she'd really wanted any. No, her body opened to his touch as his fingers found her core and his mouth brushed a nipple, and it could easily have been a dream.

Except Cam was very real, his cock throbbing against the juncture of her thighs before he'd eased inside of her.

His thighs parted hers, his hand dipping down to guide his thick shaft toward her swollen sex, the way he'd whispered to her that she was still so wet for him and she almost cried at how good all of it was.

She had, a little, now that she thought about it, had buried her face in her pillow after a particularly startling orgasm, as the tears started to slide.

She remembered whispering to him that she didn't want

the night to end. She'd wanted to remain uncensored. Careless. On the edge without rules or ties. But sleep had won out and now she was alone.

She got out of bed, grabbed fresh clothes and showered quickly, before the water heater suffered from the power loss. She turned the water as hot as she could stand it, like if she scrubbed his scent off her skin the desertion would hurt less.

She was really out of the dating game if she couldn't handle a one-night stand. With her bodyguard. Sent by her father.

Sheesh. *Way to go, Skylar.*

She viciously towel-dried her hair. She knew that a wet head didn't get you sick, but with what she was recovering from, why chance it.

She dressed in jeans and a heavy sweatshirt, dragging the sleeves down over her hands for added warmth, and headed to the kitchen.

Cam wasn't there either. Nor was he in the living room. When she glanced out the window, she didn't see any sign of him, or a car he might've arrived in last night. Her own rental was barely visible under the piles of snowy white drifts that had blown around all night.

She tried the lights again, to no avail, cursed this place, which had sworn they had generator backups, and realized she'd forgotten to call yesterday when she'd noticed there was no wood for the fireplace.

Dammit. You'd think she hadn't been taking care of herself all these years. The details were slipping out of her grasp, no matter how tightly she attempted to rein a semblance of control over them.

She grabbed the bottle of OJ from the fridge, grabbed a glass and hopped up on a stool, since she felt the cold tile through her socks. She sorted out the pills she needed and then dutifully replaced the bottles into the bag Cam had insisted she keep packed.

The snow was so high outside the kitchen windowsill, she could only see the sky—or what she assumed was the sky, since it was nearly as white; it appeared that the storm would last longer than expected.

"We're not going anywhere," she mumbled, and then took the pills with juice. The OJ was still cold, since the power had only been out about eight hours. If it lasted much longer, they'd need to buy some ice to keep the food she bought from spoiling.

"Yeah, we are."

She turned at the sound of Cam's voice, wondered how long he'd been standing there. He'd obviously been outside, although she hadn't heard any of the doors—front or back—open. But the cold radiated off him—and his jacket, which he quickly shrugged off, was wet.

His boots squished along the carpet as he walked toward her. "Pack up. It looks a lot worse than it is."

So much for the morning after. "Did you get any sleep?" she asked.

"Don't need it." He grabbed the milk out of the fridge and drained it, without benefit of a glass, and even though that annoyed her more than anything, he managed to look sexy doing it. Like a devil-may-care bad boy wrapped up in one large package.

"Look, I don't want this to be weird," she said, even though it was apparent he wasn't feeling weird at all.

"Okay."

"It's not for you, is it?"

He crossed his arms and leaned against the fridge. "No."

"I guess you do this a lot."

"Sex? Or sleeping with someone I'm protecting?"

"Both," she countered as her cheeks began to burn.

"The first, yes, but not as often as I'd like. The second, once."

How she wanted to believe him. "Really?" she asked, but he'd disappeared. She slid off the stool and headed over to her BlackBerry.

She'd turned it off last night to conserve the power. Now her emails flooded into the device, from her agent, editor, publicist. All checking in.

She also had voice mail messages. Again, publicist, agent. Too many to ignore. But nothing from her father.

She opened one of the older messages from her publicist, Pam, frantically trying to get ahold of her. Because Sky's apartment had been broken into late last night—and her publicist was her emergency contact for the alarm list. "Shit." *Shit, shit shit!*

"What's wrong?"

She couldn't speak, handed the BlackBerry to Cam, who was now right behind her, so he could read the message.

He still had his damned big boots on, yet she hadn't heard him. How he moved so silently was beyond her.

He handed her back the phone, not saying a word.

"Pam's on my alarm-code list for when I'm traveling," she told him. "I need to call or email her, let her know I'm okay."

He didn't respond to that. "Where's your place?"

"Manhattan. Upper East Side." She rattled off her address.

"Who has access to your apartment?"

"Besides the super, Pam and my father? No one. I have no reason to give my keys to anyone—no pets, boyfriends or plants, because I end up killing them. The plants, not the boyfriends," she clarified. "I don't like it that someone was inside my place, touching my things."

"I'm less concerned about the touching than I am about what they might've found."

That snapped her to immediate attention. "The address of this place. Shit. I saved the confirmation to add to my receipt for my accountant—a working vacation for a tax write-off."

She cursed herself some more for being so stupid, for not having better locks, for not living in a more secure building.

She'd never wanted to live in a fortresslike environment resembling the one she'd grown up in, both before and after her mom died. Although right now, impenetrable sounded like a good idea.

"Pack up. Now." He put her .38 Special next to her on the table. "It's loaded. Safety's on. Keep it with you all the time."

"Okay. Thanks." She stared at him for a brief second, trying to find the man who'd held her last night. But he was gone, replaced by warrior in mission mode. Impenetrable.

She grabbed the gun and headed for the bedroom. Her phone was in her other hand, and when it began to vibrate, she looked down and saw the familiar name: *Olivia.*

As an intern, Dr. Olivia Strohm had assisted in the removal of Sky's first kidney, and then had performed the recent transplant. And she was constantly checking up on her, making sure she made all her appointments. The woman was a force of nature and she refused to be ignored by patients who didn't reply to messages.

She tried to keep her tone light as she answered. "Hey, Liv, how are you?"

"You haven't answered any of my texts." Olivia herself sounded slightly out of breath, which meant that she was no doubt moving through the halls of the hospital at top speed. She had no other speed.

"Sorry—I've been working."

"You know, you might be a great liar to others. But never to me."

"I'm okay. Trust me," Sky lied. "And before you ask, yes, I've been taking all my meds and eating right."

The doctor was thirty-three, seven years older than she had been when Sky had her first kidney failure. The women had gotten close—as close as one could get to the doctor, Sky supposed, because the woman worked twenty-four seven, and Sky could appreciate why. It was Liv's tenacity that kept Sky alive, and her generous nature and wide smile that kept Sky from spiraling into depression when she was most lonely. Olivia came at her patients full-force, nursing them back to health with an urgency that made them feel well cared for.

"I hope you're at least trying to have a life," her friend teased, and Sky thought about last night and was glad she didn't have to face Olivia right now.

Liv always prodded her to get out there, have some fun.

Sky would remind her that she worked too hard to have any fun of her own either, but Liv would shrug and say there would be plenty of time for that later.

Sky wanted to tell her friend not to waste any time, that it was all so damned precious, but Liv knew that as well as Sky did. And so Sky just told her, "I'm trying. I'll check in soon, and if not, I'll see you next week for sure."

"You bet you will—you can't miss that appointment. Speaking of which, your dad missed his last checkup. I'm assuming he's feeling all right?"

"He's feeling great," Sky lied. "Talk soon, okay?"

With that, Liv hung up the phone and Sky did the same. She began to pack without really noticing what she was doing, her mind once again focused on her father.

They'd had private nurses watching out for both of them for the first few weeks post-surgery, although her dad insisted on doing a lot of the work for Skylar himself. He cooked for her, kept track of her meds. Talked with her about her books and played Trivial Pursuit and Scrabble with her.

He grumbled that she won every game, even when he tried to cheat. Somehow, he could never get one past her.

She'd missed all of that time together doing regular things—hadn't realized how much until her father had sprawled across the bottom of her bed, playing Wii... and laughing.

But then there were times during the recovery she'd find him alone, looking pensive. Planning mode, for sure, especially during that second month. She'd seen it too many times not to recognize it.

It was because of the time spent together that her hatred

of competing with his job was brought into sharp relief. She knew what she'd missed.

It was also why she didn't trust that she could have happiness for the long term. No, happiness was only for short bursts, moments in time she clung to during the long stretches when the loneliness was palpable, when she literally threw herself into her work and didn't look up for days on end.

"No matter what, Skylar, this is the best thing I've ever done, second only to having you in the first place," he'd told her.

The next morning, he'd been gone. Left a letter for her, a simple note that reminded her to eat well, take her pills, stay in touch.

I'll be there whenever you need me.

But this time, he wasn't.

Cam, however, was. And with that thought to comfort her, she began to pack.

The next morning, Dylan was still outside, by the pool.

Did the man not have a hotel room of his own? Had he seriously spent the night here? It didn't bode well for Riley, meant that he would no doubt remain until he got what he was looking for.

Riley should've kicked him out last night when she'd had the chance, but she hadn't been able to, and the whole bodily harm thing—well, been there, done that, and his hard body was very . . . hard.

She'd always melted when she was around this man. Even before she'd actually met him and had only seen him from afar, she'd managed to screw up the car bomb she'd planted, which was supposed to take him out. That was three years earlier, in Bogotá, and all because she kept picturing him while she was wiring his car.

Id-i-ot.

So yes, she'd known Dylan Scott aka Deacon Sanders could be a potential weakness from the beginning, having ended up in his bed that same night, and had confirmed it a few months later.

Two and a half years earlier—Rio de Janeiro.

She'd finished up a job, guarding a government official and preventing a planned assassination attempt. A fairly easy job—she'd been well paid...and as a bonus, Dylan Scott was in town.

She'd told herself that wasn't the reason she took the job, even though she'd known he was on an extended mission in the area, because he'd finally called her and they'd made plans to meet earlier.

"Hey, it's me," she told him now when he answered. "I finished early—thought I'd meet you at the hotel."

"Then you should hurry," he told her, his voice tinged with an impatience that made her smile.

"I'm a block away," she told him, and then the explosion sounded in her ear and shook the street at the same time. She took off at a dead run, her heart plummeting.

When she arrived on the scene, she saw that the hotel she'd been headed toward—the one Dylan was staying in—was no more than a shell. Fire ripped through what was left of the structure, the steel beams exposed and folding under the intense heat.

Now the policía *were holding her.*

"Did you see... Where are the people?" She was aware she was yelling, half English, half Portuguese—the only way to be heard among the screams and sirens and other noises filling the disaster scene.

The *polícia who* held her shook his head, said roughly, "Não sobreviventes!"

No survivors.

She yanked away from the officer and he let her go, believing she wouldn't launch herself in the direction of the building.

"Desculpa, *lady,"* he told her.

She was sorry too, stumbled away from the scene, her lungs burning from being so close to the burning building.

The only thing she could do was walk back to her own hotel in a numb fog of grief. Took the elevator, let herself into her room...

Found Dylan Scott sitting on her bed.

"Jesus... Dylan," she whispered, shut and locked the door behind her and made her way quickly toward him. "Was the bomb meant for you?"

He laughed, an oddly hollow sound, accentuated by the hoarseness of his voice. It was then she noticed that he'd definitely been near the building when it blew, that it most likely had been a very close call for him. There was soot on his face and clothes—a larage scrape on his neck and another on his arm.

She pushed the hair out of his eyes as he spoke. *"My mission's complete. They needed to think I was dead."*

"And you couldn't have warned me?" she demanded.

He took the phone from her hand and opened the back, pointed to the bug that had been placed there.

Dammit. Dammit to hell.

She'd learn quickly that this wasn't the first instance of him dying—and that it wouldn't be the last. But her reaction had been so completely visceral that it frightened her.

She'd been with him only once before. And even though she didn't want to get attached, she couldn't deny that she already was.

"I wasn't sure you'd care," he admitted.

"I don't." Of course, her retort was basically negated by the fact that she was already grabbing the back of his neck, her words nearly lost as she kissed him, a long breathless kiss intended to make him forget about anyone but her and ensuring that she'd lost her heart to him again.

But as her clothes piled up on the tumbled marble floor at her feet, she wondered why she hadn't tried to find Dylan Scott again sooner.

Liar.

Because she had tried. He was simply too good. But she would find a way to breach his walls, break down his all-too secure defenses.

Because it was all about the game.

Because it was only about being in his arms.

Now she forced herself to push out the doors and to the pool, to confront her past and her present. That was the only way to ensure he was not a part of her future.

Riley finally joined him by the pool. Good thing the cabana had all the amenities of a regular bathroom—and extra towels. Around five that morning, Dylan had showered and changed back into his clothes, prepared to . . . well, wait.

Sometime after seven, his stomach was badly protesting the lack of food and he was cursing himself for attempting to wait out a woman. And then the sliding glass doors finally opened and she stepped out into the sun, her skin darker than honey, wearing a small red bikini that most definitely caught his attention.

Dylan knew she was closer to acquiescing than even she did.

She dove into the water and swam several precision-perfect laps before stopping and pulling herself out of the pool without the benefit of a ladder.

He met her halfway to the bar, handing her an opened water with lime, which she took from him, drinking a long pull. And then she asked, "Don't you have any friends you can stay with?"

"No."

"We're in the land of beach bunny blondes. I'm sure you can find one that suits your needs."

She was in his arms before she could blink, her damp skin pressing against him. "I've never liked blondes."

She cocked an eyebrow at him.

"I haven't liked blondes since I met you," he corrected, his hand sliding over her ass and the teeny tiny bikini bottoms.

"You're checking me for weapons," she murmured.

"Always, Riley."

"I'm clean."

He snorted and kept her close. "Whatever you're into . . ."

"Is none of your concern."

"Whatever it is was important enough to shoot me over."

"Don't flatter yourself. I would've shot anyone that day, not just you."

That made Dylan's stomach clench, even though he didn't really believe her. She'd never been a good liar when it came to him, although the night of the shooting she'd come really damned close. "You had a file of intel on Gabriel Creighton the day you shot me. Now Creighton's disappeared. I want to know why."

Riley's expression remained unchanged and he had to force himself to remember that he was dealing with a skilled, trained, and deadly operative with no loyalty to him.

He was battling someone like himself. With major personal demons she refused to share.

He'd use those demons, parade them in front of her. Break her down. Make her vulnerable and use that to get the intel he needed. It wasn't easy to hit Riley where she was weak, but it was necessary to get her to spill what she knew.

"Why would you come to me?" Her voice was soft, forcing him to lean in close, unable to ignore the unrelenting heat that shot through him.

"I'm still trying to figure that one out myself, Riley. Why don't you tell me?"

The emails had gotten more detailed, desperate. Skylar's publicist had been trying to force her client to respond.

Your apartment's been broken into. I know who you really are was spray-painted on the wall. The police have been notified and they're investigating. Please get in touch . . .

The message burned on his brain. This was getting worse by the second. And as much as Cam wanted it to be the work of some crazy fan of Sky's, his gut told him it wasn't.

What the hell had he walked into?

The police would be useless in this case if, in fact, Gabriel's enemies were after Sky. Cam had been dealing with that type for the better part of his adult life, and for some of his teen years. There wasn't all that much difference between spies and criminals. You couldn't trust either group, but you could gain their respect by just being labeled either-or.

None of the men on Cam's team knew about his past. He kept a tight lid on that info, and on his emotions, and he encouraged the men under his lead to do the same. He knew that if he needed them, those guys would come and help, no questions asked, no favors needed in return.

But to involve them in this didn't sit well with him. Bad enough to have Dylan helping, even though he was already part of that world.

Bad enough that Cam had come here at all.

Focus.

He scanned the front windows. Nothing. And still, unease settled over him like a fine mist.

He'd already been outside that morning—no footprints and no tire tracks near the house, or on the roadways. The main road had been plowed at one point during the night, but several more inches covered it, and everything had been pristine and quiet for a while. And then, finally, Cam heard the familiar rattle of a plow.

He glanced out the window—it was an SUV with a

plow attached, black truck, clearing the road in front of this townhouse. Which was good.

They had to get the hell out of there, and fast. Cam had never liked or trusted *too quiet*. That's when the real trouble always started.

He was preparing for trouble, in mission mode. And when he went into mission mode, he tended to bark orders. His men might not have appreciated that, but they listened.

Sky listened, had taken the gun with her, but she wasn't happy. Mainly because this wasn't anyone's idea of the perfect morning after.

That didn't matter. Getting Sky to safety was top priority right now.

I guess that means she's safe with you.

She was safe from whomever was after her. But she was still his leverage—that hadn't changed. It couldn't. His life depended on it.

He tried not to think about her, the way she'd whispered his name, again and again. The way she'd fit against him. Hugged him in her sleep.

He was getting soft. And hard. All at the same time.

He opened the fridge and drank the orange juice straight out of the bottle, wiped his mouth on the back of his hand and froze. The perimeter alarm was a silent one, set to vibrate, which it was now doing against his chest.

In his periphery, he noted that the snowplow truck had stopped and was parked across the narrow road, its driver nowhere in sight.

At least not yet. But his skin crawled, because, fuck, they were close. Way too close.

Forcing himself not to turn around right away, he

moved as if to put the container back. His chest tightened as he fought the burst of adrenaline, forcing himself to wait until the precise moment he'd need to unleash it. Which would be in three, two, one . . .

He whirled around fast, his arm winding to smash the nearly emptied bottle against the skull of a man as tall as he, with enough force to break both the bottle and the man's skull.

For the next moments, he was pure reaction. He slammed the arm holding the gun, as the guy's head jerked to the side from the force of the original blow, noting a second man standing in the background. A shot went off, into the ceiling, muffled by the silencer, and yeah, these guys were pros. Hired killers. That type typically fought methodically—and dirty.

They would be no match for him. Cam's fury was white hot and instant—he never liked people fucking with him, surprises even less. He didn't waste any more time, held the unconscious man in front of him like a shield as the second guy aimed and fired his way.

One shot grazed off Cam's shoulder, and he turned his body so his back was to the unconscious man's. The next shot went through the first man, catching Cam square in the shoulder and not exiting, and fuck, that was going to hurt like a mother in a little while. But it was still better than getting hit in the chest.

He grabbed the gun from the first man's hand and fired back, hitting the second man before he had a chance to take cover.

The guy was down, but not out. The unconscious man's

gun decided to jam at that moment, and before Cam could grab his own, the second guy was up and over the counter.

Cam dropped his human shield and found himself on the receiving end of a kick to the face. Half-stunned, he hit the fridge and used the momentum to slam forward, taking the kicker to the ground, both of them grunting.

As they went down, he jerked the other guy's knee out from under him, and the two of them went rolling across the hard tiled floor. Cam grabbed the guy's fist, the one that held the weapon, and twisted his arm, which broke with a satisfying snap. The man howled and a mix of sweat, blood and surprise filled the air. The fight wasn't equal now—in truth, hadn't been even when it had been two against one.

Cam put his arm across the guy's throat. With one last-ditch effort, the man brought a small knife up and managed to slice Cam on his chest, before Cam crushed his windpipe.

The man's head lolled to the side and Cam eased off him, surveying the scene in the once pristine living room and kitchen.

Now, not so much. Still, two attackers, two down.

Except he heard Sky's voice and she was talking—not yelling, talking.

There had been three men—and that was one too many.

W*hy would you come to me, Dylan?*

Why don't you tell me?

"Nothing to tell," she managed. Not true, of course. There was so much Riley wanted to say, let it tumble out between them on this hot Florida morning, but common sense and training kept her mouth shut. "What hotel are you staying at?"

"I'm not staying at a hotel. And you owe me some answers." His grip got tighter...and her body continued to respond to his.

"Just because I screwed up doesn't mean we're going to play twenty questions." She closed her eyes briefly, until the picture of Dylan lying on the floor of the storage unit forced them back open.

"Sure we are. But first things first." He leaned in. "My friend's life is on the line. Because of Gabriel Creighton."

"Lots of people have grudges against spies—and vice versa."

"Including you?"

"What happened to your friend?"

"Gabriel's been screwing him royally for years. And my friend, he's not a spy. He wants nothing more than to get away from Gabriel."

Her stomach dropped. She knew what Gabriel was capable of. "That's your friend's problem, not mine," she lied.

Dylan shook her a little, held her closer. "Do you know where Gabriel is?"

"No."

"When was the last time you had direct contact with him?"

"Never. I've never met him." Her stomach clenched as she thought about what she wanted to do if she ever did come face-to-face with him. "If I had, he'd be dead right now."

"But he's not."

"Last I heard, which was yesterday, no."

Dylan looked surprised at her answer—maybe that she'd admit anything. She wanted to ask him for help, but then he'd be in as much trouble as she was. She couldn't do that to him. "Please go now. Please. There's nothing more I can give you."

He shook his head slowly with mock regret. "I know who you really are, Riley. It took some digging—you've really been wiped off the map."

She was. Her past was buried so deep, only the most skilled could find it, and only with hours of manpower. She'd had so many different names and identities, she'd nearly forgotten herself, forgotten the once happy, normal girl who didn't know guns and spies and what it was like to run in a world where you couldn't trust anyone with anything, especially your life.

And Dylan was telling her he knew everything. To admit it, let it pour out of her would be a relief—and a fast way to jail for turning in a CIA agent to a group like DMH.

Beyond that, she'd be a hunted woman. "You're not going to get what you want from me."

He traced her jaw with a pinky, his other hand on the small of her back, pulling her closer. "I already have. And I'm going to want it again and again."

She would too. Her body would admit it first—whether or not her mind would follow remained to be seen.

He was staring at her, all deep-eyed, like he knew what she'd been thinking. "You're pissed that you have feelings for me," he told her, then bent his head and gave her an intense kiss, sweeping the air from her lungs when he did. She pushed at him, but he held her in place against him, even as he slowly backed her up against the small cabana at poolside.

"You're going to learn your lesson," he said when he pulled away, his voice husky. "I'm going to show you what I'm capable of, and for once, you're going to sit back and shut up and just fucking learn something. Something real."

Yes, real, because nothing could be more real than the weight of his body on hers, the pressure of his mouth, insistent and hot against hers again. It didn't matter that it was broad daylight, that she'd thought her defenses would be stronger if she let the night pass.

She simply thanked God she had a private backyard, because she was sure her neighbors would never get over this.

Her hands threaded in his thick hair, tugging, holding, her body responding with an urgency that frightened and thrilled her at once.

"Put your hands above your head," he instructed, and she did it, without hesitating. He circled both her wrists easily with one large hand, let the other trail up her bare inner thigh, until he reached the thin slip of fabric that covered her. He caressed between her legs for a brief second and then slid his hand inside her bottoms.

His fingers—oh, his fingers began their slow, lazy exploration. Her hips rocked toward him, and stopping wasn't an option now—she convinced herself that his grip made her too vulnerable and decided she had no choice but to go along with him.

But vulnerability had never been her strong suit. "I'm not your girl."

He grinned at that and then tore her top away as if it

were paper. Before she could complain or protest, his finger trailed her already wet sex, his eyes wicked. "You're whatever the hell I want right now, Ri."

She might hate herself later. But now there was nothing but licks of pleasure as he took her with his hand, his eyes never leaving hers.

"Feel good?" he asked.

"I thought . . . you wanted me . . . to shut up." The words were punctuated by moans, and he smiled, a lopsided grin, his eyelids heavy.

His voice was thick when he spoke. "I want you to scream my name. Long and loud. And I want you to come harder than you've ever come in your life. That's what I want."

She'd never been more conflicted, but the decision to let Dylan have his way, that was easy. So easy—too easy—and as the first orgasm hit and her knees went weak, she lost any resolve to keep him out of her life.

Sky heard a thud and the shattering of glass from the kitchen, had almost peeked out to see if Cam just dropped something when she heard the muffled shot.

She'd been in the bathroom grabbing her toiletries, and she quickly closed the door and locked it. Then she crouched down inside the large tub, gun level to the porcelain ledge, barrel aimed at the door. She heard sounds of struggle through the thin walls of the townhouse and fought to keep her breathing even, to not let panic wash over her.

She wasn't prepared for this, wasn't in shape physically or mentally.

Her parents had lived it—and she'd trained at ages fifteen and sixteen and even seventeen, after her mom died and before she'd gotten sick, as if she could follow in their footsteps.

Now she only wrote about it, but still, her body reacted to the imminent threat with an adrenaline rush that had her moving.

Bathroom. Tub. Hide. Gun.

Normally, she'd have gone to a window or a door, would've run for help.

Doing so in waist-high snow wouldn't get her far, though. She had Cam—and a gun in her hand pointed at the door for anyone who got past him.

God, she prayed no one would get past him. Killing on paper was one thing...

You'll be saving your life. Remember that. A father's stern warning, not looking fatherlike at all in a black leather jacket and a scruffy beard that she assumed was part of his cover at the time, and showing her how to lock and load several different guns, from an M16 to a Sig Sauer to the .38 Special—the one that, on that day, her father deemed fit her the best.

"This was your mother's favorite as well," he'd said. It had been one of the rare times he'd mentioned her mother since her death and Sky had smiled.

He hadn't.

From then, it had been self-defense moves, well beyond the normal chop, block and run.

She tried to recall those moves now, but her mind was blank with sudden fear.

You're too weak.

It will come back to you when it's necessary.

She closed her eyes for a second and channeled her father, teaching her all those self-defense moves when she was younger. Telling her that being mentally ready was more important than anything.

She remained still, like an animal being hunted. For a few minutes, she heard nothing...and then more shots. Then she saw the doorknob rattle, the locked door given a hard jerk, and her adrenaline surged, even as she fought to remain still and steady.

Sky said a quick, silent prayer that Cam was still alive, that he was the one coming through the door by kicking it open, shattering it off its hinges and making short work of the flimsy lock.

Her stomach dropped. The man wasn't Cam. He was tall and lanky, dressed in black, his face all sharp angles under his dark hair. And his eyes—dark, piercing...mean. His gun was aimed straight at her, but only for a second, and then he lowered it and smiled.

Smiled. The man had broken into the bathroom with a gun and now he was smiling. She glanced quickly to make sure her own weapon was actually visible and pointing at him.

It was. And she wondered if she could do it, if she could kill him. She wondered why he wasn't trying to do the same, until he spoke.

"Don't be scared, Skylar. I'm here because your father's in trouble."

Her father. She hadn't heard this much about the man from total strangers in twenty-something years, and now twice in less than twenty-four hours.

"Who are you? How did you get in here?" she demanded, avoiding mentioning Cam in case he'd pulled one of his disappearing acts and the man hadn't seen him. Although judging by the earlier gunshots, that was a false hope.

The man continued to smile, kept his voice comforting and low. "Sky, your father needs your help. He wants you to come with me. I'm a friend of his. We work together. Please, we don't have the time for this." He held out a hand to her but she shook her head.

"Tell me where he is."

"I can do better, I can take you right to him. Get you out of danger. It's important that you follow his directions. You know that."

Was it true? Her instincts screamed *no,* and her mother's words echoed in her head.

Instincts, baby girl, her mother's voice whispered, fierce and clear as day in her ear. *Go with your gut instinct, it's always right.*

Still, if this man knew where her father was, killing him wouldn't help anything. "Put your gun down. I want you to call him; I need to speak with my father before I go anywhere with you."

He nodded, as though that was the most reasonable request, reached into his pocket with one hand but he didn't put down his weapon. She kept her finger on the trigger of her own gun as he pulled out a cell phone and began to dial it, and then he nodded and took two steps to her, holding the phone out.

She hesitated before reaching out to grab it...and saw two hands come up from behind him.

A palm went on either side of the man's head and twisted, and she heard a snap. The man's eyes went wide with surprise and then they simply stared out at her vacantly, before his body pitched forward onto the tiled floor. The cell phone he'd been holding scuttered along the slick marble, hitting a wall before stopping.

Cam stood where the man had been, breathing hard, blood staining his shirt. Very much alive. He stepped over the dead man, was calling to her, but all she heard was a rushing sound in her ears.

When he got close, he put his hand on hers, but he didn't take the gun from her. Instead, he knelt by the tub and just said her name, quietly. A few times, until she finally focused. And then, "It's okay, Sky—but we can't stay here."

"Why did you do that?" she asked him, aware that she sounded out of breath, even though she hadn't moved.

He cocked his head to the side and stared at her like she'd gone crazy. "He was going to kill you. Did you want me to make small talk?"

"He said he would take me to my father."

"He was lying," Cam said flatly.

She stood then, pointed the gun at him while he remained crouched on the floor in front of her. "What are the chances that my father sent that man—and you—to get me in the space of twenty-four hours?"

Cam remained unimpressed by the gun, and moved toward the dead man and began to rifle through his clothing. He patted down the guy's chest, found nothing in or under his shirt. Then he fished inside the man's pants pockets, pulled out handcuffs, and syringes that were pre-drawn.

Cam held them out to her, and she saw that they were labeled as morphine.

"The only thing this guy was going to do was take you out of here—and then who knows what else would happen from there."

She stared at the paraphernalia in his hands but still didn't lower her weapon. "This doesn't make sense. None of this makes sense."

"Until it does, we're gone." The words were a command, for sure. No more gentle talk.

"The phone—he was calling my father. Said I could talk to him." She pointed to the silver cell, still opened on the floor. And then she backed up, reached down and grabbed it. A quick glance at the screen showed that it was password protected—and that the battery was nearly drained. "I want to talk to my father. You have to get in touch with him. This guy said he would bring me to him."

Ignoring the weapon pointed at him, Cam strode over to her, closing the distance with two steps. He still held the plastic bag full of needles and the handcuffs as he stood with the barrel of her gun pressed firmly against the middle of his chest.

When he spoke, his voice was low and held the edge of a barely couched fury. "Did you tell them who you are? Did you tell them you're Gabriel's daughter?"

"I didn't . . . I asked if he was okay."

"You know you're never supposed to admit to the connection."

She nodded in agreement.

He grabbed her by the shoulders, hard, unexpectedly, surprising her. "Then why the hell did you?"

CHAPTER
6

Riley winced when Dylan pressed her back against the cabana. Immediately, he stopped what he was doing and turned her.

Her skin bore a large, purple-and-black bruise that ran along her entire left side, which made him bare his teeth viciously. It had been hidden by her arm when she'd walked out here and he had a feeling she'd forgotten about it until now.

Something—or someone—had hit her. Hard. "Ribs?"

"It's nothing. Job hazard," she said as she wiggled out of his grasp, with him somehow ending up with his back against the cabana. "And you know you'd say the same thing to me."

It's true, he would. But he still felt the urge to kill who-ever did this to her. An urge that was quickly replaced with others when Riley's hand stripped him of his low slung pants, leaving him naked in the morning heat.

"You've always been protective," she murmured. "You don't care that it came back to bite you when I shot you?"

He gripped her shoulders tight so she couldn't get down on her knees, even though he wanted her there so badly he could taste it. "You'd better watch out when you're talking about biting, Ri."

She smiled . . . always looked so damned pretty when she did that, more so now, with her hair tumbled down around her shoulders and her bikini barely still on her body. "Let me, Dylan. I promise, you'll like it. You always do."

He groaned against his will and let her sink down on her knees to the grass. In seconds, he was on the receiving end of the best blow job ever.

Her tongue played along the head of his cock as she stroked him. He had nothing to hold on to, could only lean against the cabana and fist his hands, because he wanted to touch her, even as she urged him to spread his thighs so she could cup his balls. Play with them until he realized it had been too long for him.

The truth was, it hadn't been that long—but when it wasn't Riley, it never seemed right. Always felt like he was cheating on her, although they were in no way committed to each other. Especially after their last meeting.

Riley was humming around his cock—the vibrations made him laugh and moan at the same time, guttural sounds that probably did wake up the neighbors.

He was too far gone to give a shit. And as hard as it was

not to orgasm right then and there, he didn't, managed to free himself and pick her up, bringing her over to one of the big lounge chairs with the nice comfortable cushions.

"Missed you," he murmured against her breasts, the way he'd wanted to when he first saw her yesterday. Untied her bikini top, tugged at her nipple with his teeth and listened to her swallow a moan, her body straining into his, her hands between them, guiding his aching arousal inside her.

For a split second, they both stilled when he entered her fully, as though the understanding of the symbolism of being locked together wasn't lost on either of them.

"I'm still waiting for your apology, Ri," he told her, his body taut like a wire that had been pulled far too tight for comfort. Something hard and uncomfortable balled up inside his chest as he waited for her response.

When none came, he began to move, pumping her with a rush of power. Of heat.

She clamped her ankles around his waist, her cries breaking through the quiet morning. She was disoriented. Ravaged. And when she whispered his name like a prayer right before she came, he took that as the apology he'd been seeking.

Sky didn't say anything, didn't have to. The fear was evident in her eyes, even as she held the gun against him, the metal barrel pressing his chest.

He tried to keep his voice calm, but the anger came through. "You're never supposed to tell anyone who your father is, Sky. Never."

"I know. But he mentioned him first."

"Did he give you any identifying information? Anything? Or did you willingly give intel to a man who wanted to kidnap you?" he growled. "You need to be smarter if you want to survive this."

She nodded. Bit her bottom lip to stop it from trembling, but she didn't cry.

He'd scared her and it had been exactly what she needed—and the last thing he'd wanted to have to do.

This was crazy. With Gabriel missing in action—if he was truly kidnapped, or dead—it ultimately meant Cam's freedom. There would be no reason to stay with Sky. He could walk out of this house, leaving her, and this life, behind for good.

The only thing that could keep him from doing so was loyalty. But he'd never had that with Gabriel. Only fear and debt, and if Gabriel was truly gone, that would all be erased.

If...

So much depended on one fucking little word. Because this could all be a giant test.

If Gabriel was alive, Cam had the ultimate bargaining chip in his possession. Could be a win-win situation, either way.

He stared down at Skylar, who wisely hadn't struggled against his grip, and released her. "You shouldn't trust anyone. Not even me." He took the cell phone from her hand, but left her with the weapon.

"I have to trust you. You're the only thing keeping me alive." She raised her chin defiantly, her voice shook slightly... and he wished to hell he hadn't slept with her, hadn't held her against him and let her take a piece of his heart, when he hadn't thought he had anything left to give to anyone.

Before she could say anything more, he'd hoisted the dead man's body over his shoulder and walked out of the bathroom and down the hall.

I have to trust you. You're the only thing keeping me alive.

For the moment, Sky was absolutely correct. And as he carried the body out the back door and down the deep snow on the steps, trying not to kill himself, his mind worked overtime.

These guys must've been close. Waiting all night for just the right moment.

He and Skylar could have been watched the entire time Cam had been holding her, fucking her—making love to her—and his internal radar hadn't signaled a damned thing.

Because the danger wasn't pointed at you.

Until the men burst in, he'd been cautiously hoping the letters to her publisher were the bullshit ravings of an obsessed fan, that Gabriel was pulling some spy crap with his disappearance.

Now he knew differently.

He didn't doubt that Gabriel was in some kind of trouble—didn't doubt that, suddenly, too many people knew Sky was his daughter.

And Cam already knew something about these men— they were hired guns, muscle, prepared for an easy smash and grab of Sky. And they weren't sent here to rescue Sky from him.

No, the one thing Cam knew for sure was that Gabriel Creighton would trust no one but himself with the job of keeping Sky safe, if at all possible. And the Gabriel he knew would make it possible.

Who the hell these men *did* work for was anyone's guess. And he didn't have time for guessing games. And that's where thinking stopped and rote training kicked in, driving him to action.

He dumped the first body in the woods beyond the house. Then he did the same to the other two. If he buried them deep enough, it would be well past spring thaw before they were found.

He and Sky wouldn't have the same luck staying invisible. Not if he didn't act fast.

He moved cautiously toward the front of the house—even though as of last night the houses on either side of Sky were empty—scanned the area and found the truck with the plow they'd driven. He'd already fished the keys out of one of the men's pockets, and now he slid into the driver's seat. It was still warm.

He took down the plate number, dusted for fingerprints, and scanned those he lifted thanks to a nifty gadget, courtesy of Delta. Then he emailed the intel to Dylan, because talking to his friend now could only make things worse.

The truck was most likely stolen, and so he parked it a few houses down, by the woods and away from the bodies. He let the air out of the tires, made it look like it had been abandoned while someone went for help. Naturally, it would trigger a few alarms and maybe even bring the police around, but they'd have to hunt pretty deep to find the bodies. More than likely, these guys had popped the truck from a local, who would be only too happy to have it back.

Of course, men with gunshot wounds thrown in the woods would show it was no accident, but he didn't have time or choice on his side.

By then, he and Sky would be long gone.

His shoulder ached by the time he was done. He'd worked through the pain like a machine. He'd functioned with worse wounds, although he typically had a brother in arms to take care of him.

This time, he only had Sky, and she remained scared and unsure of everything. Still, she'd packed and was waiting for him when he walked back, and that was something.

It was hot and dark and impenetrable, but Gabriel had been in this position before, many times, and he couldn't doubt his ability to get out of it. Not this time, not ever.

Doubting oneself was the first step to failing. Instead, he listened carefully, for the footsteps he knew would eventually come, an update on his status.

They would talk about Skylar again. And again, he would refuse to listen, believe or acknowledge that she was in danger. To let on was to admit weakness. He would not do that to his daughter, would not fail her.

Gabe Creighton grew up on Mercy Street, a place where he'd never found any. He'd escaped from a brutal existence as quickly as possible, using his smarts to get first a high school and then a college scholarship. From there, law school and then recruitment by the CIA.

It was exactly what he'd wanted.

The way he'd existed for the past four days? Not at all. Lying on his back, on the floor of a basement that doubled as a cement cell, he had nothing but time on his hands. Time to think.

The worst thing to happen to a CIA agent. Normally, in a situation like this, he would do something more productive, like recite Shakespeare sonnets or the multiplication tables. Anything not to go stir-crazy. To keep his mind alert so their plan to break him would fail.

But not today. No, today was best spent in the past.

A day to learn from mistakes, because he could never be sorry enough for what had happened.

There was no atoning. He'd never felt the need to do so before Mary's death. Her murder.

All the same, in his book.

Strings of endless deals, either ending in sex or death, and he was still in the game, long after his colleagues were picked off. Burned out. Quit.

He'd thrived when he was undercover with the OA. Had chosen the name Sinister. That had been one of his favorites, although he'd felt like scum for two years, had done things in the name of the job that would've collapsed lesser men.

It had only served to make him train harder. And he would've gone on happily from one job to another, had planned to...

But he'd lost his mind when Mary was killed. He'd been lucky that Dead Man's Hand hadn't made the connection to him or to Skylar, lucky that Mary had been very careful in all her missions.

She'd never seen the assassination coming. Whether DMH had gotten a tip about her as a CIA agent or just suspected, he wasn't interested in knowing. The end result was the same—DMH had killed her, and as a result he'd been trying to get close to the group for years. But his supervisors kept him off the case, told him it was far too personal a mission for him to undertake. That he was needed elsewhere.

He'd tried telling himself that he had something more important at home. That DMH played far too dirty. That he'd sidestepped a bomb when DMH hadn't realized Mary had a daughter—or a spy for a husband.

Fate would not be that kind twice.

He made it his mission to learn everything he could about DMH, to work in tandem with the CIA, using his own man to do the jobs the CIA agents couldn't—or wouldn't. The plan had cemented itself in his mind, and Cameron Moore had been a big part of it from the start. He knew the boy had smarts, was tough, and figured after two years in jail he would be ready to sell his soul in order to get out.

But Gabriel had given Cam a lot of tools to better himself. He'd given the boy a career. And in return, he'd expected payback.

Gabriel was busy with his undercover missions, but not too busy to keep up with the chatter on DMH. Over the years, Cameron Moore had worked to take out two key players in DMH, as well as thwart many DMH missions.

It had worked well, kept him out of DMH's way, even though he'd wanted nothing more than to be within their reach.

Ultimately, it wasn't enough. And so, after Sky's transplant, Gabriel resigned from the CIA, put safeguards in place to have the men and women who'd worked for him killed if he was captured, or missed a check-in. Which now he had.

And he'd infiltrated. Had been prepared to blow DMH off the map, if it took the rest of his natural born life.

He'd never thought DMH would find Sky, hadn't realized that the kidney transplant donor list would be public information. Or even semi-public. Hospitals obviously had no clue about proper security for their files.

Of course, DMH would never have discovered that he even had a daughter if he hadn't been betrayed by someone as a CIA agent.

Well, he'd work with what he had.

He'd gone back into the fire much too soon. The timing had been perfect, but thanks to the surgery, his mind and skill set had not.

And now... and now he remained, waiting to see if DMH would make good on their promise to kidnap Skylar.

She was the only thing keeping him glued to the spot.

The only thing he knew for sure, thanks to his daughter's phone call, was that the safeguards he'd put in place in case of capture or kill hadn't worked on Cameron. And so, with Sky in Cam's hands, Gabriel had to figure out a way for himself, if there was one.

His enemies knew who Sky was.

His daughter was with a man who hated Gabriel's guts.

But Cameron Moore was nothing like him. Cam was honorable.

If anything, Gabriel was sure Sky could *keep* Cam honorable.

The old saying *You can't go home again* was true. Elijah glanced around the old house that had once been the center of his entire world and felt the pervasive smell of old failures and dead dreams as surely as if he was sixteen again and everything he'd held true was falling apart.

He'd often tried to imagine what his CIA or FBI or Interpol file said about him. What profile the psychologists and other analysts painted of him. What they'd hypothesized about his childhood, his formative years.

They had probably spent months on his profile—years even. No doubt they added to it after every job Dead Man's Hand took credit for.

It was simple, really. The world was his playground, and everyone in it, his potential pawns. It was all a giant game and he was careful the way he played it, much more so than the men he'd grown up with. His vision had always been big, some would say impossibly so.

He knew better.

DMH was a homegrown terrorist extremist group born from a shared enjoyment of poker and Wyatt Earp among Elijah's father and his father's three best friends. Modern-day anarchists, the men were restless and disillusioned with the current government. Small-town men with what Elijah would now term even smaller minds. But at the time, they'd been his heroes, fighting for their freedom.

He stared around the kitchen—the old wallpaper had yellowed, his mother's ceramic utensil holder remained in its place by the stove, even though no one had used it for the past ten years.

He should've sold this house years ago, but had not been able to make the break. He hated that he had sentimentality for something that had not shown him the love he'd craved.

His mother had been strict. Religious. Overbearing. Definitely head of the household, even before his father's death, and Elijah had stayed behind, while his brother left as quickly as he could, when he turned eighteen.

Two more years, kiddo. You can do it, his brother said.

Elijah had no choice. But it was a living, breathing hell, made worse by the fact that there was no golden child to buffer him. The abuse was more mental than physical—the fact that he was told daily that he would never amount to anything because he was stupid.

It took him many years to figure out that *stupid* meant dyslexic. That he didn't have to keep his mouth shut about his ideas to bring the group more into the mainstream, to get them more power and prestige.

His older brother had been so dedicated to the cause, he'd enlisted in the Army in order to learn proper military fighting techniques. He'd planned on recruiting men from the military to help DMH realize their missions, planned on opening a training ground for their own militia, to make it more professional.

But his older brother never came back. The U.S. military killed him as surely as if one of its own soldiers put a gun to his head, and from there Elijah's entire world crumbled, like fine sand through his fingers.

The simple fact was that everyone Elijah truly loved died. And whether it was him who cursed them or he was the cursed one, the end result of him ending up truly alone was still the same.

He poured everything into DMH—all his pain—until the group was able to move locations to the Horn of Africa, which he'd correctly predicted as the new area of terrorism.

So, no, Elijah had not invented Dead Man's Hand—he'd simply taken it from a small-town, homegrown extremist group whose members talked a hell of a lot but didn't do much more than that, to what it was now—a well-known terrorist group, capable of a hell of a lot of damage. They did everything from aiding in guerilla warfare in American cities and her interests abroad, to funding terrorist training camps, to human trafficking.

He'd taken some of DMH's younger and more adventurous members with him to Africa. Used the same name and expanded the group's vision. The ones that survived were heads of various branches, managing everything from skin trades to black market organs.

It had gone from being an idealistic version of how he wanted his world to look, to a game. Every game had winners and losers—and the winner owed loyalty to no one but himself.

The CIA had been after him in one form or another for years, sending operatives to take out Elijah's, but it was only a mere drop in the bucket in terms of hurting DMH.

But Gabriel had the patience of a saint without the sensibilities of one—he might have been with DMH for years before he'd made his moves, taking down Elijah's dream without a second thought. And still, Elijah liked Gabriel Creighton, because the man understood his vision, and perhaps even empathized with his position, knew that the best way to hurt a man or woman was through their children.

Elijah would've died for his son. Whether Gabriel was willing to crack under the pressure of watching his daughter tortured would be interesting. But before that happened, Elijah had flown here, to his old house, where they were keeping the former CIA spy locked away tight, to try to reason with him. He walked to the basement, past the guard, and sat across from Gabriel. The man barely looked at him.

He'd like to think of himself as strong as Gabriel—and he would've spilled everything if it meant his son's life. Even though he was savvy enough to know that, in most cases, both parent and child would end up dead anyway.

He leaned forward in his chair casually, his voice echoing in the small concrete chamber that had been built as a weapons cache for the old DMH. "Be reasonable. If you choose to work with me, we could do great things."

Gabriel remained on his back, the thin mattress the only thing between his body and the cold floor. "You would never trust me. Besides, what's in it for me?"

"Life."

Gabriel's eyes flickered over him coolly. "Not really enough incentive."

"I figured as much." Elijah remained far enough out of reach, even though Gabriel was chained down, because he was brave, but not stupid. "Your wife was more than willing."

Again, no movement. This time, the man didn't even turn his head, but Elijah caught the clenching of the jaw.

Still in mourning for the woman, all these years later.

She'd been Gabriel's ultimate downfall—couldn't he see that?

In Elijah's mind, in his world, women were disposable. Vessels.

But children were a different matter. A son had been his future, the future of DMH. A legacy.

Mari was his equal—maybe too much so. She'd been planning on killing her newest lover that night and framing Elijah for it, hadn't expected their son to be home to thwart those plans. And she'd been smart enough to take from him what she knew would slay him, even as it cost her own life.

She hated their son because she believed that Elijah's affections had transferred. Which was, of course, not true, since Elijah knew he was not capable of loving a woman, and as such had never truly felt affection for her in the first place. Not truly, not well, not ever.

To say he'd feared her would have been closer to the truth, and what he feared had always fascinated him. Made him fly too close to the sun with no protection—he had no one to blame but himself when he got severely burned.

Gabriel would have no one to blame for the torture he would endure either.

Riley lay on her side, facing Dylan on the double lounge chair. She was covered in a towel, the bikini long abandoned. Dylan had managed to pull his pants back on, but his chest remained bare.

Neither had said anything for a long while—no, they'd communicated by moaning and coming and then silence, while Dylan held her hand, the way he had in that bed in Bogotá years earlier.

So much had changed, and yet everything was the same.

"I know what it's like to be all alone, Riley." His voice drifted over her, pulling her back to a reality she didn't want to face.

"Stop, Dylan. Don't."

"Don't what?"

"Don't be nice to me."

"Fine. I know about your mom...I know where she died," Dylan told her.

She froze, and suddenly the towel was much too flimsy. She flashed back to when her mother lay dying in a state-run hospital because Riley hadn't been able to afford to put her someplace with better conditions.

And then she pulled herself together. "So we were poor. Things are rough all over." She shrugged. "The childhood thing is really boring as hell. I'd rather skip it."

"I was twenty when my parents died," he told her. "I raised my brothers. I was already in the Army, so I got custody."

"I'm sorry."

"What happened to your father?"

She knew that question was coming, had dreaded it... and wondered if saying it out loud could make everything stop, could make all the madness and fear go away. "They say he committed suicide, but I know better."

"Who's they?" he whispered.

"The CIA. He was a CIA special agent. They told my mom that my dad was a traitor, that he sold out his country. They said he knew he'd been caught, admitted everything he'd done. And then they stripped him of every-thing—his job, his money, his life. And so he killed himself, and we were left with nothing."

"But you think the CIA actually killed him."

"I know Gabriel killed him," she spat. "I don't believe my dad was a traitor—can't believe it. And I've spent most of my adult life trying to prove them wrong." She'd learned well in the Navy—and more than she'd ever wanted to after she'd gotten out.

"I kept approaching the CIA, and the FBI, trying to get a job with either agency. But they wouldn't let me in, and I knew it was because of my dad. Of course, they never came out and said it. And the only one I can blame is Gabriel Creighton."

"So now that we've established we have a common enemy in Gabriel, we can work together," Dylan said.

"I like to work alone."

"You weren't saying that when I was inside of you."

She sighed. Mainly because it was true. "Who do you work for again?"

"Never told you." He paused. "I work for myself. I pick the jobs I want. I'm in control of right and wrong, won't be forced into a situation I don't want to be a part of. I do that so I don't end up without a soul, like Gabriel. Are you will-ing to do the same?"

She stood then, tied the towel tightly under her arms. "Don't plan on taking me with you down redemption road."

But when she tried to leave, Dylan was on her, slam-ming her body back down to the lounge chair without any of the patented gentleness he'd shown her before. "We both have souls. That makes us just as dangerous as Gabriel, if not more so."

He eased off her, but didn't offer a hand to help her up from where she lay. And she remained prone—even as he stood next to her, and long after the wind returned to her lungs—staring at the sunlit sky, thinking of her old, shitty apartment in Queens, where she'd put stick-on stars on the ceiling, because she didn't like to sleep in the dark and couldn't afford the electricity it would take to keep a light burning all night.

Heat was something else she couldn't afford, and she remembered always feeling damp and cold, and was never without a heavy sweater and extra blankets.

She realized that she did little differently today, just in case the rug was pulled out from under her.

And she'd purposely chosen a warm climate, because she never wanted to feel the cold again.

She and Dylan always seemed to connect in the warm climates . . .

They'd met up again, this time in Mumbai. Headed through the hotel lobby to her room. But when she'd opened the door, the shock of what she saw made her stumble back against Dylan.

Nothing was in the orderly fashion she'd left it. No, her room had been trashed. Invaded. What wasn't taken, like her computer and camera and iPod, was destroyed.

She fought a sob, born of equal parts anger and sadness. Because she'd vowed she would never let anyone take anything from her again. And even though she was smart enough to realize she'd only lost material possessions—all replaceable ones, at that—there was still the jolt to remind her that she wasn't invincible after all.

"Ri..."

Dylan's voice sounded far away. She was vaguely aware that he led her down the hall, to another room. His room.

She'd slept for hours—stress, fear. It was ridiculous how hard the break-in had hit her. It was, no doubt, random. There were no signs that she'd been targeted by another spy—they tended to wait around and talk to her via bullets rather than a smash and grab job.

She'd pulled off ops most men and women never dreamed about—faced her fears and had been dogged about using her position to try to find intel about her father's case. She'd been to the edge—over it—and back. And a petty thief was making her break down. In front of Dylan.

When she'd woken, she found a note from him. He'd cleaned up the mess, checked her out of that room.

And left her with a laden room-service tray, and the feeling that he'd taken her heart with him this time. Because there were also new clothes. A computer. An iPod.

iPod. She pressed the dial, discovered the sleek gunmetal gray machine was fully charged—and loaded with music.

Her music. Even the songs she was embarrassed to admit she liked.

How had he known? Out of everything, music was one of the only things that had gotten her through the years after her father died. She couldn't carry a tune worth a damn, but that didn't matter—there was something soothing about blocking out the rest of the world and letting the songs comfort her.

Besides, no one could take that away from her. Even today,

when she needed to travel light, she could still take her iPod along.

But Dylan had obviously known.

Her cell phone began to ring. Dylan. She picked it up, didn't bother with hello. "How did you know...about the music?"

"You always have your iPod with you. And you sing to yourself sometimes. You get this dreamy look when you listen to music—like you relax, forget everything. It's almost the same look you have when we're in bed together."

She felt the tears well and swallowed hard. She'd shown enough weakness in front of him for a lifetime. "Thanks. You didn't have to."

"I learned a long time ago that no matter how small it is, whatever gets you through the day is the most important thing."

She wished he was there, wanted to wind her hand inside of his, hold tight and not let go.

She wanted to tell him that he was on his way to becoming what saw her through her day—or he could be, in a very short amount of time.

But she knew she was asking for something she should never, ever want. Depending on Dylan—on anyone—was a mistake.

"You need to stay out of it completely. Go away, leave town and forget about me," she told him now.

"Way too late for that. I won't rest until I take Gabriel down. If that means taking you down in the process, so be it. But just know that I gave you the choice." His tone was fierce. When Dylan wanted to be, he was easily an unyielding force of nature, and she'd managed to conjure up a storm. "Gabriel's daughter's in danger because of you. She's an innocent and now she's going to pay for her father's crimes. Sound familiar?"

He left her lying there as he walked away, started down the path that ran alongside her house, toward the street.

Her eyes filled with tears—half-relief, half-desperation. She fought the urge to vomit, the bile rising inside of her as her head swam. "I didn't want to know that."

She thought she'd whispered those words softly into the air, but she swore she saw Dylan's shoulders stiffen slightly at her admission before he continued on his way.

CHAPTER
7

Zane's cell had been ringing all goddamned day. Unfortunately, the party he'd been at the night before had been so fucking off the hook that his entire body was still offline.

For him, time off equaled trouble, and he'd manage to find it in spades within the next twenty-four hours unless otherwise occupied. During leave from his SEAL team, he found himself looking for more action, more risks.

And so even though he wasn't happy with the phone shit, he was hoping there was an interesting proposition on the other end of the line.

He checked the messages. Six of them.

Dylan.

Dylan.

More Dylan. Cursing at him so fluently it actually sounded like a foreign language.

Zane could appreciate that, but not so much when directed at him. He ignored the remaining three messages and dialed Dylan's number.

"Nice of you to wake yourself," Dylan bit out.

"I thought my job getting intel on Riley was done." Zane poured a large mugful of coffee and decided it needed to be black for it to work. And in IV form, but that wasn't really an option.

Or was it? He stared at the old IV bag he'd used to give himself a dose of glucose the other morning, and wondered if an invention like that would be viable.

"This call isn't about Riley," Dylan growled.

He'd been there when Dylan fell apart over Riley, even though Dylan hadn't asked. Mainly because he got it—much more than Caleb would've.

"Why would she shoot me over Gabriel's files?"

"She either loves him or hates you," Zane said. "It's why a woman does anything. Yeah, and fighting turns them all on."

"How do you ever get a date with all that shit you talk?"

"Date?" Zane raised a brow. "You're really old school."

Again, Dylan looked as if he was fighting a strong urge to kill him, saying only, "Please go."

That's how Zane had known Dylan was on his way to healing. Of course, his idea of healing would have been not to hook up with the same woman who'd put a bullet through him, but hell, Zane got it.

"... you even listening to me?" Dylan was demanding on the other end of the phone, sounding suspiciously like a boss, or a girlfriend, and Zane didn't take to either of those well.

"Ya. Listening." He shoved the IV bag in the garbage, wrote down the info Dylan gave him and grabbed a to-go coffee on the way out of Virginia, knowing he'd be stopping for many more on the drive down to Florida.

But there hadn't been enough coffee in the fucking world to help him deal with what Dylan wanted. No, whiskey might've helped instead, because a visit to a goddamned jail was enough to shrink a man's balls.

Nothing like the last assignment, which involved a lot more fun. And women, all of whom needed nothing more than a drink and an orgasm, and not necessarily in that order.

But he'd squeezed the Riley Sacadano well dry, and he'd need to be mission-ready for the SEALs come next week. He'd be doing his six-month tour with Team Twelve—and who knew what hellhole they'd be visiting this trip.

Speaking of hellholes, he pulled into the prison's parking lot and stared up at the large, gray buildings that stretched at least a mile long and three stories high. He'd been in some fucked-up situations—the threat of capture was always real—but this, humans trapped in cages, always made him feel claustrophobic.

Forcing himself out of the car and into the visitor's waiting area, he flashed the dummied fed ID Dylan had given him years ago.

The bars slammed behind him, and even though Zane was only visiting, he still had the urge to turn and take down every guard to escape.

He'd probably been watching too much of that jailed-abroad show on the National Geo Channel. Yeah, way too much time on his hands lately.

"Down this way, sir. Private visiting room number four." The guard pointed to the heavy steel door. "The prisoner will be escorted in through the second door."

Zane walked into the closed room, complete with a table and chairs, all nailed to the floor, and hooks where the prisoners could be chained by both hands and feet.

The guy he was visiting was a sixty-year-old Outlaw Angel lieutenant doing time for drug trafficking. It hadn't been easy, finding an OA who wasn't a lifer.

Lifers won't talk as easily as men who thought they had something to gain by giving intel. Especially if they thought the man in front of them was some kind of special agent, which Zane had led the OA to believe in order to get a meeting with him.

Zane whipped out the ID and let the guy named Boz stare at it for a while.

Boz tossed it back at him, his mouth pulled in a permanent sneer thanks to a scar that looked like he'd nearly had his nose and lip torn off. "I don't talk to feds."

"I need to know about a man in your chapter—a Howie Moore," Zane said anyway.

"I ain't no snitch."

Yeah, sure, buddy. Dylan would've given the guy money. Zane preferred to work through fear—way more effective in the long run. "But you are a snitch. Or at least the guys in your local chapter will think so when I'm done."

Boz lunged, but the chains would only let him go so far, and he was pulled back into the metal chair. "Little fucking asshole."

"Not so little, Boz. I'm sure your chapter's president won't be happy to hear you're talking. And I do believe his brother's on your floor in this lovely establishment."

Boz looked around, like his gang was waiting in the wings to beat the shit out of him. Finally, he leaned forward and said, "Howie was killed the night of those murders."

Zane leaned forward as well. "I heard the men were FBI agents."

"I heard the same rumor."

"Who killed Howie?"

Boz paused and for a long moment Zane figured, same old, same old—that the man wanted to seem like he knew everything, but a lot of these guys had gotten left in the dark when it came to matters like murdering chaptermates.

Finally, Boz spoke, his voice so low Zane almost missed it. "Sinister."

Sinister. *Sinister?* "Who the fuck is that? No one I've spoken to ever mentioned an OA named Sinister. Stop fucking with me," Zane growled.

Boz held up his hands. "It's the truth, man. We're not supposed to talk about the guy. Ever. He was OA from the Miami chapter. A chief. No one would've gone against him. He told us that Howie was the traitor, that Howie killed the FBI agents to set all of us up." Boz shook his head in disgust. "I never believed it. Howie had your fucking back, man, no matter what."

Sinister. An OA. *Fuck.* Zane knew how much this meant to Dylan—and to Cam—and leaving here with an answer like the one he'd gotten didn't sit well. And still, he pulled out of his pocket the picture of Gabriel he'd printed out earlier from his email. "Know this guy?"

"What is this, a fucking joke? That's Sinister," Boz growled. "How the hell did you get that picture?"

Zane smiled. "You let me worry about that. You're sure this man killed Howie the night of the double murder?"

"Damned sure. Sinister killed Howie. I saw it happen. Got more to lose by telling you than I do by lying." He paused. "Howie was a good brother. Didn't deserve what he got in the end. I never believed the story that Howie was double-crossing the OA."

Yeah, neither did his son. Zane felt the walls begin to close in on him and was just glad he didn't have to be the one to break the news about Gabriel to Cam.

Sky had followed Cam into the kitchen, still shaken, watched him carry the body out the back door. That's when she saw the blood on the refrigerator, the two other men lying dead, and realized that the time for questions was not now. And so she turned tail and packed fast, grabbing anything she could get her hands on and then dragging the heavy suitcase out of the bedroom and into the living room. From there, she packed the computer and her phone and grabbed her bag with the pills and stood there dumbly, waiting for Cam.

He was still outside and he'd taken the other two bodies with him. Immediately, she felt better, but still cursed herself for leaving information lying around her apartment, and then realized how stupid that was. It was her place—she should be able to leave things lying around in her own home.

Never leave important personal information sitting out where people can find it, both parents would lecture.

Her doing so was complete rebellion, coupled with a sense of safety.

The thought of people inside her apartment, rifling through her things, was less upsetting than the fact that they were tracking her. That this wasn't over—not by a long shot.

And if Cam hadn't been here . . .

No, she couldn't think about that. Wouldn't worry that, as of now, she and Cam would both be wanted for questioning, and she wondered if the CIA could help them. She only knew that calling the local police for help wasn't any kind of option.

Don't trust anyone, Skylar. Her father's words. Always, his words.

But she had to trust someone. There was no way she could handle this herself, alone.

There was broken glass, and blood, on the kitchen floor, and she grabbed a pair of rubber gloves from under the sink and paper towels and carefully wiped it all up.

"Sky."

She looked up at Cam, who was watching her crouched on the floor, putting the last of the mess, including the gloves, into a garbage bag. "We can't leave it like this."

"I know. But I would've done it."

"I'm in this just as much as you are," she told him as she stood.

He was on her with one long stride, took her shoulders in his hands. "No, you're not *in* anything. You're not doing anything wrong."

"I know. It just feels that way." It felt the way it had when her mother had been killed. She remembered the men in dark suits. The too-clean kitchen.

The fact that all the pictures had been taken away, including the photo albums. Her life before the age of sweet sixteen pretty much erased.

Her father's assurances of *You've done nothing wrong, Skylar.*

God, she missed her mother.

"Sky, we should go." Cam had grabbed her bags and the garbage. She pulled on her coat and he helped her down the back steps toward a large, waiting black truck that looked more than capable of getting them through anything.

No more than fifteen minutes had passed since the men had broken in—although it felt like much longer, like everything was moving in slow motion.

It was so quiet outside. She thought about people in their beds, sleeping, or just rolling out for coffee, thinking about skiing and fireplaces and hot chocolate.

She was thinking about *bodies.* Fine for fiction, but freaking her out in real life.

Keep. It. Together.

She pulled her jacket tight around her—the jeans and sweater underneath doing nothing to help keep her warm as she walked toward Cam's truck, him right behind her.

"Be careful, it's slippery," he told her, his voice calm, cool and collected, like they were going on a morning drive. Like people hadn't just tried to kill them.

Like he didn't just hide three bodies in the snow.

Stop it, Sky, she ordered herself, and stepped aside so Cam could load their stuff into the truck.

It was only when he turned his back to her to throw the bags in the backseat that she noticed the blood soaking through the back of his shirt—good enough reason for him not to be wearing any jacket at all.

He turned to her, motioned to the passenger's side door. "Get in."

"You're hurt. Do you have a first-aid kit?"

He didn't answer, just opened the door and waited. But she didn't climb in. Instead, she put a hand lightly on his shoulder to try to get a better look at exactly how bad the wound was.

"At least let me help you stop the bleeding..."

"I'll tend to it later. Leave it." He ground the words out, and that pissed her off, because the wound looked bad. Bright red, fresh blood, and he was pale—although, granted, still capable of saving both their asses.

But Cam wasn't having any of it. "I need to get you out of here. In from the cold, and away from whoever the hell is looking for you, Sky. And if I have to tie you up and throw you in the truck to do that, I will."

His eyes blazed with anger—she was pretty sure her expression matched his as she pushed past him. "Fine. But I'm driving while you stop the blood. Because if you pass out while driving, we're both screwed."

He grabbed her biceps—an iron grip that somehow didn't hurt—and steered her back in the direction of the passenger seat. "I've lived through much worse than this," were his last words to her before shutting the door.

And then he was in the driver's seat, pressing the gas on the massive machine, and she felt the power of the car surge under her. Indeed, it smoothly pushed aside the massive amounts of snow from its path and she felt much surer than she had before as he drove away from the townhouse and out toward the main road.

"If you want to, you can try to pack the wound while I drive," he told her.

"Gee, thanks, chief," she muttered, even as she rifled through his glove compartment, where he was pointing. She pulled out a first-aid kit and heard his low snort.

She looked up, saw many guests' cars buried underneath large drifts, as her rental was. And then her brain began to work. "Wait, did those men have a car?"

"Yes. I took care of it."

"Maybe if we ran the plates..."

He shot her a glance. "Good idea."

Which meant, of course, *Been there, done that.* He'd gotten rid of the car and was trying to trace it and she wanted to ask him how he did it all so effectively and so quickly. "You had time to run the plates?"

That made him smile a little. "You'd be surprised what you can get done in fifteen minutes if you put your mind to it."

"Something to strive for," she muttered. "When will you know anything?"

He didn't answer her for a long moment, just watched the road intently, and then, "They'll come back as stolen."

He turned right, out of the main complex and onto the service road that would lead them to the highway, and she unbuckled her seatbelt so she could get a better angle to help with his shoulder.

The heat blasted, enough for her to feel comfortable taking off her heavy coat. She put it in the backseat and noted that Cam's truck looked and smelled brand-new. Clean, perfect and huge—big enough to put a mattress in the back once two rows of seats were down.

Cam was rifling one-handed through her bag. He pulled out her phone and began to dial.

"Who are you calling?"

"The manager of the resort. You're going to tell him you've been called away for a family emergency. The last thing I need is the local police on our tail because a well-known writer disappeared on vacation."

She nodded, because the resort sent out someone to check on the guests daily, and she took the phone from him. He'd put it on speaker. When the manager answered, she explained that she had a family emergency and had to leave last night, before the storm got bad. "I took the keys with me, by accident. I'll mail them back."

She managed to sound appropriate during the call, slightly panicked, fatigued, as someone having a family emergency might be.

"That's not a problem, Ms. Slavin. We'll go inside later when the roads are clear and check the place out. I'm sure you'll get your deposit back. How much trouble could you get into in twenty-four hours during a snowstorm?" he asked.

"Right," she said, choking back a sound that was somewhere between a laugh and a sob and knew she had to end the call before she lost it. "Well, thank you."

She clicked the phone off and handed it back to Cam but he reminded her, "You've got to call your publicist too."

Of course; she'd forgotten about that. "What do I tell her?"

Cam thought for a second. "Ask her what the police found. Tell her that you're fine and that she can reach you on your cell phone. Let her do most of the talking, okay? That way you don't have to lie. Because you suck at it."

She opened her mouth and then closed it, because she couldn't decide if that was a compliment or an insult.

His expression didn't give her any indication.

She pressed the speed dial key, the phone still on speaker, as he drove onto the highway, which was mercifully clearer than the side roads had been, although not by much.

As usual, Pam answered on the first ring, flying at one hundred miles an hour, which never did leave much room for Sky to talk. "Skylar, where have you been? Oh, my God, I've been freaking out about this—your apartment, they looked through everything. The police were here, they have no leads—they think it's related to the notes, but they're not sure . . ."

Pam kept talking and Sky shot Cam a quick look. He continued to stare at the road, but she swore his eyes had glazed over.

"Pam—Pam, I'm fine, okay," she managed to break in. "Thanks so much for taking care of everything for me. Please keep me updated—I'm going to stay here and keep writing."

"That's probably a good idea, stay out of town," Pam agreed.

"I'll talk to you soon," Sky said, and then ended the call with the press of a button. Her battery was just about dead and she turned her phone off and grabbed the charger from her bag, plugging it into the AC outlet on Cam's dashboard.

"Is there anyone else who'll worry?"

Her throat tightened. "Pam will tell the necessary people."

There was silence for a few moments, then Cam said, "I wouldn't have many people worried about me either, if that makes you feel any better."

She nearly laughed at the unexpected comment. "It does...and it doesn't. What about those men—what did you do with them?"

"No one's finding them until spring thaw." He was stripping off his shirt now, finally ready for her help. The car weaved a little as he shifted in order to get completely free, and she took the shirt from him and tossed it into the backseat.

It was then she saw the wound along the top of his shoulder. It looked like a ridge—canyonlike. Not pretty at all.

"That's just the graze. Go lower," he instructed, and holy crap, there was a hole. The skin around it was swollen and raw, clotted with blood.

"Deep breath, kid. We don't need you fainting."

"I won't faint," she muttered, and then wondered if you could actually will that.

She guessed she'd find out. As she went back to checking his wounds, she heard herself say, "You were shot."

"Yes."

She'd been hoping it was anything but a bullet wound. "Is the bullet...still in there?"

"Unfortunately. I'm clean, Sky—I get tested regularly

for my job." He was talking about his blood, worried about her again—when he should be worried about the freakin' bullet in his shoulder.

She pressed gauze against it—thankfully, the bleeding had slowed. Shifting her gaze back to what was in front of her—a long, empty stretch of white—she asked, "Shouldn't we find you a doctor?"

"Probably. But I'm not stopping right now." He was checking the rearview mirror and she did so too, wanting to see if they were being followed, and that caused another surge of panic inside of her. She fought it, because there wasn't time for crap like that. And still, the words escaped her before she could stop them. "You're not going to die on me, are you?"

"You're not going to keep asking me questions like that, are you?"

"I'm freaking out here. And I get that you're all trained and stone cold, but you weren't last night." Sometimes, she really wished she could keep her mouth shut.

Cam handed her his water bottle. "Drink. And breathe."

She did both.

"Pack as much gauze as you can, and then put the pressure bandage on it and buckle back in, okay?"

She nodded. Did what he asked. "It's just that you put your life on the line for me. I know that's why my father sent you . . . but I never expected this. Any of it."

"It's going to be okay, Sky." His voice was still rough as gravel, but she figured that must be from pain and stress.

She wanted to ask him how the hell he knew they'd be

all right, but didn't. "How far are we going?" she asked instead.

"As far out of town as we can."

"In this weather?" She glanced at him, saw his jaw clench. "You've got to get that shoulder looked at long before that."

He ran a hand through his hair and then checked his GPS. "There's a motel not too far from here. We haven't been followed. We'll stop there for the day so I can deal with the wound myself and then move out tonight."

He mounted the portable machine to where she could see it and prepared to let it guide them through the snow-covered roads, toward their safety.

The drive to the motel took just under two hours. Sky's hands were sore from literally white-knuckling it, even though Cam—and his truck—seemed in control of the road the entire time.

He appeared fine, but that didn't stop her from continually checking to make sure he was okay.

"Why do you keep staring at me?" he asked at one point, his gaze straight ahead, focused on the seemingly invisible road.

"I'm just . . . looking," she said lamely, and noted that a small grin pulled at the corner of his mouth, as if against his will. "Sorry. There's not much I can do beyond sit here like some weakling who needed saving."

"You're not frail or weak, Sky. You handled yourself well at the house."

"I held a gun on you. I didn't trust you."

"I told you not to trust anyone."

Yeah, him and the great Gabriel Creighton.

The GPS beeped, signaling they were approaching the motel. The lot was pretty empty, with large snow drifts indicating a recent plowing.

Cam parked in the small lot—pulling on his jacket while she noted fresh blood on his shirt and the seat—and checked them in while she waited in the idling truck.

The room was around back—ground level—small and not fashionable, but it was clean and warm.

He dropped their bags, locked the door behind them and headed straight for the bathroom, stripping his jacket off as he went. She sat on the bed, then realized she was too jacked up to remain still.

He'd left the bathroom door open and she caught sight of him—his back to the mirror, looking over his shoulder at the ugly wound and attempting to poke at it with a metal instrument that looked like a pair of curved tweezers.

He cursed, then cursed again, under his breath this time, when he saw her. And then he focused his attention on his shoulder.

She watched for a few moments before telling him, "You're not going to be able to get it out that way."

"Stating the obvious isn't helping."

He's pissed because of the pain, not you. She reminded herself how completely balls to the wall bitchy she'd been sometimes at the height of the kidney failure. In comparison, he was as tough as nails. Even when he seemed relaxed, she got the sense of a coiled snake, ready to strike if the need arose. But now he needed her.

She took the instrument from his hand. "No, but I will."

He blinked, stared at her over his shoulder. "You've done this before?"

"No. But I seem to be your only option."

He smiled. "You're a lot tougher than the woman I met last night."

"Amazing what nearly being killed will do to a person."

"Does a kidney transplant hurt?" he asked suddenly.

"Like a bitch," she said as she gazed at the wound, and then met his eyes again. "As I'd imagine this does."

"Now I know where Violet comes from."

She paused, instrument in the air. "You've read my books?"

"One of them." He mentioned the title and she nodded. "So Violet's in the book you're having so much trouble writing?"

"Yes. She has to choose between falling in love with the guy or killing him," she said, and then, "Now tell me what I need to do."

"Get the bullet out," was all he said.

She clenched her teeth, held her breath and braced her free palm on the curve of his shoulder while pushing the instrument gently into the wound. She noted the ends were thin and serrated like a large tweezer, and she kept them slightly parted as she delved inside the opened skin.

He jerked, muttered something unintelligible under his breath.

It didn't deter her—and finally she felt the tips of the instrument scrape against something hard. Praying it was the bullet and not bone, she clamped the metal around it and pulled, slow and steady until the instrument was out, a single bloody bullet in its grasp.

Cam drew a long, shuddering breath and she took one of her own.

He sank back on his hands, his face pale, and then slowly the color returned. "Good. That was good. Thanks."

His voice was hoarse from pain.

She dropped the instrument and the bullet into the sink, where it landed with a loud clank. Then she grabbed fresh gauze and pressed it against the wound to stop the bleeding. "What now?"

He waited a beat and then said, "Feel like learning to stitch?"

CHAPTER
8

Cam guided her through the process of using the needle holder on the wound, showing her first on the thick skin of his fingertips how deep to stitch.

Sky stood, one hand still pressing gauze to his shoulder, her body brushing his thigh, her forehead scrunched intently.

She was close. Really close. He'd barely let himself process the closeness he'd felt to her last night, but this was altogether different, and yeah, you'd think a bullet wound would take the rise out of a guy.

He could go on the record by saying it didn't. Despite the pain and stress of the day, the close proximity was definitely affecting him, especially when her breasts brushed his back, and her free hand traveled along his rib cage as she stitched.

Yeah, he was pretty much ready to ask her for a sponge bath.

Whether she noticed or not, she didn't say anything, just continued to work, stitching slowly and carefully, which hurt more than a fast and dirty job.

Still, he was grateful for the help. He was damned impressed with how she'd handled herself. He just hoped she hadn't seen the third wound, on his chest—a long thin opening, courtesy of the freakin' paring knife the guy had grabbed from the counter.

But she noticed, traced a finger down along the slice, lightly assessing the damage. "This needs stiches too."

"I'm fine," he said before she could say anything. He took the needle from her—or tried to, but she took it back, saying, "Let me."

And he did, because he knew that in a situation like this, helping made one feel less helpless.

He could tell Sky hated being helpless.

When she was done, she cleaned the area with antiseptic and watched him give himself a healthy dose of antibiotics via a needle in the arm. And then he picked up the bullet in the sink and rinsed it off before studying it. "Favored by spies—quick and deadly."

"Funny, I tend to think of all bullets as deadly," she muttered.

He didn't respond, tossed the bullet in his bag and began to wrap up the bloody gauze, because no need to freak out housekeeping.

But she wasn't going to drop it that easily—in fact, he'd

been surprised she'd held it together so well on the ride over.

"Cam, I need more information about what's going on. Please—you must know. And I have to. I think those men have my father—or at least I think they know who has him."

He didn't say anything just then. Letting her speak and spill was far more effective in finding out intel about her father—about anything she might know, and she did continue.

"Do you think...well, it makes sense that whoever's after me, whoever's sending letters, would want me for leverage."

His own words came rushing back to him, because that was how he was supposed to see Skylar. *Leverage.* Nothing more, nothing less. And hell, how did this get so complicated? "It makes sense," he agreed finally.

"My father must've had a contingency plan. We've got to get in touch with someone. Can't you call anyone about this?"

Could he? Sure, and get into even more trouble. "His contingency plan is me, Sky."

"Look, I know you're Special Forces. Delta, probably. You have contacts," she persisted. "I won't sit here and do nothing. They're not going to stop looking for me." She stared at him, the fear shining through her previously calm gaze, the pulse at the base of her neck fluttering. And all the calm control she'd portrayed since leaving the house was fading fast.

"You keep...pulling back. Like there's something big

you're not telling me." She paused. "It's about the danger I'm in, right?"

"You know what I know, Sky. I'm on the bodyguard end, not the investigatory one." All true, since Dylan was the one doing the actual investigating.

All true, mixed with an equal amount of lies. A perfect blend.

And Sky's instincts wouldn't let her buy into it. She'd continue to fight him for intel in the most unassuming way. And he didn't blame her one bit.

But if he let her in on the truth now, there was no telling what she'd do—she might run, call the police . . . put herself in more danger.

He was her best choice right now.

He wanted to be her best choice for a long time. "Your father never mentioned any recent threats to you—or even not so recent ones?"

"I told you, I haven't seen or talked to him in months."

"But before that—was there ever a time you were threatened?" he persisted, and he saw it, the crack in the foundation. She turned away and walked out of the bathroom.

Still shirtless, he followed her.

She sat on the brown comforter, pulled her legs up to her chest, as if protecting herself from some invisible force. He sat next to her, said her name quietly a few times until she responded.

"I don't want to talk about this anymore, Cam."

He didn't push her. Something was there and it would come out eventually, but he'd learned a long time ago that forcing someone to spill wasn't the most effective way to keep their trust.

He wanted her trust—and not for the same reasons he'd wanted it two nights ago, or even last night. No, the look in her eyes when she saw he'd been hurt, the pure concern . . . he wanted that to be real.

It's all going away when she finds out the truth.

Yeah, well, he'd let it play out. For now, she was safest with him.

"I think I need to rest," she said. "I'm still . . . I get tired a lot."

More mental than physical at this point, he supposed, but no matter which, she needed the shut-eye. "Go for it. We'll most likely leave when it's dark—roads should be clear and we can make tracks without worrying about being followed. I don't want to stay in any one place too long."

"What about you?"

"I don't sleep much."

"Yeah, I noticed. A job requirement, I guess."

She wanted more information—more from him than he was ready, willing or able to give—but he simply pointed to the pillows and said, "Sack out."

She scuttled backward willingly and pushed the covers down so she could get under them.

It didn't take long before he noticed the easy breaths of a deep sleep. As he'd noted last night, she was a heavy sleeper, which was good for him.

She looked pretty—and peaceful. He slid outside, closed the door gently behind him and dialed Dylan's number. "You got my texts, I'm assuming."

"Yeah, I got them. I love hearing in a text message that you've been shot," his friend said.

"Hey, I used code."

"What the hell, Cam?"

"Creighton's in trouble."

"And we give a shit about this why?"

"Because Sky's life is also in danger. There was a break-in—probably from the same men who have Gabriel. They were going to kidnap her. Told her they would bring her to her father."

"Did you believe them?"

"They were carrying enough morphine to tranq a small horse."

"Shit."

"Yeah, that pretty much sums it up."

"How badly are you hurt?"

"I took care of it."

A long sigh and then, "I've got the intel—Zane ran it for me. Plates were stolen, so's the car. There were four sets of prints in the car—one didn't show up in the system, probably the truck's owner. One set of prints belongs to a Jess Jones. He's done time for voluntary second-degree manslaughter. Pretty long rap sheet. Hired gun. The second guy is wanted too—selling military surplus, being looked at for some arms trafficking. Third guy must be new, or really good—there's nothing that comes up for him, but he's listed as a known associate."

Cam leaned against the building and stared out into the gray day, remaining mostly hidden by his truck, just in case.

He'd already changed the license plate to one of the

many he kept in the back. They wouldn't be able to trace him through that.

"Do you think Gabriel knows you're with Skylar?"

"I don't know how." Then again, how the hell Gabriel had found him two nights earlier was a bit of a mystery. Cam had come right from the post, so it was likely Gabriel tracked his missions and his comings and goings that way . . . but still, the thought of Big Brother watching him—especially these past five months when he thought he'd been truly free, for the first time since he was seventeen—was unsettling.

"So what now?" Dylan asked.

"Dylan, I can't do this . . . not the way we planned. Sky's not in danger from me, not anymore. I'll keep her with me, yes. She's still my way out of this mess with Gabriel. But in the meantime I'm going to do everything I can to keep her safe."

And then he waited for the fallout.

You've gone from being her kidnapper to being her rescuer in less than forty-eight hours. Jesus, Cam." Dylan rubbed his head, tried to be pissed, but was secretly relieved that his friend wasn't a hardened fuck.

Apparently, neither was he, even though he'd always thought of himself as one. Because, somehow, everything had seriously shifted and he needed to put his assigned game face on and figure out what the hell Riley knew about Gabriel. At least before she tried to put another bullet in him.

He rubbed his chest where she'd shot him. It had left a

massive bruise below his heart that had hurt like a bitch for weeks. Sometimes, he swore he could make it ache by just thinking about her.

"I like her," Cam said quietly. "How the fuck did that happen?"

"It happens." Dylan paced the small space in front of the sliding glass doors and the view that overlooked Riley's house. Because how could he tell his friend that he was wrong, that it was simply lust. Fucking.

Cam was way more cautious than that. He was no sucker. And this situation had gotten more complicated than Dylan could have ever predicted.

Cam had nearly killed him for not telling him about Sky earlier—could Dylan really keep what he'd learned about Gabriel and Howie a secret for now? And what the hell good would it do?

His friend would need to learn the truth eventually. "Gabriel will probably have you killed for making contact with his daughter in the first place. For even knowing she exists."

"I know that—but, like you told me, you're my backup." Cam's voice got fierce. His *You can't talk me out of this so don't fucking bother trying* voice.

Dylan knew the tone all too well. His friend's resolve was legendary. He had to respect the man's morals even if he didn't agree with them. And now was the time to tell him what he'd found out from Zane.

I've got some intel for you, on Cam's father, Zane said when he'd called, his voice hard and flat. Not like Zane's usual party-in-a-box drawl.

He'd tell his friend fast—yanking off the Band-Aid so

the shock factor stopped the sting. "Zane met with an OA who knew Howie. Said he saw Howie get shot by another OA the night you were arrested."

He waited, heard the sharp intake of breath on the other end of the line. And he continued to wait, could picture Cam standing there, his face set in stone, refusing to admit any of this bothered him.

Dylan knew better.

Finally, Cam spoke, his voice choked. "He was sure it was the night of the murders?"

"Very sure."

"So my father couldn't have come for me," he said quietly. "All these years, and I've hated him as much as I hate Gabriel."

"Howie should never have allowed you into his world. You and I both know that. It's no place for a kid, and that's what you were. And I think Howie finally realized that." Dylan wished he didn't have to do this over the phone.

"You think Howie was sending me to safety, that he knew something was about to go down and he was sending me to the FBI agents so they could help me?"

"It makes sense. But there's only one man who knows for sure." Dylan paused and then, "The OA said that a member named Sinister killed Howie. And when Zane showed the guy Gabriel's picture, the one you took from Sky..."

"Sinister and Gabriel are one and the same," Cam said dully.

"I don't know whether to say I'm sorry or not, man. You've been waiting for this intel for so long."

"Where do they all think Sinister's at now?"

"Killed by the police."

"Yeah, I'll bet," Cam muttered. "And Gabriel got off scot-free for his part in the mission."

"According to the OA Zane spoke with, Sinister was working with a Colombian cartel, making big deals before the huge CIA bust. The FBI was involved and there was a rumor that an ATF agent had infiltrated the OA and was killed then too, along with the two FBI agents."

There was such a long silence, Dylan thought they'd lost the connection. Finally, Cam spoke. "It's not Sky's fault."

"She's his blood. If she's going to choose . . ." Dylan trailed off, not wanting to push too hard. "I'm still following a lead on Creighton."

"Through Riley?"

"She knows where he is. Claims that, as of yesterday, he's still alive."

"You'll follow her."

"Yeah. What about you?"

Another long pause filled the line and then, "Nothing's changed."

But they both knew that wasn't true at all. "You could call the CIA. Let them know where she is. And then get your ass to the house you built and disappear. No one knows about that place. It's secure."

His friend let out a long sigh on the other end of the phone. "She had a fucking kidney transplant less than six months ago. She's strong. But scared. And she doesn't deserve this."

Son of a bitch. Dylan had no more points to argue. Cam clicked off the line and Dylan stood there for a while, staring at nothing in particular.

"He was supposed to fuck her, not grow a conscience," he finally muttered to himself, fully realizing he was projecting.

Riley had gotten in. Granted, it had taken longer than two nights, but Dylan had always known Cam would fall hard once he finally did fall.

Why it had to be now, with Gabriel's daughter, was something that the fates could have a good laugh about. With Zane. Who was too fucked up to fall in love.

Enough. It was time to pull his focus back to Riley. It was apparent she needed his help as much as Cam did—maybe more.

He'd dragged himself away from her early that morning. Although she'd admitted her connection to Gabriel to him, he knew she'd never let him help her. No, he'd have to do that the old-fashioned way—by sneaking around and doing so behind her back.

After Cam hung up with Dylan, he remained outside. He stared down at his own arm, where the OA tattoo was nearly gone, but he could still see it, clear as day.

Three days before the murders, he'd sat in the chair with his father and gotten it permanently marked into his skin. He'd been scared as shit, because he knew what it meant: that he was an OA for life.

He hadn't signed on for that. He'd been told, when he moved in with his father, that he just had to play the game and go to school. But somehow, the deeper his father got pulled in, the deeper Cam had to go, just so he wouldn't let his old man down in front of the other men.

Your father didn't sell you out... he'd been trying to save you.

Howie hadn't left him in jail to rot after all. But Gabriel had. And Cam would find the reason why, or die trying.

To have suspected it was one thing. To have it confirmed, after all this time, it made him want to grab Gabriel by the throat and not let go.

He'd been waiting thirteen years to hear that, and still, the victory was hollow as hell. His father was still gone, as were Cam's late teens, and he'd let Gabriel consume most of his twenties.

It was time for his freedom. *His* needs.

He'd done so much good work with Delta Force and the Rangers—important work, work that saved lives. And maybe what he did for Gabriel saved people too, but the not knowing was killing him.

Eventually, Sky would learn all of this. But his gut nagged that the timing was wrong, that he didn't know enough yet.

He remained outside, telling himself he was simply collecting his thoughts, when really the idea of going back inside the way-too-small room with the very beautiful woman who'd managed to get him worked up while stitching him made him worry.

Mainly because she was already freaked, and climbing into bed with her was really tempting for him.

It was also tempting to go in and talk to her, spill his guts. And he had a lot to process.

Sky was innocent, but not in the way other men might think. Counting her as such would prove a liability he neither needed nor wanted. Because Skylar Slavin was smarter than most of the operatives he'd worked with; she might be recovering physically, but her mind, and her instincts, were sharp as shit. He'd seen that immediately in her writing, as he'd read the book at Dylan's house the night before he'd met up with her. The way she'd drawn the deep, dark undercover world was too good for someone who wasn't acquainted with that way of life. It wasn't firsthand knowledge, but it was as close to it as it got.

She'd be as hard to fool as her father, and about as trusting as Gabriel too, once she got her bearings back.

He was just lucky she was still in recovery mode.

Finally, he went inside, shutting the door quietly. She didn't stir at all, remained on her side, facing away from him, her hair loose on the pillow, her body tucked into a near-fetal position.

You could lie next to her and still control yourself.

He did, waited for her to say something, but all she did was turn—in her sleep—into his arms.

He held her cautiously, holding his breath, waiting for her to say something, but she was still in deep slumber. Her face nuzzled his chest and she gave a soft, contented moan as she shifted her legs under the covers, which brought her body closer to his.

The easiest thing would be to kiss her. Run a hand over the soft mounds of her breasts, teasing her nipples until her flesh was warm and supple under his touch.

She shifted, but he didn't have the heart to wake her, no matter how badly his dick wanted him to.

Her shirt had ridden up high, exposing her stomach, flat, with the softest skin he'd ever touched...or tasted.

He rubbed his fingers together, imagining her taut, pink peaks between them, her sighs of pleasure in his ear.

She sighed then, her leg rubbing his, as if she was inside his head.

When she found out why he'd come for her in the first place, how much he despised her father, she would hate him. But he didn't do pretend well. No, he was all about living in the real world, but the stark bite of reality would suck beyond belief.

Nothing perfect ever stays that way. The fact that this had taken a momentary turn in that direction should've set the alarm bells ringing in his head much sooner than this.

God, he felt like shit, physically and emotionally. He probably had a mild concussion, maybe a broken rib and his shoulder throbbed.

He'd let the bullet stay in longer than he should have. If he hadn't had antibiotics with him, he'd definitely need to be in the ER. And still, a chill ran through him, a warning that he'd overdone it.

A warning that maybe spending the night here, rather than attempting to go to another location tonight as he'd planned, might be the smartest thing. And lately, nothing he'd done was fucking smart.

CHAPTER
9

As a light rain pattered against the hotel balcony, Dylan remained with his head on the pillow as if an outside force was stopping him from rising out of bed and staring out toward Riley's house.

He'd set up a watch on Riley's place from his penthouse room a block over, with the help of a telescopic lens. He'd also planted a few bugs throughout her house, but he had a feeling she'd swept for those immediately after he left.

Then again, she was smart enough not to talk business in her house.

She was too smart for her own good. And he couldn't get the way she made his body hum with satisfaction off his mind.

She hadn't left her house so far that day. He'd begun to get antsy as hell, wondering if he should just give up on the surveillance, and on Riley herself. He was wasting time here—she didn't want his help and Cam did. The choice was easy enough.

He could help one without the other.

But he couldn't shake the feeling that Riley knew a lot more than she'd told him, that she was the key to successfully answering all the unanswered questions that kept popping up.

He shifted to his side, trying to get back into the restless nap he was taking, until his cell rang. Expecting it to be either Cam or Zane, he was more than happy to hear Riley's voice on the other end of the line.

"Hey," she said.

"Hey." His hand fisted around his cock, instantly hard at the sound of her voice.

"Are you alone?"

"Are you?"

"Not anymore."

Yeah, that was nice—both her words and the feel of his hand gliding up and down his erection, imagining it was her hand. Her mouth. Her . . .

Her voice washed over him, a sleek, soft blanket of warmth. "If you were here, Dylan . . ."

"What would you do to me?"

"You'd be naked. Because I like you that way."

He groaned, because he sure as shit didn't mind it either. And he'd been beyond frustrated after being so close to her and not doing anything at all about his own throbbing needs.

No, their fight had taken care of that.

Now Riley wanted to make up, and he was more than prepared to let her.

"Roll on your back, baby," she murmured, and he followed her directive, spreading his legs. "I like looking at you—all spread out and hard for me."

If he concentrated hard enough, he could feel the warm, wet drag of her tongue along his rigid length. Feel her hair caressing his thighs as her mouth worked him.

She was touching herself too—he could hear the catch in her voice when he told her, "I would be fucking you so hard right now, taking you from behind, the way I wanted to last night."

"I would've let you."

Her voice intoxicated him better than a shot of Jack, Johnny, or Jäger. He held himself in check, his body on a taut wire, set to explode—all it would take was one word, one final stroke.

Sweat glistened on his chest and he could barely hear her. "Fucking wish you were here, Ri," he growled.

"I am...taking you inside of me. Can't you feel how tight I am, how wet I am for you? All for you?"

That was it. He was pretty sure he cursed as he came, hard, panting, like a twelve-year-old who couldn't control himself.

He had plenty of control, but there was no point in abusing it. Instead, he kept his eyes closed as he jerked and groaned, his body twitching from the aftermath of the orgasm.

Momentarily spent, he remained in the same position—hand on his cock, phone pressed to his ear. And waited.

She had something more to tell him. She always did this—used the phone to distance them . . . but somehow it always ended up pulling them closer.

He had a feeling that would be the case this time as well. "I'm listening, Ri."

Her words came out in a hot rush, and he found himself sitting up in bed, still as a statue. "My dad, he'd told my mom, *If something happens to me, it's this man's fault.* And he gave her a name—Charles Sullivan. It took me years to track a CIA agent with that name, only to find out it was an alias. One of many." Riley's voice shook—anger, pain, fear, all mixed together and tumbling through the phone line. "And this man . . . He didn't just take my father's life. He took everything, every cent my father ever earned. His investments. Our house. The cars. It was all gone. My mother and I were living in a homeless shelter. Applying for welfare. We slept in a car until my mom got enough steady cleaning jobs to put us up in a rat-hole hotel. He took away my past . . . my whole life up until that point. I didn't even know what end was up anymore. I was fifteen and helpless. Watching my mom get sicker every year. I worked long hours after school, stayed up all night studying because I knew the only way out of the squalor was to get a scholarship."

"What did you think I would do, Ri? Just because I found the files—"

"It wouldn't have been the first time you screwed up my plans, Dylan," she told him, and yeah, that was true. One-upmanship had played a big role in their relationship until that point, with him going out of his way to win at all costs. Even against Riley, the woman he was falling for. Or maybe he wanted to win *because* he was falling for her—a way to put distance between them, to prove to himself that he could still do his job.

A way to prove he didn't need her.

"I couldn't let you have this one, Dylan. Couldn't let you start poking around, because you'd find things out. Maybe even try to stop me. And if I didn't finish that last arms deal the night I shot you, I never would've gotten that lead on Creighton's whereabouts."

"How did the arms dealer know?"

"Former ATF agent gone way south of the border. Found there was a lot more money—and fun—on the other side of the law. He'd gotten intel on a really badass new guy in DMH."

"Dead Man's Hand," Dylan said, his throat tight. They'd started out small about ten years earlier—in the last few, they'd expanded from mere menace to major threats. The expats involved were the worst traitors of all, and some of the meanest too, selling any and all intel they had on the United States to known terrorist groups. "How did you find out it was Creighton?"

"About five months ago I heard a rumor that he'd resigned from the CIA. And disappeared, for all intents and purposes. And then he got sloppy, probably for the first time in his career. When I started piecing things together and seeing if it could really be Gabriel who'd infiltrated DMH, I knew there would have to be a reason why he had such a hard-on for them."

"Was there?"

"DMH was responsible for the murder of his wife, who was also an agent. She'd been trying to infiltrate the group."

"That'll do it," he muttered. "What the hell did you do?"

"I contacted them, told them they had a traitor in their midst."

"You outed Gabriel to DMH as a CIA agent."

"Yes." She paused. "I thought that would be the end of it. That they'd kill him. Maybe torture him first. I lied and told DMH I was in it for the money. But DMH traced me. And now—"

"They want you dead."

"They want me to work for them," she corrected. "Which really is the same thing as being dead."

And then she made a sound that was half laugh, half choked sob. "I wanted Gabriel Creighton to pay, and all I've managed to do is dig myself in deeper." Neither of them said anything and the silence hung between them with the weight of her words and deeds.

Finally, he spoke. "We can work together. You don't have to give DMH what they want."

Riley went silent and he willed himself to believe that she was considering it. The only other thing he could think to say was, "Please."

Even before she cut the line, he knew that wouldn't be enough.

The call had come in less than an hour ago, summoning her. Riley had been waiting for it for a couple of days now, prayed it wouldn't happen when Dylan was with her.

It was a big part of the reason she had called him instead of going to his hotel room, letting his voice wash over her like a mini-redemption. And then the confession had poured out of her so easily. Always did after Dylan brought her to orgasm, whether with his hands or his dick or his voice alone—this time, it had been her talking dirty to him, bringing him to the brink. Then and only then did she drive away from her house, sure he was far too distracted to notice.

The plan had worked, but now he knew everything. Knew that revenge had shrouded her every move since she'd realized she had the power to set her world right.

Earlier, she'd disposed of the listening devices he'd planted in her house and car and cell phone. Still, it would be a neat trick for her to stop him from following her, because the man had supersonic tracking abilities and an uncanny sixth sense when it came to her.

Nine months earlier. Russia.

Bullets rang overhead. Riley's hiding place was behind a metal dumpster in the alley; the Russian gang she'd just stolen blueprints from would close in on her soon.

Her only salvation was that she'd hidden them already. The man who'd hired her would pick them up later.

Of course, that meant no one cared if she lived or died at this point. Or so she'd thought, until a pair of strong arms hauled her up from the ground through the window of an abandoned warehouse, moments before the Russian men descended on her now-defunct hiding place.

She whirled around, to find Dylan was the one holding her. "What are you doing here?"

"Saving your ass." He ground out the words, and he was the

angriest she'd ever seen him. Because she'd almost ruined his op . . . and he'd certainly ruined hers, but in a much different way. Because she couldn't stop thinking about him, wondering if they would continue along this path for years, hooking up when fate randomly brought them together . . . until one of them got killed.

"You trying to get yourself killed?" he demanded.

"Yes, Dylan, it was a suicide mission," she shot back. "I didn't ask for your backup."

"You sure as hell need it."

In the dark, his body pressed to hers, she felt the familiar urge. Wanted to give in to it. Wanted to run her fingers through his thick hair, let him take her against the wall, or back to his hotel, and not emerge until they were both sated.

Dammit. She pulled out of his grasp, remembering she had places to be. Needed to collect the money for the job she'd just completed, not hanging around with Dylan.

The worst part was that she'd been grateful that he'd arrived. Had actually thought about calling him for help.

She'd shoved away from him and hightailed it down the stairs and away from the abandoned building. Maybe she could still salvage this mission, could still grab the men, make the deal with the stolen maps, as planned.

"Riley." *He'd caught up to her, a hand wrapped around her biceps. An unrelenting grip, and she'd wanted to scream with frustration.*

"Let me go."

"You'll do something stupid."

"That's none of your concern." *She bared her teeth and finally he released her.* "Don't you understand, Dylan—I am none of your concern anymore."

She'd walked away, determined not to make contact again. And she hadn't, until he'd shown up in her storage locker.

But now he knew about DMH. Her role in everything. The fact that she might actually be employed by DMH, an organization that was for most of what Dylan fought against these days. If he still wanted anything from her, he was definitely a crazy man for aligning himself with someone a major terrorist group wanted, dead or alive.

Neither option appealed to her, but they'd made the choice seem so simple—work for them or they would kill her. Maybe her life was meant to be lived this way, a punishment for seeking revenge, for trying to play God, judge and jury.

What will you do?

She didn't know what fate she'd choose, not until she opened the door. From there, she'd go on instinct and not think about Dylan Scott and his many offers of help.

She didn't need help. She needed to confront her demons. And if she chose DMH, there would be more to follow. Perhaps, after a while, she would stop feeling. Killing would make her a rote machine, her conscience erased.

The nervous thump of her heart told her that pipe dream was over.

So. Over. Which was why she'd needed no further instructions when the familiar voice called with a time to meet.

DMH would come for her if she didn't show up. And, since Dylan was watching her house, Riley couldn't afford that.

She wouldn't involve him further. Bad enough she'd

spilled her stupid guts like some kind of weak-willed woman. She thought she'd pushed that need out of her, stomped it down hard enough that it would never show its face again.

She didn't want to need, and she held on to that control with a fierce and hard hand as her convertible veered off the highway and headed toward the address the man she knew only as Rocket had given her.

The private, underground garage nearly brought on an attack of claustrophobia, which was only made worse in the elevator. She longed for air and light and space, nearly stumbled in relief stepping off the elevator, into the long hallway that led to the steel door.

She'd only spoken with the man called Rocket by phone, all three times. The first was her reaching out with intel. The next two were from him, even though she'd made sure to block her number when she'd called.

She'd made them think she was giving them Gabriel Creighton on a platter for money. They'd made her realize the price of dealing with DMH was higher than she'd ever thought.

The key to the penthouse was along the top of the door on the heavy molding—she pulled it down after running her hand along the cool steel and took a calming breath before opening the door, letting herself in without the courtesy of a knock.

They were waiting for her anyway. Prepared, thanks to the myriad of cameras positioned from the parking garage right up to the door she'd just opened.

There was a man sitting on the couch. She took note of another man, behind her, big and beefy.

A thin trickle of sweat ran between her breasts, despite the frigid air-conditioning in the penthouse, as she shut the heavy door, the key still clutched tightly in her hand.

The seated man nodded in her direction and she immediately recognized Rocket's voice. "Great to finally meet you, Riley. Your information was invaluable."

She didn't say anything, simply nodded and listened.

"He's still alive, in case you were wondering. We've got plans for him." Rocket put his hands together, fingertips touching as well as thumbs, forming a diamond shape. "We've got plans for you too, Riley. Although my orders say differently, I think you can be of great use to our organization."

"And just to be clear—if I refuse?" she asked, kept her voice firm and steady, her hands equally so. Her insides were jelly, undecided as to fight or flight.

He sighed, but when he spoke, his tone remained affable, his hands unchanged. "We kill you. The choice is yours."

Riley realized that it always had been. For the first time, she might actually choose correctly.

She was surrounded by angry, armed men. Trapped in the tub, Sky was paralyzed as they came closer . . . closer.

"Come with us, Sky . . ."

She reached for her gun, but it wasn't there. She was alone and they were coming for her. And she was fighting, her hands clenched into fists and making contact—

"Skylar, baby, you're dreaming. Wake up—you're safe."

Skylar, baby.

She *was* safe, pressed against Cam with his strong arms wrapped around her. She uncurled her fists against his chest and let her breathing get back to normal as he rubbed her shoulders.

She had no idea how long he'd been lying next to her, but her body was warmed by his and it was officially dark outside. "Sorry. It was so real. They were after me and I couldn't get away. Do you have dreams like that?"

He pulled back from her a bit. She could make out his features in the dark as he stared at her, the dim ceiling light dappling his skin. "Yeah, sometimes. Hazard of the job. Not something you should have to deal with."

His tone was decidedly casual, and that made her unreasonably angry. "That man's face, when you killed him." She pressed her palms over her eyes in an attempt to block out the image but instead succeeded in burning it deeper into her memory. "How does this not affect you?"

"Who says it doesn't?" His words were quiet and somewhat gruff, as if she'd forced him to admit something shameful. "There's blood on my hands, Sky, and there always will be."

"This time, it's because of me."

"None of this is your fault, you have to know that."

She did, but that didn't make anything easier. "My father is always pretending to be someone else for his job... does he feel that way too? That there's blood on his hands?"

Gabriel had blood on his hands, but whether or not he cared was something about which Cam refused to speculate. Cam had been unable to get his own father from his mind, thanks to the earlier conversation with Dylan about the OAs.

Cam had always wondered how his father had done it, pretended to be someone else. Had it been easier to really become an outlaw, or had Howie Moore simply found his true calling? He'd seemed to like being a rough-riding, hard-talking biker, a man people with half a brain were afraid of.

The ones with less brains than that never fared too well under his father's fast moves. Howie had been known to kill indiscriminately, although that could never be proven. They called him Dark Angel—no one ever saw him, but whenever vengeance was necessary, Howie was at the center of it. "My dad was a dangerous man. Trained ATF agent and a biker. I know he scared the shit out of me. And he was always in character. I don't know if he would have ever been able to separate himself from that last job."

Growing up, Cam hadn't brought friends home—or girlfriends. Howie was a serious body builder on top of everything else—big, thick, tattooed to the hilt. Smart. And angry.

The man was always angry. He couldn't have had too much peace with himself. At least that's what Cam would tell himself when Howie was knocking the shit out of him a few times a month.

Sky didn't say anything to those admissions—and Cam felt himself sticking up for his father, inexplicably. "He was under a lot of pressure."

She gave a low, raw laugh. "That's what we tell ourselves, right? Stay out of their way, they've got an important job." She turned to him. "I get it—but why have children, then? Those jobs are much better suited to independent, unattached men and women."

"I guess they fell in love, couldn't help themselves." He'd said it almost flippantly, nearly said, *Probably couldn't keep out of each other's pants,* but went with the slightly more romanticized version.

She made a soft noise, and for a second, he thought she was crying. She might've been, because when she spoke again, her voice had an odd, hollow quality to it, couched in a steely resolve. "My mother was killed when I was sixteen. My father told me that it was someone looking for revenge on her—I don't know much more than that. I was supposed to be home—would've been too if I hadn't snuck out back to visit at the neighbor's house. When I came home hours later, everything had changed. I was taken away, my last name was changed and I was guarded for about six months until they determined no one knew I existed. My parents set it up that way. My mom was an agent too."

I know who you really are. This was what she hadn't wanted to tell him before. She might not have been threatened before, but her family had certainly been a target. "I'm sorry—I didn't know."

"Dad never talks about it with me, so I can't imagine him mentioning it to someone else. I was always coached, taught to tell people that my parents were executives, that they traveled for work. But my parents never talked about me, didn't carry pictures of me. Didn't claim me on their taxes. I always had a different last name. When I was growing up, for the longest time, I had this strange sense that I didn't exist."

Her words explained the haunted look that shrouded her face at odd moments.

"There wasn't a funeral. It was, like, one day she went

to work and never came home, and I wasn't supposed to acknowledge it. I went on with life, being raised by a string of housekeepers who disapproved that my father worked so much," she continued. "I shouldn't be telling you all this— I never tell anyone."

"Everything you tell me helps me protect you more effectively," he lied, and she gave him a wan smile.

"I hated feeling so scared and helpless. It was such an awful time and I really thought I was past it . . . and I don't know if I can get through this."

"You can—you will. You held it together today." He paused. "Did you tell me about your mom because of what I told you earlier?"

"I don't know. Maybe. Maybe I was going to tell you no matter what. I've kept it inside for so long . . . it's tiring."

"Yeah, I know."

"I already told you that I hated my father sometimes. His job. I wondered, how can he do something so dangerous, how can he put me at risk like that? After my mother . . . didn't he care enough to quit?"

He didn't say anything—what was there to say?

And then she reached out, touched his cheek, spoke to him . . . implored him. "How do you do it, Cam? You have a dangerous job too. What's that like? How do you get yourself back?"

He had no idea how to answer her.

I know who you really are, Sky—but you have no fucking clue who I am. Or why I'm here.

Would it ever come down to telling her? Dylan was right—he could call the CIA, let them know where to get Sky. But that wouldn't solve the problem of Sky eventually telling the CIA—and, by extension, Gabriel—that Cam had been with her.

If Gabriel was even alive. "I already told you, Sky— I have blood on my hands."

It was so quiet. The TV wasn't working. The lights kept dimming, even though the worst of the storm was over.

And still, Sky knew both of them were used to this, for such different reasons. Cam, with the military training— watching, waiting in semi-darkness for the danger.

Or hunting it down, she supposed.

Her danger had once come from a different source. She remembered sitting there in the hospital, watching her own body betray her. Wondering what she'd done wrong. How much longer she could hold out. Even now, she stared down at her inner arms, ran a palm down one of them, remembering IVs and blown veins, black-and-blue marks.

There was still a light scar near her collarbone from the central line. Cam had run his fingers over it the other night—and then he'd kissed it, even when she'd closed her eyes tight and tried to forget how many scars her body held.

Too many for a woman.

She turned from him on the bed, because she'd already revealed way too much, too fast, and this whole thing was crazy.

When he'd asked her earlier about whether or not there had been other threats made to her before this one, she hadn't wanted to go there, revisit the past. But he had to know, whether or not it applied to the current situation.

It was something she'd never told anyone. Somehow,

sharing secrets in the dark seemed safer, even though she knew it wasn't, that everything could come back to haunt her.

You have to trust someone, Sky.

Instincts, baby girl.

She lay on her side, head on the pillow, facing the window. When the next words came out of her mouth, they surprised even her. "Was there ever anyone special? I mean, could there be?"

"I don't think it's possible. Not with my job. Don't get me wrong, plenty of Delta guys do it. But it's hard on them, hard on their families."

"Their wives must get used to being alone. A lot."

"Yeah."

"I'm alone a lot too. I used to tell myself that it was by choice."

"Same here."

"Are you alone because... because you don't want to hurt someone the way we just talked about?" she asked finally.

"Maybe. I never really thought about it like that."

"I think I'm alone because it's easier. They told me that, even with the transplant, there are no guarantees."

"There never are, Sky." He paused, and then, "You said you started writing when you got back."

She nodded. "It was like, I had everything to lose, and nothing to lose. I could get lost in something else, didn't worry about machines beeping and nurses and transplant lists." She paused, aware of how strident she sounded. "I'm not alone when I'm writing, if that makes sense."

"Yeah, I get that. That's why you were so upset when you couldn't write."

Even though he seemed to understand her, to get her in a way she never thought possible, she still couldn't bring herself to turn back to him when she asked the next question. "Do you ever see it changing? The alone thing, I mean, whether you're out of the military or not?"

"We should get out of here," he said abruptly—and okay, point taken. Especially after he dropped his hand from her shoulder and rolled off the bed, without so much as a backward glance.

And yeah, she'd checked over her shoulder.

Even though he'd consoled her after the dream-slash-nightmare, and he'd lain down beside her, he hadn't tried to so much as kiss her again. Or touch her in any way that couldn't remotely be considered chaste.

She drew her arms over her chest as if to protect herself. Last night had obviously been nothing more than a mercy fuck, and although it had gotten her battery charged . . . the knowledge that it had been a one-night stand was almost too humiliating to bear.

The fact that he was saving her life? Well, that made her plan on sticking it out despite all of the humiliation.

She heard Cam mutter, "Shit," saw him holding on to the wall for dear life.

Instinctively, she grabbed on to him and helped him over to the bed. He didn't argue, let her lead him back into a sitting position on the edge of the bed.

"Thanks. Dizzy," he said finally.

She realized he was shaking, and sweating a little. She reached up and wiped his forehead. "You've got a fever."

"I'll be okay—the antibiotics will kick in soon."

"Do you think it's shock, from the blood loss?"

He snorted. "A few stitches and suddenly you're a doctor."

"I've spent enough time in hospitals to pick up a few things myself." Add to that the research she'd done for her books, and yes, there were times she wished she didn't know as much.

But he had antibiotics in him. That in itself was a huge relief. Now if she could just make him more comfortable . . .

"Sky, I'm going to be fine. Won't let anything happen to you, okay?" he murmured, his voice strong and soothing. "I've dealt with much worse and survived."

She touched his cheek, stroked the rough stubble for a few seconds. "Let me help you get the fever down."

"I'm okay."

She heard the irritation in his voice, but she ignored it, left the bed to wet some washcloths and grab dry towels as well.

He'd remained with his arms propped on his thighs, and so much for the tough-guy routine.

"Cam, come on," she said softly.

He didn't argue any further, winced slightly when he sat up straight. Let her help him ease his T-shirt off.

She checked the bandage, looking over his shoulder. "I think the bleeding's stopped."

He simply nodded, but his color was already better.

"Come on, get into bed." She'd propped pillows up against the headboard and he leaned back against them, sitting on one of the towels she'd laid out so the sheets wouldn't be damp when he went back to sleep. "I think maybe we should stay here tonight."

"No. I'm okay."

"You're not ... but I know you will be."

"I told you that already." But his protest was gone, his eyes heavy-lidded and his arousal ... well, there wasn't a problem with that. She hadn't realized that in the effort to get him leaning back, she'd sort of ... straddled him.

And Cam, of course, didn't seem to mind. And maybe, just maybe, he wasn't lying when he'd said that the scar wasn't a problem for him.

Or maybe it was simply a horny male response.

Staying in place, she ran the cloth along his face, holding it for a few seconds against his forehead, and he closed his eyes and leaned into her hand.

Her free hand stroked his hair away from his face. "I've got you, I'll take care of you," she murmured as she began to move the cloth across his forehead and cheeks, pushing his hair out of the way, then working the washcloth down his throat and chest.

He sighed a little. "Feels nice. Thanks."

She brought the cloth to the back of his neck. And then she pushed back off his lap and unbuttoned his jeans and began to push them down over his hips, trying her best to ignore the arousal she found there.

He helped her, lifted his ass off the mattress so she could pull the soft denim down his long legs and push the jeans aside. He wore black boxer briefs, and they didn't leave anything to the imagination. She remembered all too well what he looked like without them.

She continued the exploration down his chest, the

image of what she'd seen last night in the shower, the feel of him on her in bed still so fresh in her memory, threatening to erase everything, including common sense.

And now, even though he was down, he was in no way out. She noted that sinewed biceps, the muscled pecs... noticed that he was still hard as a rock.

"Problem?" he asked, with just enough innocence in his voice for her to know he was anything but at that moment.

"No problem at all." Instead, she rubbed his chest down again while he bent a thigh up, trapping her somewhat in place. "You look better."

"Just a momentary lapse. I'll feel better once I get something to eat—shouldn't have gone that long without anything." He closed his eyes for a second and then opened them, the brilliant blue back, his gaze sharply focused on her. "How are you feeling?"

"I'm okay," she assured him. He nodded, his thigh rubbing her side, his eyes locking her in place. She saw so many things there. Anger. Pain. Lust.

All she wanted was the latter to override everything.

CHAPTER

10

Rocket didn't move and the fight rose up in Riley suddenly and inexplicably and she knew without a doubt that DMH would not control her.

She'd rather die. But she'd fight tooth and nail before she let that happen either.

Rocket smiled, as if he knew her choice. Hands came from behind, pressing her throat as she'd expected, and she let her body go limp, her eyes focused on the gunmetal gray walls of the penthouse for a moment.

She tried to sink farther to the ground, but the brute wasn't letting up on his chokehold.

She dropped the key to the penthouse to the floor, and Rocket watched it fall as the breath squeezed out of her.

Spots swam before her eyes and she forced herself not to panic, because—no matter the outcome here tonight—she would be free.

In her other hand, loosely held, was a Chinese star, carefully laced with just enough poison that even the slightest hit with a point would cause near-instantaneous death. And as she sagged against the man holding her from behind, she released the spiked gold metal with a practiced flip of the wrist and watched with satisfaction as it hit its mark right beneath Rocket's Adam's apple.

She saw the surprise in his face as he clutched at the star, even as the man who held her loosened his grip, unsure of what to do next. But she knew; she turned hard and brought her knee up to his balls, because that always worked to bring even the biggest man to his knees. But he was up quickly, slamming her first across the side of the face and then landing another blow on the top of her head, hard enough for her to know she'd have a concussion. On top of that, breathing was still not easy—she heard the painful wheeze coming from her throat as she attempted to draw in air.

From behind her, she heard Rocket groaning, cursing—he stumbled over the coffee table in a last-ditch attempt to grab her, his own weapon in his hand.

All she needed to do was duck and roll to elude the shot—his bullet hit the man in front of her and then both men were down, dead and unmoving.

She was down for the count as well, collapsed to the thick carpet. Her phone was ringing and she grabbed it, answered with a hoarse hello.

A calm voice simply said, "You killed my men."

"Impressed?" she managed.

The man chuckled. "You might be worth more alive than I thought, little one."

She fought the urge to gag. "I've already given you a major piece of intelligence. All I wanted in return was money. I didn't ask for any ties to you."

"You found us. That alone ties you to us. I thought you were smart enough to know that," the man said. "You'll get what's coming to you in due time. Make no mistake about that."

The line went dead and her vision began to blur. She managed to dial her phone because she couldn't drag herself out the door and to the elevator, and she could only pray that Dylan found her before other men from DMH did.

Sleeping with Sky now would be wrong. Cam knew that and somehow couldn't shake the ridiculous notion that she could somehow heal him. Fix the pain inside.

Unbreak him.

The way she looked at him told him she wanted that job, had already in part taken it on. "There's so much about me you don't know."

"So tell me."

Yeah, tell her—tell her what you just confirmed about Gabriel. Because that'll really make her understand everything.

And maybe it was the blood loss or the exhaustion . . . or Sky's earnest look, because he knew he *would* tell her. Not all of it . . . but something.

"What I told you before, about my dad . . . I didn't tell you the whole story," he said. "I never knew what happened to him, not until recently, and I hated him all these years because he left me to take the heat for him."

"What do you mean?" She sat back on her heels, watching him so intently that he almost shrugged it off. Wondered why the hell he'd started telling her anyway and decided it was the fever and the gunshot.

And the proximity to her. And the way she touched him.

Son of a bitch. "It's complicated."

"Always is." She tightened her hands around the washcloth and moved to leave the bed.

"He's dead. At least as far as I can trust the source." He ran a hand through his hair, realized just how fucking exposed he already was and figured he might as well go all the way. "I told you before that your father helped me."

She nodded. "And that you don't like him."

He didn't bother asking how she knew that.

"You hate my father—and yet, you'll do what he asked," she continued softly. "Why is that?"

Jesus, could he tell her? Could he really share that secret and keep the other ones from her?

Before he could think it through further, he said, "Your father got me out of jail."

"Jail?" she repeated uncertainly, her words clipped. To her credit, she didn't move from his arms. "But you're Army. I didn't think—"

"Again, your father. He wiped my record clean and helped me enlist, to start a new life."

"Why were you in prison?"

"I was serving two concurrent life sentences for murder."

She shifted, but she didn't leave the bed. "I don't . . . you don't . . . You're one of the good guys."

He swallowed, hard, unable to voice how much her words of confidence meant to him. "I know everyone says they're innocent, but I really am. I didn't commit the murders I was convicted of. For a long time, I figured it was my father's handiwork, but I had no way to prove it."

"My God, Cam," she breathed. "You really think . . ."

He took a staggered breath and then, "I knew my dad had gotten so deep in his cover that it was hard for him to know right from wrong anymore—maybe I even understand it a little bit better now. But then all I knew was that I did what my father asked me to do and ended up in jail, for what could have been the rest of my life."

Sky's eyes were softer than they'd been before, and she'd moved closer to him. "What makes you think your father would do that to you?"

"He came to me—it was three in the morning—handed me keys and told me to let myself in through the back door of the neighbor's house. Not to ask questions. And I trusted him, so I did. Then I saw them—dead, on the floor in the kitchen. I bent down to check on them, getting blood on my hands. And I ran out of there, left the keys in the door and my prints everywhere, and I got on my hog and sped off, even though I heard the police sirens behind me. And they chased me until I knew I had no choice but to pull over. I thought that my father would come and straighten everything out. But no one came. The public defender said he looked for him, but our house had been all packed up and he'd left no forwarding address, either at his fake job or with the ATF."

"And the ATF wouldn't help you?"

He shook his head.

"My God." She put a hand on his arm and he jerked it away fast.

"Sorry. Shit." But he still didn't touch her again. In fact, he actually moved away, as if his pain was contagious. "It was fucked up."

He didn't want to go back there, even to convince Sky—but he had to. Within seconds, he was back in that small room, his hands cuffed behind him, his legs chained to the chair, waiting to see who'd requested a meeting with him.

His lawyer had given up on him a year and a half ago, claimed he'd exhausted all the possibilities. And when the tall, good-looking guy in the suit came in and told the guards they could take off the cuffs, Cam had wondered why a suit would take that kind of chance.

"I could take you out with one hand," Gabriel told him when the guard left, as if he'd read Cam's mind.

Cam had been living in fucking hell, fighting tooth and nail for his own life, and he'd learned a hell of a lot about survival.

He'd later realize he'd learned nothing at all, not compared to what he knew now. But, for a nineteen-year-old, he'd been pretty sure he could take the suit.

"I knew your father," the man said, introducing himself as Gabriel Creighton, and Cam's world shifted and then righted. "I promised him that I'd keep you out of trouble—and by the looks of things, I'm a little late."

"Do you know where he is?"

Gabriel shifted in his chair and then looked Cam in the eye. "He's gone, Cameron. But I'm going to get you out of here."

"I'd figured my dad was a drug addict or riding his Harley cross-country. That he'd fucked me over good. I was so angry . . . and scared," he admitted. "I'd done what my father asked me to and I ended up in prison. And I had no idea where he'd gone. And I've bounced between hating him and wondering if . . ."

He'd forgotten who he was speaking to for a second, and so he pulled back. "Tonight, I found out that he was killed the night of the murders."

"And all that time, you thought he was alive, and that he sent you into that house to get you caught by the police on purpose," she said softly. "Cam . . . it had to have been a mistake. My father's a hard man, but he'd never do anything to hurt me. I can't imagine yours would either. He probably would've—explained, helped you."

"I hope so. Thing is, I don't know if he would've. I don't really know anything except I never want to go back to prison."

He'd received a certain amount of protection in there, thanks to his association with the OA, but that didn't mean he didn't have to fight. There was so much confusion surrounding what happened with his dad that no one could truly say the man had been a traitor.

That was probably the only thing that saved Cam's life.

But there were plenty of other hog gangs, dubbed *one percenters* because they were among a very small grouping considered outlaws of the motorcycle culture, who'd thought the young man was a perfect toy to play with.

And so he'd fought. Over and over. Barely slept. Watched his back. And when he'd gotten some level of respect, he still hadn't let his guard down.

He'd never stopped feeling guarded. Maybe he never would.

"I keep thinking about you in jail," she told him. "And I can't see it. You were so young, a baby..."

"I wasn't that innocent. I held my own," he said.

"Yeah, you're a tough one, Cam. I knew that from the second I met you."

Her voice was soft, without a hint of sarcasm, and his arms tightened around her. "After each fight, I was put in solitary. I spent a lot of time there—just me and the four walls. And lots of time to think, when that was the last thing I wanted to do. And I sat there, most of the time wishing I was dead."

"I guess jails and hospitals have a lot in common, then," she said. "Except I spent most of my time praying I would live."

Cam had never imagined that telling a woman about this would make her actually seem to like him more. To understand.

To believe him.

Shit.

"About last night..." Sky started hesitantly, and then took a deep breath. "I think you regret what happened. And I wish you didn't. I mean, you just met me. And I never expected..." She trailed off and motioned between them.

He wanted to tell her that it was all a result of the danger. The adrenaline rush. That it wasn't—couldn't be—real. "I didn't either."

But whatever had happened, it *was* real. And the ultimate irony couldn't be ignored. There was an expiration date on whatever was unfolding between them. But, for now, she was his haven. "I didn't thank you for helping me. You were a trooper. Didn't faint at the sight of blood or anything."

She smiled at that. "Yeah, well, it wasn't that hard once I got the hang of it. Not that I'm looking for a repeat performance."

"I'm not used to having someone help me. I mean, I have the team, but..." He drifted off, because damn, he'd told her more than he'd wanted to. And he continued. "Well, let's just say I learned a long time ago to count on myself because I wasn't sure anyone else would be around to help. And I've been doing that for so long, sometimes I forget it's good to let people in."

"I've been on my own for a while now too," she said quietly. "I make my own money—don't actually count on my father for anything. He would be there for me, I know it, but I can't help but feel like... I need to do it on my own."

"Why?"

"Because someday I'm going to be really alone. And I'd rather get used to it now than have it come as a shock later."

It was like having his own thoughts repeated back to him. Her body held a fierceness, as if daring him to tell her she was wrong, and he couldn't.

He could only tell her that in this instance, she did need help, no matter how badly she wanted to do things by herself. "Kiss me, Sky."

She straddled him, one hand on the headboard behind

him, the other winding in his hair. She blushed, but she was initiating all of it. He enjoyed watching her take control for a while, because she was so obviously enjoying herself.

"I thought you were ready to pass out," she murmured.

"Yeah, not so much now."

CHAPTER
11

Riley was gone and Dylan cursed himself for thinking with his dick. She'd played him perfectly—let him play with himself until his brain was mush and then hit him with the DMH punch to the gut.

He'd struggled to the sliding glass door to look through the high-powered scope pointed at her house, but he'd known it was futile. She was long gone, and his chest tightened.

She would, no doubt, claim leaving him behind was for his own good. For hers too maybe, but the thought of her in debt to DMH made the bile rise in his throat.

She'd probably found all his bugs—in her house, her phone and her car. He'd be flying without a net going out to look for her, and still that hadn't stopped him from getting dressed and hauling ass to his car.

It wasn't the first time he'd followed her when she was headed for trouble. And even after she broke off contact with him after he'd saved her gorgeous ass in Russia, he hadn't stopped.

And fuck it all, Dylan Scott did not do things like that.

Bad enough the fucking iPod thing had nearly cost him any and all street cred. Mainly because he'd had to call Zane to figure it out fast.

"I'm too busy to screw around with iPods," he'd ground out *while Zane had laughed in the background.*

"It's like being back in the day, making a mix tape for the girl you liked. When I was in sixth grade," his brother howled.

So when he heard through a friend of an arms deal involving Riley and an ATF agent, Dylan made sure to get involved. To stop her, because the feds were on to the deal. And when he'd tailed her, found her rental space and went through the files she kept there, he had the ultimate surprise finding the intel on Gabriel Creighton.

He knew he was partially to blame for what happened in that warehouse—he'd pushed and she naturally pushed back. Hard. His side ached just thinking about it. Scar tissue that yanked at him at the most inopportune times.

There was nothing left to do but wait for her to call.

She would. Had to.

In the meantime, his other source came through, the one he'd called in a special favor from. Because until Riley had closure on what happened to her father, she would never fully heal.

It wasn't the news he'd wanted to hear, but it was the truth.

And when he'd been driving around downtown Miami for the better part of an hour, his nerves screaming, the call finally came through—he fumbled for the speaker button and ran a red light, ignoring the steady scream of horns and screeching tires that followed him.

He could barely make out her voice, but he knew it was her.

"Riley, say that again," he urged as she rasped out an address. He punched it into the GPS while telling her, "I'm coming for you. Try to stay awake with me, honey—I'll be there in five minutes."

"Cameras everywhere," she croaked as he took a turn on two wheels in order to make a green light and shave a little off the time it would take to reach her.

"Are you alone?"

"For . . . now."

"How badly are you hurt?" He got silence in response. Her phone was still on, though, and he continued to talk to her in a steady and reassuring tone, knowing full well that she might be able to sense him even if she was unconscious.

The address belonged to an old commercial warehouse turned into luxury apartments. He parked his car next to hers—a Mercedes convertible that was as sleek as Riley herself—in the underground lot and headed for the elevators.

Cameras everywhere . . .

He forced himself to tamp down everything but his professionalism, to treat this the way he would any other mission. To make it too personal was to fuck it all up, which he'd seen happen time and time again.

As he walked to the elevator, he presented like any busy man, with his head bent toward his BlackBerry. He tried to run a quick check to confirm who lived at this address—who could possibly be the Miami link to DMH.

It was only when he got into the steel box and went to punch the numbers that he realized she hadn't given him a destination other than the building itself.

There were only three floors—two sprawling, loftlike apartments on each.

He took a chance and went to the top floor—people always wanted the prestige and privacy of the top floor, criminals and businessmen alike.

When he stepped off the elevator to a silent hallway, he checked the intel being returned to him on his BlackBerry.

The names triggered nothing in his memory—businessmen, two legitimate, two not so legit, none of whom he could easily connect to Gabriel Creighton or DMH, and two semi-famous D-listers.

Living on the top floor—the actress and one of the legitimate businessman.

He'd decide how legit the man really was.

He didn't hear anything through the steel apartment doors. He ran to the door on the far left, his gun pulled, pressed his ear against the cold metal, tried the doorknob.

Locked up tight.

The door on the far right was a different story—it gave easily against his touch, and he cautiously pushed it open, his weapon still drawn, but at his side.

A large man sprawled facedown on the rug, with no obvious signs of bleeding. But he was dead just the same.

There was silence and then a small groan. Female.

He stopped dead in his tracks and looked left, found her wedged behind the couch, where she'd obviously dragged herself for some cover in case unwelcome visitors came in.

Please let her be okay. Please.

He closed the distance between the doorway of the apartment and Riley's prone body. When he got to her, he noticed a second man, a few feet from her—he was faceup and most definitely dead, judging by the fact that half his skull was blown off.

Gingerly, he moved Riley's hair and felt her pulse. Thready, but it was there.

She stirred, turned her head a bit.

Shit. "Riley, talk to me. How hurt are you?"

He saw a small bruise on her temple, which was nothing compared to the angry red marks that spanned along her neck.

Someone had tried to strangle her, but she was still breathing and she didn't appear to have been shot. Nor had she done the shooting—her own weapon was still holstered.

Her phone was next to her cheek—he shoved it in his pocket as she stirred and looked at him, her eyes squinting.

"Get me out of here. Please. Fast," she murmured before she slid into unconsciousness again. He checked around for anything that could easily identify her as having been here, like a purse, and saw nothing. She'd traveled light.

And as much as he wanted to run with her now, he rummaged through the clothing of the dead men for identification. He took both their wallets and stuffed them into his jeans—then scooped her up and took the stairs, hoping he wouldn't run into anyone. By the time he got to the garage, she was moving in his arms, muttering something, over and over, but he couldn't understand it.

He managed to get her into his car without incident, and squealed out of the lower lot. Mainly because they were no longer alone.

"Dylan." Her eyes were wide as she stared past him out the side window, at the SUV heading straight for them.

"I see them, sweetheart. Buckle up—I can't tell how bad this is going to be." He shot forward as she did so, and heard her small gasp of pain. He really needed to get her some medical attention.

Cameras everywhere.

He pulled out of the lot and into the street, his small car bouncing on its struts but then blending easily into the nighttime downtown traffic. There were a million small black expensive rental cars like his, all with darkened windows.

He checked the rearview and saw no sign of the Bronco that had threatened to plow into them back at the garage. That didn't mean it wasn't far behind but it gave him breathing room.

Breathing was good. "Riley, stay with me. I'm going to take you to a hospital."

She reached over and squeezed his arm hard. Reassuring. "No. Take me someplace safe."

He could do that, and if necessary, would call a doctor who would ask no questions.

Sky leaned in, and even though she was the one on top, Cam's mouth devoured hers with a deep, hot kiss that flooded her body with immediate heat.

His hands remained on her hips, which she realized were rocking against him, rubbing his hard shaft against her jeans, but she wanted more. Needed the sensation of his hands on her again, making her realize that it wasn't a dream, that she was alive. Really, truly, spectacularly alive.

She'd felt his pull from the second he'd stood in her doorway and it hadn't lessened, even with what she knew now.

She shoved her jeans down impatiently. He was kissing his way down her neck and her hand sought the hard column brushing between her legs. She heard him mutter against her skin as she wrapped her hands around his arousal. The sound got louder as she stroked—his thighs shifted under hers and he suckled the soft flesh along her collarbone.

Hail began striking the windows again, the lights shuddered and dimmed, but none of that mattered at the moment.

"Not going anywhere now," she told him.

He nodded in agreement, his mouth quirked to one corner as he watched her watching him, her eyes sweeping the shadows along his chest, noting her hand play with him—and his obvious pleasure.

He reached forward, lifting her shirt to expose her bra while she stroked him deftly. "Take your clothes off, Sky."

His voice held the touch of command, enough to make her obey him almost instantly. Refusing to let go of him, she used her free hand to pull the shirt over her head, and he helped with her bra, reaching around the back and unhooking it with a swift, confident movement.

She fought the urge to hold her arms over her breasts, same as last night, but the way he looked at her again...

The way he needed her.

"Keep going," he said, and put his hand on his own arousal when she took hers away to unbutton and shimmy out of her jeans and underwear. She watched him stroke himself slowly as she lowered herself back down to his thighs, and his gaze moved up and down her body as sensuously as a touch.

Her breasts felt heavy, ripe, despite their small size, the nipples already puckered taut, as if readying for his lips or to be suckled between his teeth.

Hesitantly, she dragged her own hand down her body and let it rest between her legs.

"Go ahead," he urged, and she did, rubbed herself the way she had so many lonely nights, when she'd close her eyes and try to picture a man who could handle everything she had.

Now, with eyes wide open, she realized that she might actually be looking at one.

Both of them had their ghosts—neither was perfect, or unafraid—but maybe, just maybe...

"Don't think," Cam was saying, his voice husky. Gruff. His fisted cock was purple at the head, and he hissed then, as if he was trying his best to hold back.

His hand joined hers and she did the same as they simultaneously worked themselves and each other, until their breathing was rapid and she was sure her eyes were as glazed as Cam's.

Embarrassment washed away as she rode the taut wire of wanting this to never end and needing relief.

But he stopped before she could come, took his hand away, and hers too, and he slid down farther, unmindful of the wounds on his shoulder and back.

She knew what he wanted.

Last night, he'd taken her with his mouth, his tongue, and she wanted that again. He urged her over him and she felt her face flush as he positioned her hips over his face and buried himself in her.

A blast of heat ricocheted through her—his tongue penetrated her in the most demanding fashion, dragging her over the edge to an orgasm that rushed through her body and left her weak and panting . . . and oh so satisfied.

The tension left her body instantly, replaced by sheer bliss.

She shifted, moved back along his body until his thick erection pressed between her wet sex. She leaned forward, elbows on the bed on either side of his head, spent, but so willing to accept and give more pleasure.

"Condom," he murmured. She'd nearly forgotten, her head so fogged with the heady smell of dark, tangy spices that surrounded them. "In the pocket of my jeans."

That made her smile. "Planning ahead?"

"Hoping."

"Me too." She took the package and opened it, rolled

the condom onto his arousal while he watched. And then she lowered herself onto him, slowly.

He remained still, letting her have her way, allowing her to set the pace of how fast she let him inside. When she'd settled her weight onto him, she took a moment to simply breathe and let herself adjust to his girth.

With her sex clamped around him, and with his hands pushing and pulling her hips, she rode him, faster and faster, until another orgasm was imminent, until he groaned and called her name, a guttural, fierce sound that pounded through her like a fierce moving storm, drenching her with its dominant beauty.

The time had ticked by. It was dark outside and for a second, only that much, Sky allowed the horrors of that morning to rise up before she beat them back down with a fierce resolve and the notion that Cam would keep her safe.

But reality summoned. She had to go into the hospital, to Dr. Strohm, for her bimonthly test at the end of next week. Had to keep her fingers crossed and her hopes high.

Beds were for sleeping, for being sick and recovering in. For her, they'd never been connected to pleasure. Until now.

Maybe if her character, Violet, could fall in love, so could she. Maybe it wasn't all bullshit and hormones.

Maybe all of this was real. Cam felt real under her, his breathing shallow, since he remained awake, his body warm against hers, like a living, breathing heating pad, and this was so much nicer than waking up without him this morning.

Her hands molded along his sides, her fingers reading him like Braille, trailing between the ridges of hard muscle and rib, careful to avoid the bandaged area.

There were other scars, lighter and older. She wanted to explore them all, to ask about them. To hear all his stories, no matter how scary.

She had plenty of her own stories to tell.

"Before last night . . . it had been longer than two years." Longer than three, most likely, if she bothered to count, beyond the releases she'd given herself. They weren't nearly as satisfying as this . . . and neither were the few sexual encounters she'd had.

There'd been too much to worry about with her health for casual sex, and conversely, her health had gotten in the way of having anything more than fleeting relationships.

Contrary to popular belief, hospitals were not a good place to meet a doctor, especially when you were a scared, sick woman, lying in a regulation hospital bed.

They'd treated her clinically, hadn't worried about her emotions. Probably because she'd always acted strong. It was easier than having people fawn, though she'd long suspected that the nurses could see right through her.

"I guess you're making up for lost time." He tightened his arms around her, even as his shoulder began to throb again—from overuse, he was sure. A good kind, and nothing he regretted, but he had to get his mind back on his job.

"I thought . . . I thought maybe you didn't want to do that with me again. God, that sounds stupid. I mean, I know we've been a little busy, but—"

He cut her off with a thumb to her bottom lip. "I

shouldn't be kissing you. Shouldn't have done anything with you in the first place, Sky. It was unprofessional. I let my guard down, and I can't let that happen. Not now."

She nodded, looked confused, and yeah, join the club. "So . . . now what?"

"Let me keep you safe. And then we'll figure out the rest, okay?"

"I might actually believe you mean that."

He couldn't help but smile. "I do, Sky. But there are other things . . ."

"There are always other things." Her voice held a wistful quality, and it was just them and their secrets in the small room. And the secrets were all out.

In a way, they were two stray, scared tough kids who'd found each other. And Cam wondered if either of them would ever be the same again after all was said and done.

He was getting closer to her. It would only make things harder when he had to leave her.

When she left him.

She wanted him—he could tell by the way she touched him. And it killed him that she thought he didn't want her.

That couldn't be further from the truth. It was more that his gut told him that moving on, despite the storm outside, was the best course of action. "We really do have to go soon."

She nodded, but neither made a move to leave the bed.

He pulled her close, because hell, he wanted more time with her like this. "Are you sorry you know about my prison time?"

"Not at all. I'm glad you told me. I understand, Cam."

"Yeah, I guess in a weird way, you do." He shifted so he wasn't pressing on his shoulder. "It's not exactly something I share. Ever."

You could tell her now . . . tell her what her father did.

"I don't think less of you. It was out of your control. It wasn't your fault," she murmured as her finger traced a circle over his bare nipple. But he didn't want to deal with that now, wishing he could bury himself in Sky again, as deep as he could, just to hear her cry out in passion.

He fought the urge to simply roll her over and take her. Claim her, the way she just had him.

Instead, he said, "I could've done more over the years to look for him."

"It sounds like you did."

"After a while, yeah." After Gabriel's promises fell through and Cam began to realize that if a top CIA agent couldn't get answers, something was really wrong.

"Do you know who killed him?"

The million-dollar question. "Yes. I've suspected for a long time, but I've just gotten some new information that points to the killer. It's unconfirmed, though."

"It doesn't sound like you've had anyone on your side."

"A few people, but it's been difficult."

"You need people on your side who can help bring him to justice." She paused. "Did you ever ask for my father's help?"

Tell her. "That wouldn't be appropriate."

"Screw appropriate. He has connections, Cam. And if he's the one who sprang you from jail, and he knew your father, why didn't he help you? I don't understand."

"That wasn't his priority. Or maybe he felt I was better off not knowing. It was a highly classified case."

"So you're going after the man who killed your dad yourself?" she asked as she held him tightly.

He drew a deep breath. "Damned straight I am."

"Do you think that's a good idea, Cam? This isn't the Wild West ... revenge isn't a great motive for murder."

He wanted to laugh at her assessment, wanted to tell her that she was absolutely fucking one hundred percent correct, and that he was going to do it anyway, and fuck the consequences.

But he'd already fucked all the consequences and look where he was now.

Before he could say anything further, she spoke again. "I'm sorry. But you know I understand. I lived through it. Don't you think I don't wish my dad had gone after whoever killed my mom? But maybe he did, maybe he has and can't tell me ... though I'd never want him to get in trouble for it. Call the authorities, Cam. Let them take care of it. And then let it go."

Her eyes looked fierce, primal in the half-light coming in through the blinds, and for a second he imagined her protecting him, which was ridiculous. She was the one who needed protection.

Dylan drove for what seemed like hours. Might've been, but Riley wasn't sure. She had been going in and out of consciousness, waking only when he shook her and called her name.

Her throat was killing her—no doubt her trachea had been bruised. She was lucky to be alive, she knew that. She'd been stupid to think she could handle this on her own. Her luck had finally run out, and skill alone hadn't been able to carry her through.

The safe house Dylan borrowed from a friend who was also in the private contracting business was on a quiet street, in the middle of suburban Florida—a raised ranch with an attached garage, and the relief hit her when the mechanical door closed behind them.

The adrenaline from the car chase was waning, and she'd been primed and ready for the come-down. It arrived sooner than expected, though, prompting the decision to have Dylan carry her from the car to the small house.

Still, she fought him as he tried to get her out of her seat, wanted to walk in the house on her own. Didn't need him to help her, to survive . . . did not.

"I know you don't need me to survive, Riley," he murmured, and she realized she'd spoken her thoughts out loud.

"I do . . . you fucking bastard. I started to need you. And I wanted take care of myself—always could before."

"You shouldn't have to. No one should have to."

Those words made her lose it. "I didn't want to like you, to love you," she spat, wiped tears from her cheeks with an angry fist. "I didn't want to need a man. Not like my mother did. She collapsed without my father. Didn't say, *We'll make it, Riley. Don't worry—I'll take care of you.* Instead, she told me, *I'm nothing without a man, no woman is.* And then she proceeded to die a little every single day for three years until there was nothing left of her but skin and bones. She died because there was no man to take care of her—at least, that's what she thought despite the official diagnosis of cancer. And I promised myself I would never be in that position."

She shook after that admission, actually felt her body tremble. She even held out a shaking arm, palm raised as if to ward him off.

Dylan didn't move a muscle, didn't blink—just absorbed her rant and her pain, took it all...didn't leave. Which meant that, after all this, he probably never would.

The tears were unstoppable and she didn't even try.

In three seconds, despite her protests, her feeble attempts to push him away as he tried to pick her up, she curled in his arms, her body heaving against his from her sobs. Heavy. Choked.

All those years of surviving in a man's world—first the Navy, and then in the heady and dangerous world of black ops. Proving time and time again that she didn't need anything but herself to survive.

After a few minutes of comforting her in the poorly lit garage, Dylan pushed off the side of the car and opened the door to the house with her still in his arms. He managed to disarm the alarm and lock them in before bringing her to the couch in the small living room.

She collapsed on it, every part of her body aching, as if the lack of oxygen tore her strength away. Her head pounded and her throat was swollen—but all in all, she'd definitely live.

He left her for a few minutes. She heard him making a phone call and then rifling around in the kitchen. When he came back, he had tea for her and an ice bag. "So the bull-shit's over—you're going to let me help you now?"

"Why would you want to, after everything? After what I did, I was honestly waiting for you to ... humiliate me. To get me back."

He gently pushed some stray hair off her forehead. It always amazed her that such a strong, deadly man could keep his caresses light enough to make her shiver. "I don't want to humiliate you. And yeah, I'm angry as hell at you, confused. But you were in big trouble. You still are, and you're kidding yourself if you think you can handle it alone."

"I had a choice to make, Dylan. And now I have another and I need to handle it alone." Her life from age fifteen on had been less about choice and more about reaction. Crawling and scratching and fighting her way from the fear that she'd lived with for so long, that everything would be taken from her again one day, without notice. That people she loved would disappear and there was nothing she could do about it.

He pressed the ice bag on her head, and she winced.

"I knew Gabriel would never have cleared my father's name. Never. The best I could do was get revenge," she whispered.

Dylan was staring down at her, the conflict in his eyes unmistakable. "I called in a favor, found out that Gabriel Creighton was following an order to kill a double agent who'd compromised U.S. security and was behind two terrorist bombings on our overseas embassies. That agent was your father."

"So it's true, then." Her voice was hollow, shoulders

sagged. "All this time, I've been trying to clear my father's name. I've put everything on the line—including my life—and he really was a traitor."

"Money and power have a strange effect on people, Ri." His voice softened on the next words. "I didn't want to be the one who told you about your father."

"You told me the truth—that's all I've ever wanted, to know the truth, even if it's not pretty." She sat up, a brief look of pain crossing her pretty face. "Is DMH after Gabriel's daughter now?"

"Yes."

She wiped away the stray tears from under each eye. "What can I do to make this right?"

"You can help to get Gabriel away from whoever's got him. We have to bring him to the CIA—from there, it's up to him to deal with the consequences."

"Or not."

"Or not," he agreed.

"After what I did to you, why would you want to help me clear my conscience?"

"Because I love you, Riley. I goddamned, no holds barred, can't not admit it any longer, love you!" he yelled. Probably wasn't the most romantic declaration ever uttered. But it had been honest.

She didn't say anything for a long moment—wanted to, but the words stuck in her throat, bogged down as if by thick molasses. No, she couldn't say the words back to him, even though she felt the same way.

The light in Dylan's eyes didn't diminish—it was as if he hadn't expected her to declare her love. "It's okay, Ri. I was invested the second I took you to bed, Riley, and I don't plan on changing that anytime soon."

"I don't know who to believe. I've been living on broken promises for so long, I don't know what's real anymore," she admitted, and Dylan swore.

"I'm real, dammit. And you know it."

CHAPTER
12

After quick, separate showers—because Cam didn't trust himself anywhere near Sky naked again—they were ready to leave the motel for the next location.

The crappy motel had been a good sanctuary, and leaving had been the last thing he'd wanted to do.

Somehow, they had...meshed, when he hadn't been paying attention. Folded into each other. And he was content. Comfortable. Both were odd sensations for him, and it was no wonder he hadn't been able to recognize them.

He'd wanted her to help him forget everything—everything but her.

Even so, he'd forgotten who she was.

And when she learned the truth of why he'd come to her, what the hell would she do?

No matter, the danger lurking out there was real, and both he and Sky were targets. Until they got to the bottom of it, discovered why she was being targeted, he had to keep both their asses out of the line of fire.

He watched her check her phone. It hadn't fully charged on the ride there, but she'd plugged it in when they'd arrived.

"Full battery," she told him as she scrolled through her messages. "Nothing important," she said with a shake of her head, and she sounded disappointed.

He wanted to tell her that no news was good news, but really, that expression was bullshit. "Let's move."

She nodded in agreement, even though her face was set in a serious expression. "Did you ever find out who the men were back at the resort house?"

He shook his head and slid ahead of her, said over his shoulder, "Like I figured, the car was stolen."

She tightened her coat and walked out of the room behind him, into the cold, dark night. And then she asked, "Why don't you let me drive for a while? You didn't rest and I did. I mean, you don't have to keep constant watch on me in a moving vehicle."

She was right—and sleep would help—even a light one. But his resolve and his pride resisted, because if he had to remain awake, he could. "I'll be fine."

When she touched his chest and said, "You need sleep to heal," he almost lost it. He'd revealed more about himself than he ever had before, all while keeping himself a secret.

He was confused. In pain. Alone.

And he was with a woman who'd touched him in a way he'd never thought possible. "If you're sure."

"It would make me feel better, like I was doing something. I don't do helpless well, Cam."

It was those words that won him over, and he couldn't help it, he grabbed her and he pulled her in for a kiss— a long, hot one that threatened to overtake them both and make him carry her back into the room.

She held the front of his shirt in her fists to keep him close, and his hands wound in her hair. She'd loosened it before going to sleep, and now his hands ran through the silky strands as his tongue dueled with hers.

"Jesus, Sky," he said when he pulled away.

She smiled. "Right. I'll just drive, then."

Unlike last time, he didn't argue, simply opened the driver's door for her and helped her in. She turned the engine over while he walked around to the passenger's side and hoisted himself in, tried not to wince as his shoulder hit the seat.

Then he set the GPS for the next location. "We're ready."

She nodded and pulled out of the space, obviously comfortable with the big truck. She looked cute driving it.

Cute.

Fuck.

Idiot.

Her hands gripped the wheel. She was stronger physically than she looked. At one time, she was probably in pretty prime condition, could no doubt get back there again when her recovery was complete.

He could help her. Make her feel stronger. But she looked damned fine to him . . .

"Why do you keep looking at me?" she asked, her voice teasing as she repeated his earlier words back to him.

"Because you're hot."

He noted with satisfaction that her cheeks pinked up appreciatively and a small smile played on her lips. He wanted to keep bringing the smile to her face.

He pushed his seat back a bit and closed his eyes and tried to get some sleep, the way he'd been taught during Ranger School and then Delta training, getting the most bang for the buck in the shortest possible time. A twenty-minute nap could hold him two days, if necessary.

But the damned dream—the one he could never wake himself up from—hit him out of the blue. It was like swimming through the murk while the bars clanked and he felt the men ganging up on him, the way they'd promised.

He smelled hot asphalt and tar and sweat . . . the metallic taste of blood in his mouth. Somehow, it was him against at least three men.

If he went down completely, more than three would be on him. But for now, the others were content to watch and clap. Called him baby boy. Told him what they'd planned on doing with him once they'd pinned him.

The rage and frustration fueled him. It had been nine months of grief and fighting, and Cam was prepared to do anything it took to keep these men off him. The jeers and the yelling flooded his ears, until he couldn't hear his own thoughts.

His head pressed against the hot ground—the jarring, mind-numbing pain as the knife sliced along the back of his ear. The realization that they were actually attempting to saw his fucking ear off.

He roared, threw the man off him, watched him slam to the ground and felt satisfaction when the guy howled in pain. One of the others grabbed his arms from behind, leaving Cam open to hard punches in the gut from another inmate.

He managed to leverage himself against the man holding him, got his legs in the air and wrapped them around his attacker's neck, squeezed until his face went blue.

And then there were shots fired in the air—more yelling, guards dragging him off after hitting him with nightsticks.

Infirmary. The nurse's face swam in front of him. Getting stitched without Lidocaine and not feeling any pain. His adrenaline was pumping too hard to give a shit about much of anything.

And hours later, he woke in solitary, where he remained for weeks. Was told that the man he'd stabbed, the one who'd started the fight, had died of an infection stemming from the wound.

A danger . . . lethal. A lifer. What did you expect?

And then Mariana's face, and the face of her son—both swam in front of him and he desperately wanted out of this dream, but he'd been pulled in too deeply. The pain sizzled through him as if all of it was real, like this *wasn't* a nightmare he was desperately trying to crawl out of.

And then she was pushing him, hard.

He locked her wrist in his hand, gun pulled, pointed at her. And in that moment, he truly woke and saw the fear and concern on Sky's face—Sky, not Mariana—and realized he could've easily hurt her.

Just because she'd woken him.

Fuck. "Sorry." The word was so inadequate. Always had been. Simultaneously, he put the gun down and dropped her wrist.

"Yeah, me too." She took a deep breath. "You were talking in your sleep. You said a woman's name."

"It's not what you think."

"You didn't sound happy."

"Maybe it is what you think, then." He wiped the sweat from his brow and forced the memories out. "Is that why you woke me?"

"No. We're being followed." Her voice was terse, her posture stiff.

"You're sure?"

"At first I thought they were traveling smart, just using our tracks, but..." She shook her head and glanced in the rearview mirror.

"For how long?"

"Fifteen minutes."

They'd only been driving for half an hour, according to the clock on the dash.

When they'd gotten on the highway, there had been a few other trucks around them—they'd passed them quickly, as his truck seemed to have no problem handling speed, despite the conditions.

He watched this particular one in the side mirror for about ten more minutes, the heavy feeling settling in his gut that it was trouble.

Trouble now coming closer.

"Do you think they're following us?" Sky asked. "I could just be paranoid...although I have pretty good reason to be."

"We're going to find out. Don't check your mirror. Eyes straight. Keep driving—keep the same speed," he instructed. "There's a truck stop ahead. Pull in and act like you're going to park. And then floor it the hell out of there."

"Won't they know we're on to them?"

He glanced at her. "I have a feeling they already do."

Sky prepared to follow Cam's instructions, trying not to panic as he locked and loaded a rifle and a shotgun. If they pulled into the rest stop and the truck behind them kept going, they were all right. If the car followed them into the parking lot, and then out again, they were in trouble.

"You'll do fine," he told her, his voice kind and commanding at the same time. "All you need to do is drive. I'll take care of the rest."

He'd taken care of her before—she had every reason to believe he was fully capable of doing so again. And so she pulled off toward the rest stop.

"He's following," he said.

She drove through the near-empty parking lot and faked a right turn into a space, before gunning it. The pavement was slippery, even with the dual aid of thick tires and four-wheel drive, and she concentrated on what she needed to do.

And breathing.

"Nice, Sky," he murmured. She didn't dare turn to look at him; instead, she pulled back onto the four-lane highway as fast as she could...and sure enough, there were the brights of the truck shining in her mirrors.

And they were getting closer.

"They're not going to just let us keep driving for much longer."

"I'm counting on it. When I tell you, pull over. Jerk the wheel hard and spin the car."

"Spin it?" This time, she did dart a quick look his way, and saw he was dead serious.

He confirmed it with his next words. "Yes, spin it. The truck will balance itself."

She swallowed hard and didn't ask what he planned on doing.

The road was deserted, save for the truck following them. The lights on this route were few and far between, and she tried to keep her mind clear.

You can do this, Sky. You told Cam you hated being helpless.

She thought about the way he'd kissed her back at the motel—her toes had literally curled, and she knew he felt something for her, that he was fighting the fact that he'd never gotten close to anyone before. And how in such a short time...

It was the same on her end. Thrilling and scary at once. And it would've been a lot better if someone weren't trying to kill her.

"Now, Sky."

She followed his directions without hesitation. The truck—and her world—spun out of control, the screech muffled by the blanket of snow covering the blacktop, but it did nothing to silence the sound of gunfire.

She was pretty sure she screamed. Several times. She

held on to the wheel tightly, and Cam told her, "*Drive*. Pick your head up and drive."

She did. There were spiderweb cracks in the windshield, which thankfully was in one piece. Which meant Cam's truck had bulletproof glass.

She wanted to pull over and throw up. Actually, pulling over wasn't even all that important. The snow was coming down harder and she realized she was driving the wrong way.

The truck that had been following them was off to the side of the road, where it had slammed into a tree.

And there was a man facing them down, pointing what looked like an AK-47 at the truck.

"Go!" Cam called, even as she panicked, easing off the gas. She didn't want to get closer to the man with the gun, bulletproof glass or not.

Cam grabbed the wheel and slammed his foot on top of hers, flooring it. She struggled, even as Cam said, "Close your eyes."

She did—felt the impact of bullets slamming the seemingly impervious metal with a rat-tat-tat, and the car hitting the body with a viciously hard thump.

After what seemed like an eternity, Cam's foot eased off hers. Instinctively, she hit the brakes and he didn't complain.

She opened her eyes when the truck came to a complete stop. She was shaking and sweating and she kept hearing the sounds of squealing tires over and over in her head.

She heard Cam say, "I'll be right back."

Before she could respond, he was out of the truck. She

looked in the rearview mirror, saw him running toward the body lying in the middle of the road.

The silent sobs started then, racked her body until her chest hurt, even as she watched Cam move from the man to the truck he'd been driving, checking everything, she supposed, for clues.

She prayed no one else would come upon them—how would they explain this?

She'd just killed a man.

Self-defense. You did what you had to do.

That man would've killed her and Cam, and still . . . She wondered when her hands would stop shaking.

It was hard to keep his footing—the snow was sandwiched with ice both above and below its layers, and Cam half slid to the man in the middle of the road.

He stood over him, watched the man struggle for breath. The gun the man had been holding had jammed itself into his own chest, thanks to the car's impact.

"Who sent you?" Cam demanded, his breath a white mist.

The man said nothing, just wheezed through blue lips. Cam glanced back at his truck; even though he couldn't see inside, he knew Sky was watching him in the rearview mirror.

He knelt by the already dying man and jacked the piece of lodged steel hard. No mercy. Fuck mercy. The man jerked, groaned, and Cam tried again. "You piece of shit, who sent you?"

No answer.

"The cold will keep you alive a lot longer than you want it to," he assured the man. "You give me the information I want, I'll end your suffering."

The man stuck his tongue out to lick his lips, which were no doubt numb. And then he spoke, his voice so low and garbled that Cam had to bend lower to hear the words.

"Didn't have a real name. Only know him as Bullet. There was another guy with him . . . Pig's . . . Eye."

But Cam didn't care about the second name. He had stopped listening. He'd heard enough.

Bullet. That name would fucking haunt him for the rest of his life. He'd always known that, but he certainly hadn't expected to hear it now.

That was the name of the man he'd left Morocco without killing—the uncompleted part of his final mission.

The man drew a labored breath, bringing Cam's attention back to him. "Where are they? Where is Bullet?"

"Don't know. Met them at . . . rest stop."

"Where?"

The man coughed—hard—his face turning blue, and Cam shook him, putting a hand behind his neck and lifting his upper body away from the snow.

But it was all Cam would get, because the man's eyes rolled back. Cam didn't have to keep his promise to end his struggle.

He let the guy's neck drop and went through his pockets, but it was perfunctory. This man, and the ones from that morning, they were all hired. Not part of the group with Bullet and Pig's Eye.

If he'd finished it that night—manned up, stayed in Morocco and taken care of business—this wouldn't have happened.

Question was, was Bullet coming for him or for Sky?

Suddenly, Cam was opening the driver's-side door, telling her, "Move over. I'll take it from here."

Sky was all too grateful and ready to give up the driver's seat. As she scrambled over the console in between the seats, Cam shoved his way in, shut the door and began to maneuver the vehicle onto the right side of the road.

He was going back the way they came.

Sky was trying not to hyperventilate.

They didn't stop, drove until dawn along back roads, where a car riddled with bullet holes wouldn't call attention to itself.

Finally, she spoke, staring straight ahead, her words coming out softly. "We could've avoided him. Just kept driving. He wouldn't have caught up to us."

"Maybe not him, but someone else would've."

She was shaking—fear and anger and cold all balled up inside until an unwelcome sob racked her body, escaping despite her clenched teeth. "You made me kill him."

Cam eased the car onto a service road, slowed down enough to turn his head and tell her, "*I* killed him. Me. I held the wheel, put my foot on the gas. You had no choice in the matter. Remember that."

"Let me out of the damned car."

His refusal was silent, save for the grinding of the gears as he pushed the truck faster.

Soon, the car was moving along the snowy road at a sickeningly fast pace, given the snow. The truck shimmied, and that, combined with everything else, made her want to throw up. And then run. Maybe not in that order.

She leaned forward, dizzy.

"Put your head between your knees," he ordered, reaching his hand around and pushing on the back of her neck until she did so. "Now, breathe."

She did, until she got her equilibrium back. For a few seconds, Cam's strong fingers were gently rubbing the tender skin—he'd suckled back there the other night and she'd been amazed at how sensitive the flesh was.

Suddenly, as if he'd realized what he was doing, he stopped. Slowly, she sat up and then took the water bottle he offered.

And then he was talking, more to himself than to her, she thought. "How the hell did they find us? I checked this car for tracking devices."

She fumbled for her phone. "I'm calling the CIA, telling them what's happening, who I am."

He put a hand over hers. "No, you're not."

"Then you'll call. My father has to be in big trouble— hurt, unable to get to me. He'd never let things go this far otherwise. We need help, Cam."

Cam didn't answer her, continued to drive along the service road, and for the next half an hour there was total silence between them.

She continued to check the side mirrors to make sure no one was following them, fully aware that Cam was doing the same.

And then suddenly, he began to speak, and her world turned upside down.

"I don't know who those men are, or why they want you. I only know that three nights ago, your father sent men to try to kill me, and I came looking for you in order to ensure that never happened again."

CHAPTER
13

For a long moment, Sky said nothing. The roar between her ears got louder, the stress of the day taking its toll on an already fatigued body and she literally wanted to fall into a deep sleep and pretend none of this was happening.

But it was way too late for that now. "Who the hell are you? Is Cam even your name?"

"Everything else I've told you is the truth."

"Sure, because you wouldn't lie to me. Not when you're actually kidnapping me."

"Things changed. Now I'm saving you, Sky."

"How can you prove that those men weren't sent by my father to save me from you?" she spat.

"I can't prove it, but I know."

"Yeah, okay, I'll trust that. And you. *Not in this lifetime.*" She could barely sit still, wanted to get as far away from him as she could.

And still . . . still, he'd saved her. She couldn't keep that thought from running through her mind.

He saved you.

Or else, he killed your rescuers.

And her father could be in serious trouble. "So you didn't talk to my father a few days ago."

"No. And not for five months before that. Your father has no idea we're together."

"That might not be true," she whispered.

He cut a sharp gaze her way. "What are you talking about?"

She held up her phone. "I called him a few hours after you arrived. Left him a message that you were with me."

Cam grabbed the phone from her hands and shut it down. With one hand on the wheel, he took the battery out of the phone, cursing under his breath the whole time. "That's how those men tracked us when you placed your call, the tracking device linked to your phone. As long as it's on and the battery is charged, they can find us."

"I'd apologize, but I guess I was right to be suspicious."

"You almost got us both killed."

"You bastard." She fought the urge to shove him— mainly because he was driving, thus holding her life in his hands. Literally now, it seemed. "Stop the car."

"No way. It's too dangerous to stop." He paused. "And before you think about it, I took the ammo out of your gun earlier. I know you hate me now, but you need me alive if you want to stay alive too."

"Stop the car—*stop the damned car!*" She lunged for him, grabbing his arm, the wheel, and he was cursing, forced to brake to deal with her.

She pushed the door open as soon as the car stopped and she jumped out. She couldn't be sure if they were really on a road or not, the ground blanketed for miles around with a white powder that would've been blinding had the sun been up.

But she didn't go far—a few steps and she leaned forward, dizzy, her hands braced on her thighs.

She had no one to turn to, except the man who'd just admitted kidnapping her. Right now he was coming to her side but she shook her head, barely able to breathe, the mix of anger and fear sitting heavily on her chest. "Don't. Don't touch me."

"Sky, please—it's freezing. I don't want you to get sick."

"Why do you care what happens to me? Why should I believe anything that comes out of your mouth!" She yelled the words into the night sky. The area appeared so deserted—she was completely, utterly alone.

Cam didn't come any closer, just stood there, watching her, concerned. "I showed you my ID the other night. Except for why I came to find you, everything I've told you is true."

"How can I trust you, or anything you say?"

"Why the hell would I lie about kidnapping you?" he demanded. "Who the hell does that?"

God, this was crazy. Off the wall, out of this world, she-had-no-one-to-turn-to crazy. "Why would my father try to kill you?"

LIE WITH ME   237

"Long story."

"I need to know."

"Right now, the only thing you need to know is that you're safest with me. I didn't want to tell you like this. Didn't expect to have to tell you at all."

"What were you going to do?" Suddenly, her eyes blazed with the realization, but she still demanded, "Tell me."

When he didn't answer, Sky did it for him. "You came to find me to . . ."

She stopped, couldn't say the words they both knew she'd been thinking.

To hurt me. Kill me.

"I'm not going to hurt you. I never would have, Sky. I know you don't believe that now, but—"

She was backing away from him—slowly, as if he wouldn't notice. She was scared of him, and disgusted, and his gut burned with shame and anger.

"For all I know, you set me up with those letters, the men."

"No."

"For all I know, you've killed my father. I can't believe this—I can't believe you've been lying to me. And I helped you kill someone who was sent to help."

If Gabriel was alive, not being held hostage somewhere, he would know that Cam had his daughter. Could all these men have been sent by Gabriel himself to take out Cam and bring Sky to safety?

He had no way to be sure, but his gut told him no.

Gabriel was cleaner than that. The men that came were willing to bring in a woman by drugging her.

They wanted Sky alive and he was pretty sure the first men hadn't had any idea they'd find him with Sky. "Your father wouldn't come in like this. Those men were low-level thugs, Sky."

"And you're no better than the men you saved me from. You're no better." Those last words were repeated loudly, accompanied with her hands fisted down by her sides, clenched so hard they shook a bit, like her voice had. Puffs of icy air escaped from her mouth, and why the hell he'd told her then, in the car, why he hadn't waited to tell her . . . Dammit, why the hell did he choose to grow a fucking conscience at the wrong goddamned time . . .

He had to get her back into the truck and away from here. Had to keep her safe. Because now both their asses were on the line.

She'd believe him sooner or later.

Within seconds, he had her, pinned her arms behind her back and lifted her with an easy arm around the waist. She fought, but she was no match for him, and she knew it.

Fatigue, the illness and recovery, stress and exhaustion all took their toll at once, and Sky went limp as she passed out.

Cam wasted no time getting her back into the truck and getting her warm. He put a blanket on her, felt her pulse and rubbed her cheeks until she began to come to.

For a long moment, she stared at him, in her eyes a combination of anger, fear and disgust.

Nothing like the way she'd looked at him just hours ago. "You need to rest. I'm taking you someplace safe."

She licked her bottom lip and when she spoke, her voice sounded raw. "I'm not safe with you—I never was."

"I'll prove you wrong, Sky, if it's the last thing I do."

He'd have to tell her everything and prayed that it would be enough.

He didn't trust Gabriel Creighton—this could still all be one big game. In the puzzle of the world of spooks, figuring out the hows and whys was not only impossible, but he'd learned that ultimately, those reasons didn't matter.

He tried to remember why he started this in the first place. And he turned it over in his head again, as if the puzzle could be solved. Whether Gabriel knew Cam was with his daughter or not was irrelevant—because someone knew, and they wanted Sky.

The men had been surprised to see Cam, hadn't been prepared for him. But still, they were trained. Deadly. The type of men Gabriel would send.

None of this made sense anymore.

Sky was staring straight ahead, almost zombielike. Stressed.

"Sky, listen to me—I'm going to take you someplace they won't be able to track us anymore. And then I can get more help if we need it."

"Where?" she asked finally, her voice sleepy.

There was only one choice, and it was the last place he wanted to take her. His refuge. His ultimate plan A, B and C.

His new life.

Motherfucker.

"Home. We're going home."

Elijah watched the interrogation from the open doorway. He had two of his best men working the spy over. For added measure, Gabriel remained chained to the steel chair, helpless to stop the proceedings.

Unless, of course, he talked.

Don't kill him was Elijah's only condition. Because this torture, this was for fun. There was no way Gabriel would talk, not until they had his only child laid out on the rack in front of him, her limbs in danger of ripping away from her body as she screamed.

Screamed with a brutality that would make the walls nearly shake and echo around Elijah like a warm blanket. Elijah was sure that then the words would pour out of the man, faster than they could write them down. Because Skylar might've eluded them, but that didn't mean he didn't know exactly where she was.

Timing was everything.

"We're going to have a lot of fun with your daughter. Maybe even more than we had with your wife," one of the men said.

Gabriel remained stock-still. No change in facial expression, except for a small smile on his face. One that said, *I know something you don't.*

Cold-blooded bastard.

The ringing phone interrupted Elijah's thoughts. He watched Gabriel even as he said hello.

"Rocket's dead. Bodyguard too. Place is a fucking mess," the man Elijah called Ace reported, his disdain clear over the phone. "Taken down by a woman."

Mariana's face flashed before his eyes and he turned away from the scene in front of him in disgust. "Dispose of the bodies. Put the apartment up for sale."

"And find Riley?"

Elijah sat back and drummed his fingers on the scarred antique desktop in front of him. "Not right now—we have other problems to deal with. We need Skylar Slavin. And after a few days with us, she might not be in the greatest health, considering her condition with the recent transplant. We also need a doctor here who can keep her alive, if necessary. We don't want Skylar dying before we get all the pertinent intel from her father."

He scrolled through Gabriel's phone until he hit on the right name, and he smiled and gave the information to Ace. "We've needed a doctor anyway, and a transplant doctor will suit our purposes. It works out well for everyone. She'll be useful, even after Skylar and her father die."

"We can't make her perform surgery," Ace pointed out.

"You cut a patient open in front of a doctor, and it's her duty to help them. She won't have much of a choice."

She'd started the morning crying for fifteen minutes in a utility closet after her teenage transplant patient died before the liver donor came through.

Now Olivia put her pager into the pocket of her scrubs and grabbed her bag from the locker. It was after midnight—she had been sorely tempted to just stay in the on-call room, but her brand-new bed, supposedly the top of the line, promised a good night's sleep. The mattress was three months old and she'd slept in it only half that time.

Tonight, she needed the sleep.

She started the car and it turned over easily, the familiar hum music to her ears. But when she tried to reverse out of the space, it wouldn't move.

She checked the gas—not the problem. And then she leaned her head back against the seat and sighed.

She was a damned capable woman. But at times like this, having a man to call for help might actually be nice.

She closed her eyes for a second and wondered about the possibility of sleeping right here. She'd crashed in worse places during her residency. Worse since then even. And after today's near crash of the hospital's helicopter—on the way back from picking up a donor liver, two hours away, in heavy winds—*crash* was probably not the best word choice.

Following that, she'd had a six-hour surgery in which the liver did not pink up, resulting in Mr. Johnson going back on dialysis, yet another disappointment for his family. Add to that a staff meeting from hell, a new pack of residents following her around the hospital like they were chum circling, and yeah, she needed to go home. Definitely home.

Didn't matter that she had to be back in less than seven hours.

She opened the door to check behind the car, but that yielded no results. And when she turned back around, she stiffened as she discovered a man sitting next to her. Pointing a gun. At her.

"Dr. Strohm?"

She swallowed. Stared at him, and wondered, if this was a robbery, why he was using her name?

It's not a robbery.

"Where is Skylar Slavin?"

"Why the hell are you in my car?"

He raised the gun and asked the question again, and okay, she got it—he had the gun, questions need to be answered.

"Skylar? I don't know." Why were they asking about her patient? A patient who had been discharged months ago. "Is she okay?"

"You're going to have to be the one to tell us."

She looked to the left—there was a man standing outside her window, a gun tucked into the pocket of his jeans. Without thinking it through, she slammed the lock shut with her elbow and then turned back to the guy sitting next to her. "Get out. Or shoot me. I'm not going anywhere with you."

The man grabbed for her arm and she went limp and then brought her hand up for a nice chop to his throat. Hanging out with the cops who always seemed to be in the ER for one reason or another did have some benefits. Next, she sprayed the mace on her key chain directly into his face. The man howled and she managed to bring her legs out from under the wheel and kick at him until he was scrambling out of the car.

It wouldn't stop them for long. The phone—where the hell was her phone?

She fished in the pocket of her scrubs, yelling as she dialed—Skylar's number was in her phone, as were all her current patients'. She had to warn Sky that something bad was happening—because 911 wasn't going to get here fast enough to save her. Even now the glass shattered on the passenger's side. She ducked and tried not to scream and then she spoke as fast as she could into the phone.

"Skylar, there are men asking about you—they're taking me, kidnapping me, I don't know what they want—" She yelled as they dragged her out of the car and across the near-deserted rooftop parking lot, into a waiting car.

She opened her mouth to scream again, but one of the men carrying her backhanded her hard across the face. She saw zigzags of light and fought to stay conscious—the second slam across her face put an end to that.

CHAPTER
14

The night remained quiet at the safe house where Dylan had taken her a few hours earlier.

He'd let Riley rest for a few hours. And she'd slept deeply—part stress and exhaustion, he was sure, part not wanting to face up to what had happened. To what she would have to do.

Dylan called Cam, left him a message that he had intel. That Cam and Sky were in deep to some serious shit. That he couldn't say more because he knew Cam's cell wasn't secure, but that he'd be with them by the next afternoon, if not sooner.

When he heard the shower running, he unpacked the take-out Chinese food. And when she came out of the bathroom, wearing one of his T-shirts, which reached down to mid-thigh, her eyes were slightly puffy and the fingerprints around her neck were red. Raised.

Made him want to go caveman and kill the guy who did it. Except for the fact that he was already dead.

"I'm okay," she told him, a palm pressed to her throat. "Don't go all motherly on me."

"I'll show you motherly," he muttered, and realized he was actually dishing out her food for her. "Fuck it, get it yourself."

She giggled—a good sign at the moment—and then sat next to him and began to eat.

For a while, there was contented silence. When she'd finished her meal, he told her that he'd booked a flight for them to New York. "There are new clothes in the bedroom—you should find some stuff in your size."

"When do we leave?"

"First flight out in the morning." He would bring Zane along—his brother had a week before he had to report in.

"And from there, we find Gabriel, using the intel I've got about DMH. At least I can help with that." She shook her head at the irony of it all. "I thought turning Gabriel in to DMH would be so much better. I figured I'd feel relieved. Lighter. Instead, I stopped sleeping. And when I did finally fall asleep, I had nightmares. I'd see my mom wasting away, and I'd walk over to the bed to comfort her, and it's my face I see, not hers."

"It's almost over."

"But it's not. Dylan, I'm in trouble. They might not stop looking for me." She rubbed her palms over her bare arms until he wound a blanket around her shoulders and tightened it around her.

"Maybe you should think about looking for them. Maybe they should be fearful of you. You're a force to be reckoned with, Ri. And I'll fight DMH—with or without you . . . but I'd rather it be with you."

She shifted uneasily as he continued.

"You've been running from me—from us—for three years. Finding out about your father, about Gabriel Creighton were big factors, but they were also a really convenient excuse to keep distance between us. I'm not your father and you're not your mother. I'm sorry she died from a broken heart, sorry you had to go through that. But she loved him, she was in love. You can't fault her for that."

"Love shouldn't make you weak."

"I don't find you weak."

No, she wasn't. And Dylan, even when he was saving her ass, hadn't made her feel that way. "I want to start over. Not in Florida—someplace completely different."

"You don't like the cold, or I'd offer you the perfect place."

She felt the smile curve her lips. "You know, I don't think the cold will bother me all that much anymore."

She dropped the blanket and let Dylan gather her in his arms instead.

Sky slept for well over an hour. For the first few minutes after she woke, her brain was still fuzzy, the gentle shifting of the truck lulling her into believing that the warm, well-rested feeling would stick around.

But she remembered quickly what happened before she'd dozed, and her body chilled. She glanced over at Cam, his profile stoic in the dim lights of the dashboard, the silence between them a taut rope neither was willing to cut or cross.

I'm not scared of him, she told herself fiercely, but she was pretty sure she was lying.

She couldn't stop replaying the events of the day, over and over, until her head spun and her stomach hurt.

Her father was in trouble—and so was she, according to Cam. But not from him . . . not anymore.

Still he had a lot more explaining to do.

As she shifted, coming fully out of sleep, she knew it was time for her to take her medicine. Even in crisis, her body's internal clock reminded her as surely as if an alarm went off, and that's why she'd woken in the first place.

The nighttime meds tended to make her groggy, not think straight. But risking her health by not taking them wasn't an option.

My God, what was she going to do? Those men Cam killed, were they truly sent to rescue her? And what did Cameron Moore really have planned for her?

He'd kept her alive this long, but the unease of what he'd said about her father settled deep into her chest.

The way Cam touched her . . .

She shook her pills out of the containers even as she felt his gaze dart between her and the road, palmed them and took them with a full bottle of water. She knew, despite the sleep she'd gotten, that the combination of the meds and today's events would lull her back to sleep, no matter how hard she fought.

She wasn't sure how much longer they'd driven when she woke again, but the truck had slowed slightly.

With a swift, right-hand turn, they were on a hidden, obviously private road. Cam actually shut off his headlights before turning onto the road. Halfway up, he stopped the car, got out and walked back. She shifted to watch him get rid of the recent tire-track marks close to the road, and she thought about climbing into the driver's seat and backing up over him.

But that would solve nothing. She'd be in the middle of nowhere with enemies she couldn't name.

And with Cam, who might be the biggest enemy of all.

When he got back into the car, he drove the truck through the snow, up a hill that looked like it had no road leading to it.

The house appeared modest—new, well kept... well camouflaged. It wasn't until Cam headed the truck down a slope into an underground garage that she truly understood the scope of the place.

She took quick note of a lone set of footprints in the snow—very visible and fresh—and saw he had too.

When the garage doors closed behind them, Cam got out of the truck and pressed some keys on a pad mounted to the wall. He motioned for her to get out of the truck too, and after he grabbed her bags, she followed him through a door to the inside of the house.

Home, he'd called it.

The room they'd entered was a finished basement, with more cameras and security equipment than she'd ever seen in one place, save for Radio Shack. She supposed this was what she'd avoided by living apart from her father after her mother was killed. She couldn't decide if it made her feel safer, or like a caged animal.

She stared at the monitors, which seemed to be trained on every single available space around the house, as well as the private road they'd just taken. He was paying special attention to one that was now fast-forwarding. "There hasn't been anyone around except the caretaker."

He pointed to the man leaving—the footprints she'd seen—and she nodded.

"Sky, let's go upstairs—we'll grab some food and you can rest. And I'll explain. Try to anyway."

"I don't exactly have a choice, do I?"

"No, not really."

A glance at the clock on the computer screen told her it was after midnight—no wonder her stomach was growling. She followed him up the steep stairs into a large, open room with the kitchen on one side, where he began to prepare them a meal, and couches and a fireplace on the other. A vaulted ceiling created the effect of openness, and the caged-animal feeling dissipated slightly. But still she was somewhat dazed and disoriented, as if she wasn't fully inhabiting her body, but rather, floating above it, surveying the scene.

As if she'd wake up from this bad dream. Maybe even wake up in Cam's arms, back at the townhouse, or even the motel room.

But how could she ever trust anything Cam said?

Instincts, baby girl.

Unfortunately, her instincts were crap. The someone she'd trusted had gone to prison. She knew that being in

Delta Force meant he was lethal enough. Coupled with the fact that he worked for her father, doubly so. But prison . . .

It hadn't bothered her when she was making love to him in the motel. But now, when the betrayal sat between them, fresh and oozing, she wasn't sure what to believe about anything. "My father always told me not to trust anyone. Looks like he was right."

Those words appeared to cut right through Cam, and she was glad. Wanted him to hurt the way she did. Wanted his heart to pound and his head to swim . . . and this was all too much.

He turned his back again to grab the plates, and he quickly walked to the table and served her. She began to eat the food he put in front of her—soup, sandwich. Basic and good, especially as she needed to get her blood sugar up. Keep herself strong. Sane.

"I hope the food's okay for you. I don't have much else here. If I'd known I was coming . . ." He trailed off, took the gun from its holster and put it on the counter behind him. Then he sat. "This wasn't planned."

"Not this part," she shot at him. "But showing up to kidnap me was."

"Yes, that was," he admitted, pushed his own plate away and then began his explanation. "I work black ops for your father—or I did, for eleven years. He'd call on me whenever he needed me. And I was so fucking grateful to him that I never said no . . . not until . . ."

"If you want me on your side, you're going to have to tell me everything."

"Your father blackmailed me into service."

Did he want her to know everything? Did he even want her on his side?

He knew the answer, even if he didn't want to admit it.

"You're saying my father used you as a secret assassin," she said slowly. "Something not authorized by the CIA."

"Yes, that's what I'm telling you. I thought I was finally free of him, until three nights ago."

"When he tried to have you killed."

"Yes."

"And I'm supposed to believe this just because you tell me?"

"You're supposed to believe this because, like I said on the first night we met, if I wanted to kill you, I could've done so. Many times over. Instead, I've been saving your ass. Getting shot at, and I have no idea why."

"Why don't you think it's my father?"

"Because he'd stop at nothing to get to you," he told her. "The men sent after you were good, but they're not better than me. Your father trained me."

She shook her head, pushed her food away and stared at him, as if unable to say anything.

"Dammit, I know you think I betrayed you," he continued.

"That's because you did."

"And I don't regret any of it . . . except that I thought about hurting you. But the second I saw you, I knew . . ." He swallowed. "I knew that I couldn't hurt you. And Jesus, if I hadn't been there . . ."

"You really think those men who broke in, and the ones who followed us, were trying to hurt me, not you?"

"I do. Call it gut instinct, but I've gotten by on that for

a long time. I've been trained to follow it. You're still alive, and I plan on keeping you that way."

She sat there, her hands tight on the wooden arms, her expression unreadable. Except her eyes were glittering with a pent-up anger. "Why do you live in a fortress?"

"Because of your father. And if you have any idea where he might be—"

"If I knew where he was, I wouldn't tell you. You want to kill him."

"You have no idea what he's done to me." Cam's voice was harsh, and somehow broken at the same time. And his eyes, those brilliant, piercing eyes, were dull with a memory he couldn't break.

"What could he have done to make you want to kill him? You took an oath when you joined the military—protect the innocent. My father works for the good guys."

Cam snorted. "If you think that, you're way more innocent than I thought."

"I know that sometimes the CIA has to do bad things for the greater good, but they do it to keep us safe. That's the bottom line, the reason my father's sacrificed everything—a normal life, complete with a family he can sit down to dinner with every night. So tell me, Cam, what the hell did my father do to you?"

He stared at her steadily for a long moment before he told her, "Your father killed mine."

Sky felt as if she couldn't breathe, but somehow she stood, stared at him, wanting to disbelieve but unable to do so completely.

There was nothing to say that her father hadn't done exactly that. And while it didn't make her any less angry that Cam had been planning to use her, at least it helped her understand why.

She hated herself for understanding. For getting sucked in. For falling for this man. And even though a large part of her just wanted to collapse in screaming tears, she didn't.

Instead, she moved quickly, grabbed the gun from the counter, and pointed it at Cam. "I don't believe you, Cameron Moore. I think you set this whole thing up."

"No, you don't. And that's probably why you're so goddamned angry. Because you know!" he shouted at her, pushing away from the table. "Everything I've told you about my father, the way he died, the way I lived, that was all true. I always suspected your father, but I never had proof as much as I do now."

"I'm leaving. Taking your truck."

Cam stood his ground, appearing bigger to her than he ever had, more powerful, looming in front of her as though bullets couldn't hurt him. Yet she'd already seen that they had.

"Sky, be reasonable. I'm not letting you leave here—you're in danger."

She let out a short laugh and kept the gun pointed at his chest. "That's a good one. Like I'm safe with you."

She scanned the room, spotting some rope by the back door. Short of rendering him unconscious, she knew that he could get out of any and every way she could bind him.

There was no way she could hold this gun on him for hours either. He would overpower her the second she made a mistake, let her guard down.

There was nothing left to do but challenge him. And so she put the gun down on the table and walked up to him. "Go ahead."

"What are you talking about?"

"Do what you planned. Go ahead. Keep screwing me over—literally."

"Sky." His tone was a warning but she was well past listening, her thoughts in a confused zone. He tried to take her wrist, lead her to the couch calmly, but she was beyond that gentle approach.

Her anger was palpable, heated the room with its frenzy, and even though she knew fighting wouldn't get her anything but more frustrated, she couldn't stop. This was the fight she'd started out in the snow. The one she hadn't gotten to finish before cold and fear overtook her.

That wouldn't happen now.

She took a step back and then lunged forward, surprising him. Her arm shot out again, and this time she connected, shoved his chin with her open palm. As he reacted, grabbed her wrist so hard his hand made a slapping noise as it circled her arm, her leg shot out for a vicious kick to his gut that made him groan and then curse.

She'd been aiming lower, so he had no idea how lucky he was. But he deserved what he got, with that kick and a second that left him slightly gray and out of breath. He remained still, and it wasn't until she approached him again to punch and kick and get her aggression out that she realized he'd simply been lying in wait for her.

He wouldn't come at her—he would never hit her, no matter what she did. But he did grab her wrists and hold them together, before scooping her up and carrying her to a bedroom. Which housed a huge bed.

Her kicking and yelling hadn't fazed him. No, he had an equally determined look in his eyes as she supposed she did, but he had the distinct advantage in this fight. And the handcuffs.

He got one of her wrists cuffed to the headboard. With the other hand, she ripped at his skin through his shirt and she heard him hiss. She'd hit the knife wound. Good. Because she was fighting for much more than her life.

How much could Cam take? How much would he give? God, she didn't want to be wrong, but her gut told her that, no matter how angry she was, the feelings between them were real.

He grabbed her flailing arm and held it steady. "I don't want to hurt you."

"You already did, you asshole," she ground out, and in response, he cuffed her other hand.

She retaliated by trying to kick him, jammed her legs up and slammed them against his gut. He cursed, loud and viciously, and still he was careful with her, making sure not to bump her or jostle her—but she was beyond caring, the fight inside of her was simply too great.

To have found so much—and be losing it so quickly—it was unthinkable.

He wrestled her flat. "Stop it."

He managed to force her legs down. And she was trapped, totally and completely, arms splayed over her head, taut, legs pinned beneath him; her anger remained, but had turned into something molten.

He was rock hard, shaking from exertion, from fear that he would ultimately lose her, from holding back. "I'm doing this so you don't hurt yourself. Jesus, Sky, you're in no shape to fight like this."

"Don't you dare tell me what kind of shape I'm in. Don't tell me anything."

"I know, when you get your shit together, you won't want to lose the kidney you fought so hard to get, okay? So stop. Just stop."

Her breathing was harsh, even to her own ears, and he was right—so right, dammit. And as she felt the tears slide down her face she asked, "How could you do this to me?"

"Do what? Fall in love with you? Because that's what happened. And if this is what it took to bring us together, I can't say I'm sorry."

Cam didn't know what else to do to stop her tears and his admission seemed to bring on more.

Fuck. He sucked at this. But at least she'd stopped struggling, was looking up at him with those deep, soulful eyes that had sucked him in from the second he'd seen her picture.

Haunted eyes. "Tell me what you're thinking."

She brushed a cheek against her shoulder, did the same with the other one, to try to stop the tears. "I want you to be for real. I want this to be for real. The rest of it . . . I can't deal with it right now. So help me forget it—everything but you and me."

Yeah, he could do that.

"I don't know if you're just trying to make up for coming to me under false pretenses," she admitted. "I can forgive a lot, Cam. But don't keep up the charade if you don't feel anything."

He dipped his head and kissed her neck, letting his lips linger on the soft skin there before he responded. "You melted me, Sky. I was fucking ice before this. Before I met you, things were just getting worse."

She wanted to ask him why, but the need to kiss him, to succumb to the seduction, was stronger. The brazen, open lust she felt showed in her face, she was sure.

It showed on his as well.

Her body strained toward his. He pulled her shirt up, bent his head to suck on an already stiff nipple through her bra and she attempted to stifle a cry, but couldn't.

That spurred him on. With one hand, he ripped the bra off. He sucked a nipple hard as his hands moved to pull down her jeans.

She wasn't saying no, even though her eyes still flashed in anger.

"I'm sorry I didn't tell you sooner. I didn't know how, Sky."

She was already splayed for him, and so he slid a finger inside her thong and into her warm, wet heat, back and forth, until she was rocking against his hand.

"What *did* you know?" she managed, her voice breathless—and the way she looked at him, it nearly undid him.

"That you made me feel, whether I wanted to or not. You made me care. Made me want to not let you go." He thrust a second finger inside her and then a third, watching her writhe in pleasure as she rode his hand. Because he could do that for her, make her feel good—make her forget, like he'd promised.

After that, he would untie her and face the music. Give her the number to a CIA contact who would come get her. Take whatever punishment was waiting for him.

But for now he wasn't stopping, suckled on a breast while his fingers worked.

"I want to hate you . . . need to," she murmured.

"I know."

"But I can't."

He lifted his head. "Me neither."

He slid down and took her with his mouth, buried his face against her. She squirmed at his tongue's assault, her cries a mix of *Oh yes* and *More, Cam, more.*

Her body undulated in response to his rough touch and she liked it, heard herself begging as everything shattered in a wild tumult.

And then he was loosening the bonds, taking them away so she was free. He leaned back, sitting between her spread legs as she floated down from her orgasm, unsure of what she would do now. Of what she needed.

What she needed was him.

She stared at him for a long while, then, "Make me understand."

The way he looked back at her, she knew he would—and he would make it special. Even the room felt special. The blinds were open—there was nothing but dark, moon-lit, luminous forest around them, giving the entire room a magical feeling. She watched as he grabbed a condom from the pocket of his discarded jeans and rolled it on. And then she rose up and straddled him where he sat, his palms flat on the bed for support. With a long moan, she took his rigid length inside of her, her emotions jarred, her inhibitions long gone.

Surrounded by the chaos of the past three days, she took him, claimed him as surely as he had their first night together. This was much more intense than it had ever been. More satisfying, with everything out in the open.

When he pushed his hips up hard, driving himself farther inside her, he groaned his appreciation, and she rocked against him, pressing him on.

He murmured something unintelligible. Bucked up into her, his head thrown back. And then, "I'm alive when I'm with you. Never felt so fucking alive."

She came then, and so did he, a hot shuddering rush she felt even though he wore a condom.

She knew the sun would come up, but for the first time, she wished she could will it away, keep the dark of night, where she wasn't scared . . . where she and Cam didn't have to worry about anything but spending themselves out on sex until nothing else mattered, until the anger and pain abated and all that was left was the knowledge that, despite it all, she surely did love this man.

CHAPTER

15

Sky lay across his chest, both of them damp with sweat and sex and utterly exhausted from the fray.

"I like the way you yell my name when you're coming." Cam looked down at her as her face flushed. "S'okay—I don't have any close neighbors."

"Shut up." She swatted at his chest. "I love this time of night. It's technically morning but I still call it night because it's all dark and quiet."

He agreed. It was why he'd built the big windows in his house—not to grab the morning sun, but the moonlight.

He shifted reluctantly, rolling her gently onto the mattress and rising from the bed. His bandages had long since come loose and although he wasn't bleeding again, he needed to get himself cleaned and covered.

He headed to the bathroom to do just that. "I'll do it." She came up behind him, still naked, and took the gauze and antiseptic from him. "Are you ever going to see a doctor about this?"

"No. I think you're doing a fine job."

She simply shook her head as she cleaned and rebandaged all three wounds, and a swell of emotion ran through him.

"Hey." He pulled her against him. "I'm sorry. You have to know that. And if you need some time, I'll move out of the bedroom and sleep someplace else. Because I know all of this is raw."

She smiled, although it didn't light up her face the way it used to. No, it was a serious smile—her wheels were turning. "I want you to stay. And I want to forget everything else that's happening until morning. I want this time."

"Yeah, we can do that. Why don't you go back to bed?" Because they were safe here. Because they weren't dealing with what would happen to Gabriel, how she would process what Cam had set out to do with her. He could forget the past—and in the morning, focus on the future. On their next step to figuring out how the hell to save a CIA agent who couldn't save himself.

Sky woke to an overcast day. The blinds were still pulled from the large, floor-to-ceiling windows, the mist over the trees adding an almost surreal feeling to everything.

She was naked, wound in the sheet and oh so comfortable, save for a light rumbling of hunger. And Cam wasn't there, but she heard him moving around beyond the bedroom, as he'd left the door open.

She'd drifted off to sleep sometime after five in the morning, vaguely aware of Cam padding back and forth between the bedroom and, she supposed, the security cameras. He'd promised they'd talk about everything in the morning and she'd fallen into a deep, satisfying sleep.

"Hey, how're you feeling?"

Cam was at the door, watching her carefully. After what transpired yesterday, she couldn't blame him for his hesitation.

"Better. What time is it?"

"Almost five."

She'd slept the day away, except for a brief rise to take her meds. Her body felt better—she'd learned to listen to it since the transplant, but still was pretty sure Liv would consider all of what she'd been through far too taxing.

"I'll grab you some food—how about breakfast for dinner?" he asked, and she nodded.

She watched him walk toward the kitchen, marveling at his long strides, the way he was so in command of everything.

Lying back against the pillows, she surveyed the large space around her. Like the den and kitchen, it was open and airy, with high ceilings to accommodate the huge windows. Painted a neutral, dark beige, it felt warm, especially with the dark rug and gray comforter. Warm and distinctly male, and that wasn't a bad thing right now.

Shelves lined an entire wall. Lots of books—classics, new fiction, nonfiction. Movies.

She wondered if he got to spend much time up here, because he'd furnished it as if that was his wish. And then she pulled on a T-shirt and headed for the bathroom to wash up before Cam got back.

The bathroom was large, and the shower a walk-in with sprays set at various angles, and she couldn't resist turning it on. It was warm and steamy and she got in and relaxed under the water, wondering if she was avoiding what came next with Cam, the decisions that needed to be made.

Now or never, Sky. They both had a hell of a lot of baggage to deal with—time to find out how much each of them was willing to toss.

He was waiting when she returned to the bedroom. There was coffee. Juice Eggs and toast. And pancakes. "I don't eat this much for breakfast—ever."

"You should start." He settled next to her, his hair damp from a recent shower, and she wondered if the other bathrooms in the house were as nice as the master bath. She'd investigate later. He flipped through the TV channels while she ate—more than she thought she would, mumbling to him at one point that it was delicious.

Finally, she pushed the tray away, sated. Cam put it on the table next to the bed and turned to her.

It was time to have the discussion she dreaded. And Cam, being Cam, didn't mince words. "You're in danger, Sky. I won't leave you now—can't have that on my conscience. I'll figure out why people keep coming after you and then I'll take my punishment. I'm sure your father's not going to be happy."

"I won't let my father do anything to you."

"You will not ask for favors for me," he said through

clenched teeth. "First off, I don't deserve it. Second, I would never put you in the middle—not like I have."

He wasn't capable of hurting her—she saw that clearly now. And even though a part of her was still angry at him for lying, she was more so at her father for bringing so much hurt onto Cam.

And if what Cam said was true, if Gabriel had in fact murdered Cam's father, was there any way for her and Cam to get past that? "There's something I don't understand. If he killed your father and you were taking the fall for it, why would he get you out of jail two years later? Guilt?"

Cam shrugged, ran his fingers through his still damp hair. "He let me sit in prison for two years, so when he got me out I'd be grateful. So I'd do anything he asked of me."

"You think your father's death was just part of some plan to use you?"

"Would that surprise you?"

"I didn't think anything could anymore. But honestly, yes. I know you don't want to hear this, but you don't know him like I do." She looked concerned, upset, and he hated that he kept forcing these revelations on her. Ignorance really was bliss in situations like this one. "And I know it's not over for you—not until you get the truth from my father."

"I'd like to hear his reasons from his own mouth, yes. This is more than Gabriel killing my father. Like that's not enough. But fuck, there's more, Sky. A hell of a lot more."

"Then tell me. I'm a lot stronger than I might seem. And I deserve to know everything."

He nodded, even though her words hadn't formed a question, mainly because he didn't trust his voice. She was strong but he wasn't sure he could do this—had never talked about what happened with anyone. Not even Dylan knew the details of that night.

He'd already shattered Sky's ideals about him enough. For good. And so he turned from her, went to walk out of the room, but her words stopped him.

"If you walk away now, we'll never get through this."

She was right, and so he came back and sat next to her. And still, words eluded him.

Sky reached out and took his hands. When she spoke, her words cut right to the heart of the matter. "I know you want to kill him. Literally. But I don't want that on your conscience."

"I can't let him get away with it—you know that, right?"

"I do." She paused. "If you find him, you can bring him to justice. You have to—I understand that."

"It's not that simple."

"Why not? You've been hiding things from me. It's now or never. *Tell me.*"

The silence spread between them, thick, hot, the way he could still feel the blood on his hands some days. When he spoke, his voice was raw. "The world of black ops missions . . . it's one where you think you've learned the rules, but they change constantly. There are so many things you'll never know. Shouldn't. Since the first night I met you, I never wanted you to know these things about me."

"Before, you said that you'd been like ice for months. What happened? Was it another woman?"

He wanted to laugh, because yeah, it had been another woman—but not in the way she thought.

He'd gone through some tough crap during his military

tenure. Just last year, he'd been involved in a joint task force mission that could only be described as a severe clusterfuck. They'd accomplished half the mission successfully—but only he and another member, a SEAL, had survived along with the ambassador and his family.

More successes than losses, but he'd learned to compartmentalize, to put each mission to rest in his head as soon as he could, to not think about the successes any more than he did the failures.

Overthinking either was equally as dangerous.

"You really want to know what I did on a mission your father pushed me into?" That fateful night when he'd been forced to do something that made him question everything. That made him willing to kidnap her in order to ensure he'd never be in that position again.

"Yes. I need to know."

She didn't really. Black ops was about killing and stealing. You asked no questions, told lots of lies—and if you were lucky, you escaped with your life. "I was supposed to kill a man, and in order to get close to him, I had to get close to his girlfriend. She tried to kill me when we were . . . having sex. I stopped her, but then . . . her son came in, holding the AK pointed right at me. And the woman, she was so pissed, she started screaming that she'd known when her husband hadn't come home, even though his meeting had been canceled, that she'd been betrayed. That she'd known it was only a matter of time before that would happen. That he'd turned their son against her. And fuck, I knew the feeling. I raised my gun—I was ready, but instead she swung hers and pointed . . . and she shot . . ."

He paused, lowered his head and shook it, his voice

nearly breaking when he continued. "She didn't have to shoot him. But she said, *That'll teach him to betray me. He takes from me—I take his son from him.*"

"My God, Cam..." Sky put a hand on the back of his neck, so cool against his overheated skin. "What did you do?"

"I shot her," he said, his voice hollow. "Checked the kid for a pulse, but I knew he was gone. And then I left. Left the house and Morocco, without finishing the job. First time ever. I never heard from your father again—and I was glad. Because I thought it meant I would never work for him again."

He'd lifted his head during the last words and she stared into his eyes and saw the truth there. She saw everything in those eyes, and her heart ached for him.

"I think about that kid and I see me alone and scared. Willing to do anything to survive," he whispered. "He was holding an AK-47. How the hell a twelve-year-old knew how to handle an AK..."

He didn't finish, held his head in his hands, and she fought the urge to touch him. It wasn't the time. Not yet.

"If I hadn't taken the way out your father gave me, I'd be rotting in prison for a crime I didn't commit. So I went with him and I've stayed out of jail, even though I commit acts of murder more often than the average criminal. And for what, the greater good? Maybe sometimes—I try to believe that, but I honestly don't know." His laugh quickly turned into a half sob, but he bit it back, his eyes fierce, his neck tightly corded from the effort he put into holding his emotions at bay.

"I can't imagine."

"You never want to." Sometimes, at night, he could swear he heard the clank of the barred cell door shutting, locking him in.

Small spaces were something he had to force himself into even now, which was why the house had a wide-open floor plan. There were also lots of windows, so he could see the outside from every angle. "I sat in a cell and I rotted away for two years." His voice broke, but she was pretty sure that he hadn't in all that time. He had too much control, too much pride.

But the horror she saw reflected in his eyes, that was real, stripped away.

"I was going to use you, I made you the brunt of my anger. I'm no better than he is."

She shook him by the shoulders. "You came to me with an intention of malice, but you jumped right in to save me. If you hadn't come, I don't know what would've happened to me."

"You could be with your father."

"Or I could be dead."

"I don't know if they're following me—I might've brought all of this down on you."

"What do you mean?"

"The man from the highway who tried to kill us—the one I went out to talk to—he gave me a name. It was the man I was supposed to kill. The kid's dad. And it's all come full circle."

"You couldn't have known the repercussions."

"I didn't know anything on those missions, I flew blind." He clutched his fists in frustration, and yes, it was easy to see why a capable, trained operative would hate being given an order without knowing the rationale behind it. "I was trained to follow orders, but not like that. I don't want you to see me like this—like someone who needs your goddamned pity."

"You think I pity you?" She shoved him. "That couldn't be further from the truth." She could blame him for using her, for wanting to kidnap her, for even thinking about taking her life, though. "I want to hate you. I should hate you, Cam. But you brought me back to life, and I have to believe that I wouldn't fall for someone who had a black heart. I have to believe that."

Instincts, baby girl. They'll never steer you wrong.

She knew whatever Cam would tell her about her father would hurt her, although probably not nearly as much as it had hurt him.

When he spoke again, he told her, "My friend, he'll be here soon. He's bringing someone else to help you."

"Does he know where my father is?"

"He didn't tell me, just left me a message. He's flying now. And I've got some work to do as well. Okay?"

She nodded, because he looked like he just wanted some space from her. After he left the room, she shifted, stared at the big bed.

She'd known he wouldn't stay with her—things between them were just too raw, despite how much he'd shared, and maybe even because of it. And still, she wanted nothing more than the comfort of his arms.

Why am I here?"

"You're useful. That's all you need to know for now."

The heavy doors had closed. Locked in the room, Olivia heard nothing but silence, the dead, stark space that left her reeling, with nothing to hold on to except the thin mattress she lay on. It was the only thing between her and the cold linoleum floor.

She had no idea how long she'd traveled to get here, or how long she'd been sleeping since they'd thrown her in this room.

Her dad's face flashed in front of her. Then her mom's.

They'd have no idea she was gone. How long would it take for the hospital to report her missing?

Her patients would miss her. The staff would take slightly longer—till it occurred to them when she screwed up OR schedules.

The light streamed in when the heavy door opened and she squinted to see who walked in.

She made out the silhouette of a large man before he said, "Welcome, Dr. Strohm."

A different voice than the men who'd taken her. She did not feel *welcome*. No, her body ached. She'd been jostled. Stressed. Her cheek throbbed, and she touched the tender, bruised flesh—it might be broken . . . but that was the least of her worries.

She was in much better shape than the man who was currently being tossed in with her. As she watched, they flung his limp body on the floor at her feet, and he groaned slightly. He looked like death warmed over—bruised, bloodied. Tortured.

"He's all yours, Dr. Strohm."

"What do you expect me to do?"

"Fix him."

"And then?"

"And then we'll break him again." The door closed before she could ask for any medical supplies. As her eyes adjusted to the dim light, she noted a bag in the corner and scooted over to open it.

Peroxide. Gauze and bandages. Water. Advil.

How the hell was she supposed to help this man with just that?

Still, she grabbed the light stock and brought it back to the mattress. With a heave, she turned the man onto his side, even though she ended up nearly lying on the dirty floor next to him.

Her scrubs were dusty and dirty already, anyway, and her mouth felt like she'd been eating sawdust, although she hadn't thought about it until she saw the water. She grabbed a bottle and took a long drink before she poured some on a piece of gauze and gently wiped some of the blood and grime off the man's face.

After a few moments, she recognized him, especially when the dark, intense eyes opened to stare at her. Gabriel—Skylar Slavin's father. "My God, Mr. Creighton, what did they do to you?"

"Is she here?"

"Who, Sky?" she asked, and he nodded, his finger to his lips, indicating she should keep her voice to a whisper.

"No. They came to me looking for her. Mr. Creighton, I don't understand..."

He looked like he was wrestling over an important decision. Finally, he spoke to her, his voice low, his words, quick, "Dr. Strohm—Olivia—I'm not a businessman. I've worked for the CIA. I was infiltrating this group—they're called DMH."

"You're the reason Skylar's in danger," she breathed, and he nodded stoically.

"I'm sorry you've been involved."

"Will they ever let me go?"

When he didn't answer right away, she went cold. "Give me a straight answer. I can handle anything but a lie right now."

"In all likelihood, no. But I'll work to get us out of here. I promise." He pointed to her meager supplies. "Do the best you can. I'm going to sleep now, while I can."

He closed his eyes as she watched. This man was strong, trained—and he'd confirmed what she already knew: This might not end well.

She'd have to do everything she could to keep him in fighting shape. Herself as well.

You can do this, Olivia. And she did, cleaned Gabriel's wounds as best she could, woke him once to drink water and take the pain medication, even though he initially tried to refuse it.

She was used to that, from patients, from schoolmates and co-workers too. To an outsider, it didn't seem that she'd met with a lot of resistance throughout her life. Her family was wealthy. She had a trust fund. Everything handed to her. She admitted it had been great not worrying about med school tuition. Better still, she'd tell people who questioned, was having her parents approve of everything she did. Or at least have them talking to her. She knew some people thought she wasn't as good of a doctor, because it didn't seem like she had to fight for anything, because even the rigors of medical school seemed to come easily to her.

She'd fought, all right. She'd fought every day of her life, from the time she was nine years old and taken from her family. Fought until she escaped, three weeks after her abduction.

Then fought the nightmares. The fear. The internal scars that kept her from forming bonds with most people.

And she would fight now.

She couldn't wait to be saved; she would have to save herself, the best way she knew how.

Coffee—burning a hole in his gut—and pure adrenaline fueled Cam now as he refused sleep in order to weigh his options.

Dylan would be here soon.

Dylan, who'd left him a message earlier, one Cam replayed inside his mind, hearing the couched urgency in his friend's voice. *We'll be there. Can't tell you much, only that DMH is involved. It's bad, Cam . . . really bad.*

DMH. Dead Man's Hand. He'd come across their special brand of terrorism during some Delta missions—they were no longer a small, nothing-to-worry-about cell. No, they'd fast become a force to be reckoned with, selling secrets and anything else to hurt the United States and make themselves money.

DMH is involved. It's bad, Cam . . . really bad.

He played with the slip of paper with the CIA contact's number on it he'd gotten from Dylan. One call, and they'd take Sky away to safety. No doubt witness protection, and from there, Cam might never see her again.

Then again, that might happen anyway, no matter the outcome of finding her father.

Prepping her about DMH before Dylan and Riley arrived would be a necessity. She'd have some hard decisions to make, and he honestly didn't know which direction he'd steer her in, where she'd be safest.

Witness protection didn't always work in circumstances like this. Sky was traceable, thanks to her medical condition. It would necessitate nearly constant moving around. Living a disposable life.

He flashed back to the house he'd lived in before his mom died, a house with worn-out furniture he'd come home to every day for three years, a far cry from the neat, comfortable living room that now attempted to replace the old memories.

This was his dream space—a safe house without bars on the windows. Well, not the metal ones anyway.

The last years of his dad's undercover work had been hard for his mom and Cam had watched her slip into a depression, fueled by alcohol and prescription drugs.

Most days, when he came home from school, she was still in bed or walking around in her robe, in a stupor.

At school, he was considered an enigma. He looked— and sometimes acted—like a Grade A thug, but his grades were good and his attendance spotless. Some of that was because school, as opposed to the streets, was the safest place for him.

Translation: If he'd cut school to hang out, his father would've known. And no matter how deeply undercover

Howie Moore was, he was always available to kick his son's ass.

When Cam had moved to Howie's house, it hadn't been much better. Sparse furniture and lots of time alone was what he remembered most.

The "lots of time alone" hadn't changed much for Cam. Except now.

The door to his bedroom remained open—Sky insisted she felt better that way, although he'd been more than willing to give her privacy. She hadn't bothered him since he'd left her earlier, let him decompress, or at least attempt to.

He wasn't sure what she was doing. He'd heard the TV go on at one point. But he'd shifted to look inside the room when he heard the scratch of pen to paper. She was leaning on one elbow, lip tugged between her teeth. Her body was there but her mind . . . she was totally somewhere else.

Transported.

How fucking cool of a skill was that?

He remained still so he could watch without disturbing her. Her hand never stopped moving, not for at least half an hour. The hair fell around her face and, at times, she'd push it away impatiently as her hand moved faster across the page.

Finally, she dropped the pen and lay back against the pillows, flexing her hand as if to bring back blood flow. It was then she noticed him and she put her hands in the air, as if to say, *This is what happens.*

"I didn't mean to bother you."

"Trust me, you haven't." She flipped onto her stomach, feet in the air as she looked up at him. "I got out what I needed to."

"It just wakes you up like that?"

"Yeah. Drives me crazy. When I'm on, the words, the pictures, they come through whether I want them to or not. Writing them down is my only relief." She smiled. "What's yours?"

He wanted to laugh, although there was nothing funny about the question. Because, relief? Shit, the thing he thought would finally bring him peace—getting back at Gabriel Creighton—had wound him up further. "So far, I haven't found a lot of relief."

"Maybe that needs to change."

"Yeah, it definitely does." He ran a thumb along her lower lip. "I'd like you involved in helping me. I like seeing you here, in my house. Working. Smiling a little, despite everything we've talked about."

"I'm not going anywhere, Cam."

He leaned in and kissed her. It wasn't the time to start anything, not with Dylan and Riley due soon, but he couldn't resist.

When he pulled back, she looked pleased, and shy, and he loved that she could still blush when she looked at him.

He'd fallen hard for this woman. And letting her leave his house would be to admit defeat. He'd had too many failures in his life to allow another.

Sky's cheeks were still a little flushed. "I need something to drink."

"I'll get it."

"No, you stay. I'm capable of going to the kitchen and back safely." She smiled and sprang gracefully off the bed, wearing his shorts and T-shirt. She looked damned fine in his clothes, with her hair loose and tumbled over her shoulders, her eyes bright despite everything else going on around them.

Maybe she could be happy here. He knew he could be, with her.

"Hey," he called after her. She'd reached the doorway and she turned, leaned against the doorjamb. "Are you letting Violet fall in love?"

She laughed softly. "Well, I'm more open to the possibility of it. My editor was the one who wanted her to fall in love, and at first, I didn't think that was such a good idea."

"How come?"

"I never really saw love as an answer to anything. It always seemed to get people hurt instead."

"I can see Violet falling in love."

"You can?"

"Everyone needs someone they can let their guard down with."

"I guess they do," she agreed, and then turned and started toward the kitchen again.

He glanced over to where she'd left her papers, scattered, covered in black ink, with what looked like mostly crossouts and scribbles, but there was lilting script in between.

He knew he shouldn't—she hadn't invited him to look—but he couldn't help himself. But there was nothing about Violet on the pages—nothing that was a work of fiction at all. No, she'd written down everything he'd told her, about jail, about her father's involvement with him. About his own father.

Some of it was in note form, some in neatly written paragraphs. In places, just a few words with arrows dotted the margins. But it was his life, written out like so many plot points of the latest action-adventure Hollywood block-buster.

And yeah, it would make a great movie. Because it was all fucking unbelievable... unless you'd lived it.

Sky cleared her throat and he found her back in the doorway, a glass of juice in hand. Shit.

He put the papers down, wanted to apologize, but the anger rose up too quickly. Before he could say anything, she spoke.

"It's the way I process things. I'm trying to make sense of it all," she explained. "I didn't write it to show anyone."

He believed her immediately. "That's what I get for in-vading your privacy. It's just... It's bad enough to talk about it. But to see it laid out there..."

"I can rip it up if it bothers you."

"No, it's okay. I'm just not sure how that's going to help."

"I am," she said quietly. "Is it possible to check my mes-sages?" She held up her BlackBerry, which no longer had a battery.

"I can have them transferred to my phone," he told her. He got online, clicked a few buttons and then he was dial-ing his own phone, putting it on speaker.

She typed in her code when prompted and listened. He knew she was hoping for some kind of message from her fa-ther. He couldn't blame her—a message from Gabriel would uncomplicate some things... and make others worse.

The monotone voice announced, "One new message—yesterday at twelve-forty A.M." And then there was a long pause, followed by a panicked woman's voice that made both of them jump.

"Skylar—there are men asking about you—they're taking me—kidnapping me—I don't know what they want..."

The woman's voice trailed off into frantic screams that continued until the phone clicked off. Sky remained frozen in place.

He shook her gently and pressed a button so the message could be saved and replayed, if necessary. Just not in front of her. "Sky, who was that? Was it Pam, your publicist?"

"No...not Pam. That was Olivia Strohm."

"A friend?"

"My doctor—she did my transplant. Why would they take her? Why, Cam?" She felt herself going over the edge again, the nightmare of the past days coming back to strangle her.

"It's going to be all right."

"Tell me why they'd take her. She has nothing to do with this, she's just my doctor—" She stopped, because suddenly, she knew why. She broke out in a sickening sweat and Cam's embrace was the only thing holding her up. "Whoever took her...they need her there to keep me alive, once they've got me."

"No one's going to get you. Do you understand that? Never." Cam's voice was fierce and she saw the warrior rise up behind his eyes. It made her feel protected as hell. And she believed him.

CHAPTER
16

An hour later, still shaken, Sky heard voices and knew that Cam's friends had arrived.

She'd pulled herself together, for Liv's sake, because her friend and doctor needed her help now. Sky showered and pulled on a too-big flannel shirt of Cam's and some sweatpants before padding out past the small security station off the bedroom, and down the hall to the kitchen.

The man was dark-haired; the woman with him was really pretty, dark hair and eyes, despite the bruising along her cheekbone and a split lip. She was exotic-looking. Curvy. And when Skylar walked into the kitchen, the talking stopped and Cam moved to her side.

"Sky, this is Dylan and Riley."

"Hey, Skylar." Dylan stepped forward to shake her hand, and Riley simply nodded, her bearing more guarded than Sky would've expected.

Then again, she didn't know anything about either one of them, didn't know if they were spies or military or what. She just knew they would tell her who was after her. Who had her father. "No offense, but can we cut through the small talk? Because I'd really like some answers."

Dylan nodded. "I understand. Skylar, the men who are after you are part of a group who call themselves Dead Man's Hand."

"DMH," she whispered, her knees weak, because it was far more insidious than she'd thought. "No . . ."

"You've heard of them?" Dylan was asking as Cam steered her gently toward the couch, with a hand on her lower back. He sat next to her, a steady hand on her leg, while Riley brought her a glass of water.

She took a sip, her hands shaking. She was hot and cold at the same time, and it was like that day, that fateful day, expecting to find her mom waiting for her in the kitchen and instead being told she was dead. "My mother . . . DMH is responsible for killing my mother."

"Did Gabriel tell you that?" Riley asked her.

She shook her head. She remembered that day, listening to him on the phone, talking in some kind of code when he thought she couldn't hear.

At the time, she hadn't understood anything except the letters *DMH*. The extensive research she'd done about the group had yielded next to nothing. A mention here and there, but mostly what came up were references to the dead man's hand in poker . . . an association she'd assumed had something to do with why the group had chosen its name. "He didn't know I overhead him talking about it. I assumed they were just a militia group my mother had been trying to infiltrate."

"You were right." Riley moved with a quiet grace that didn't hide the fact that she was just as deadly as the two men. "DMH are terrorists. Killers. And they'll sell their services to the highest bidder, as long as that bidder isn't the USA. The man who runs it is an ex-patriot who took a grass-roots extremist group and turned them international."

Sky pulled her sweater tighter and Cam's hand on her leg steadied her, made her feel safe even as her world got more out of control. "They sound horrible—much worse than I thought."

"DMH is involved in everything from selling U.S. secrets to child trafficking," Riley continued. "They're like an octopus, constantly branching out in different directions, too slippery to catch. Their operatives are nearly impossible to trace—many of them are disposable, used for specific jobs and then let go . . . or killed. Getting close to the inner circle is nearly impossible."

"And you think my father has."

"I know so," Riley confirmed. "Cam and I have as well—we just didn't know it at the time."

Cam's head snapped in Riley's direction. "What the hell are you talking about?"

"I'm assuming Sky knows . . . about the work you did for Gabriel?" Riley asked, and Cam nodded slowly. Tension rose to a palpable level in the room as they waited for Riley to explain.

Riley faced Sky when she spoke, but her words were meant for Cam. "I have reason to believe that most of those missions involved taking down DMH."

Cam stiffened and rose. "How the hell can you be sure?"

This time, Riley looked at him. "The last man you were sent to kill was Bullet, aka Elijah Killoran. He's the ringleader of DMH."

Riley was referencing the job Cam had told Sky about, the one where the boy was killed.

"I was that close to the head of DMH and I let him go." Cam's fists clenched, his voice tight as he stared out one of the windows, not making eye contact with any of them. "You're fucking kidding me, right? And because I didn't do my job then, this is coming back to bite Sky on the ass."

"How could you have known that?" Dylan demanded fiercely and Cam turned to look at him. "Jesus, Cam, you can't take the weight of the world on your shoulders. Besides, sometimes when you cut the head off something, the body still functions."

"Gabriel had already started his plan to infiltrate before your mission failed." Riley perched on the edge of one of the chairs across from the couch as she spoke. She rubbed the side of her bruised face gingerly. "As far as I can tell, he officially went in about three months ago, although it seems he was making inroads well before that."

"I'm confused," Sky said. "If my father's working undercover . . . then am I not really in danger?"

Riley smiled, but there was not a lot of warmth there. No, she looked . . . nervous. Took her hand away from her face and abruptly stood, paced a few steps. "You're in danger. DMH made your father. Because of me. I turned him in to them."

"And you brought her here? Are you crazy?" Cam demanded of Dylan. "She let DMH know about Sky."

"I didn't do that," Riley told Cam, then turned to Sky. "I mean, yes, I turned Gabriel in but I never thought any further than that, that they might use his family. I thought . . . I thought they would kill him and that would be the end of it," Riley said, the pain shining behind her imploring words. "Skylar, I was trying to avenge my father's death. I don't expect you to understand—"

"Get her out of here," Cam told Dylan through clenched teeth, but Sky stepped in front of him.

"Stop, please. It's done. She's here now—and if Dylan, your friend, the man you most trust, trusts her, then we have to. The most important thing now is what we do next." She paused, letting her words sink in. Cam held up his hands in a silent surrender, but he didn't look happy. "Why does DMH want my father alive so badly?"

"They could use him to gain access to places they couldn't get—he knows how to work the system," Riley offered, but Sky shook her head.

"There's more to it."

"He'll never tell them anything that would compromise American lives, Sky. Which is why it's so important for them to get to you—you're the only reason Gabriel might possibly spill what he knows. Like the safeguards he helped design and put into place working alongside Homeland Security to make sure something like 9/11 never happens again. If he knows the safeguards, he knows the flaws. Intel like that is worth billions on the open market, and DMH would be only too happy to sell it to the highest bidder. Even a small amount of true intel from your father would be invaluable."

She'd paled at Dylan's words, but they were what she needed to hear. It was real. She understood. "They want to use me as leverage to make my father talk. They want to threaten me and see if he'll spill his secrets when my life is on the line."

"Yes."

She swallowed. Hard. Not doing a great job of pretending she didn't care, that she wasn't scared.

She'd been pretending for so damned long that it had become second nature. And somehow, Cam knew that, because she'd been stupid, had let him in that first night and he hadn't let go since.

"Why should we go to DMH?" Sky asked, holding up her cell phone in one hand and the battery in another. "Why not put this back together and let them come to us? To me?"

"Because I won't risk that." Cam's voice shook from anger and the strength of his resolve. "They're going to want to bring you to your father—torture you in front of him to make him spill whatever secrets they think he has."

"But they would take me to him—and you could follow me," she insisted. "And you can save my father from DMH, then report him to the CIA, or whatever you want to do. But I won't leave him in the hands of killers."

"Sky, you don't understand," Dylan said gently. "The only way DMH will ever leave you alone is if your father's dead."

Sky let the truth of the words sink in—and they did, slowly and painfully—and for a second she was sure her throat was closing.

Her father's life for hers. Another risk he'd take for her.

He'd done bad things. She knew that. Was under no illusions that he'd abused his power in terrible ways and had damaged at least two people she knew of because of his need to avenge his wife's death.

Her mother's murder.

"So we let DMH kill him?" The words came out as more of a challenge than a question. Cam and Dylan looked somber.

"He would never want you given to them, Sky," Cam told her.

"Are you sure they'll kill him?" she persisted. "You said yourself that he's valuable. That they'd keep him alive until they found a way to make him share his intel."

"He's a pro, Sky. He'd consider…" Cam stopped and then, with a shake of his head, continued, "He'd consider taking his own life before…"

She blinked, her body numb, mind reeling. There seemed to be no good way out of this. "In the meantime…"

"You'd be safest in the CIA's hands."

Watching Cam, his face couched in shadows, unshaven, his eyes focused, she was aware of just how big the man was. How strong… how deadly, when the situation called for it.

Shadow. On the fringe. Warriors in a dangerous game

where right and wrong depended on the team you played for.

She wrote about these men, yes. Had grown up with one. But seeing it play out in front of her—this was nothing she'd ever wanted to experience.

Delta Force operators were no angels. But black ops were altogether different. Deadly. They could rip the soul from a man if he wasn't careful . . . and in the course of writing her books, she'd spoken with men who hadn't been careful.

"I need to be alone for a little while," she told him.

She walked to the bedroom without looking back, heard the dead silence in her wake, which she attempted to close out with a firm push on the bedroom door.

Once inside, she sat on the bed, pulled her knees up to her chin and wrapped one of the quilts around her, because she was shivering again.

DMH has your father—and they're after you.

This world she was thrust into was like the dream she'd once had of plunging into a frozen lake and finding herself trapped underneath the ice. No matter how hard she pushed or swam, she could only see the world through the ice, couldn't breathe . . . couldn't get warm.

She'd been surrounded by terror, literally frozen with fear when she'd woken—ironically, drenched in sweat even as she shivered.

It's the meds, her first doctor had assured her.

And Sky had that dream, on and off, for the next five years, even after switching medicines.

But it appeared it was a harbinger of things to come. She was being stalked by a secret group of trained assassins.

And there was another group who claimed to be on her side—who remained just outside her reach on the other side of the bedroom door.

All she had to do was decide where she'd be safest.

All she had to do was figure out if the man she'd fallen in love with was the real deal.

Cam knocked on the door to his room after an hour. He didn't think Sky would invite him in, but she did, calling to him through the closed door.

She was sitting in the middle of the bed, blanket pulled tight around her. He jacked up the heat on the thermostat before he sat next to her.

"I know it's a lot to take in," he started.

"So I was right. DMH wants to use me as leverage," she said slowly, her eyes averted—staring at the carpet or her toes, he wasn't sure which. "And he'll die before he lets that happen. Like Dylan said, if he's not dead, they'll always be after me. Do you know what a horrible feeling that is? What a horrible choice?"

"It's not your choice, Sky. It's your father's."

Her voice shook as her gaze lifted to meet his. "Cam, whether he talks or not, they'll kill him. And he's got to know that."

Cam didn't deny it. "The only thing I can do is keep you out of harm's way. It's what he'd want—that much I know."

"And you'll do that, even though you hate him."

"Make no mistake about it, Sky, I'm doing this for you. Only for you."

"I can't let them kill my father."

"There's nothing you can do about that. I'm sorry."

"But there is something. You can save him—I know you can."

"First of all, I don't even know that. Beyond the fact that saving him puts you in direct line of fire—forgetting that for just a minute, based on everything else we've talked about, how can you ask me that?"

"Because you're probably the only one who can help him now."

Her words were a cross between a demand and a plea, and the anxiety welled up inside of him. "You have no idea what you're asking."

She touched a hand to his cheek. "But I do. And I'm asking anyway. I wouldn't be able to live with myself if I didn't."

"Sky—"

"He risked his life for me."

"Of course he would." He paused. "Wait a minute, you don't mean . . ."

Realization dawned as she began to speak. "I know where my father was five months ago."

She'd lifted her shirt and was pointing to her scar.

When they'd landed, Dylan found a message from Cam about a missing doctor and immediately put Zane on the case.

"If DMH has her . . ." Riley began, and then trailed off. "Never mind—see what you can find out."

And so Zane headed into Manhattan while Dylan and

Riley rented a car to drive the last three-hour leg of the trip to the Adirondacks. He'd meet them there when he was done.

First stop, the hospital. Zane drove around the large, underground lot until he found the doc's car easily enough—broken into, for sure, and roped off by hospital security, but the assholes hadn't done anything smart like call the police.

"We paged the doc, figured she was in surgery," one of them said with a shrug.

No one had reported her missing. The doctors in her hospital were pissed she hadn't shown up for her shift, the nurses said it wasn't like her. But her patients, they were worried. Upset. And that told Zane everything he needed to know about what kind of woman Dr. Olivia Strohm was.

Next stop, the doc's apartment. Across town, an odd choice for someone who worked as much as she appeared to. It was a doorman building, but he got in easily enough—slid past the guy while he was helping someone hail a cab.

She lived on the third floor. She had no deadbolt on her door, which helped him immensely.

Her place was . . . clean. Stark. Probably the best piece of furniture was a brand-new, king-sized bed, which looked comfortable as hell. But otherwise, there wasn't much in the way of decor beyond a standard couch, a small TV . . . and not a hell of a lot of food in the fridge.

Doc didn't spend a lot of time at home. Well, hell, neither did he. He knew what demons he was trying to outrun—wondered if Olivia Strohm had the same issues.

Just then, his phone began to ring. He expected Dylan, and groaned out loud when he saw it was his other brother. The human lie detector and moral compass of the entire free world. Straightlaced as hell, like he had a stick up his...

"Hey, Cael."

"What are you balls deep into now?"

Cael was like the father Zane never really had, because their father had lived his life much closer to Zane's way of doing things.

Where Cael was strict, old school—where it came from was something Zane wondered every once in a while, especially when Cael pulled that daddy shit. "Things are cool."

"What does Dylan have you involved in?"

"Nothing you need to worry about."

Zane stared at the picture of the young woman, flanked by what looked like her parents, then moved on to a more recent one of her standing next to her mom, although whoever took the picture focused on her.

Her eyes were dark, piercing, like they held a million secrets tight and still they managed to shine like diamonds. And she was laughing.

Her perfume lingered over the entire apartment, even though it was by no means anything more than a light scent, citrus-based. He hadn't noticed that before, but now he knew it would stay with him after he left.

His fingers brushed the back of the picture frame—noted that the cardboard felt as though it bulged. Although he had no right to, he justified checking it out with the reasoning that he was trying to save her life.

It was a newspaper clipping. It looked well worn, as if

she—or someone—had read it a thousand times. As if she couldn't stop thinking about it. Worrying about it.

It was dated twenty-four years earlier. *Abducted Girl Escapes Her Captors After Three Weeks.*

Olivia Strohm, aged nine.

Jesus H. Christ. His heart thudded in his chest.

"I always worry when you're not working. Military work," Caleb added. "Not working for Dylan."

Zane felt dizzy, managed, "He keeps me honest."

Caleb laughed, a short, biting sound. Zane slid the picture out of its frame and flipped it to see hand writing. Last year's date and the words *Laugh more. Love, Dad.* He slipped it into the inside pocket of his jacket. They'd need to show it around, and it looked recent. "Got to go, Cael," he told his brother, hanging up before Caleb could impart more words of wisdom.

He was dialing Dylan as he let himself out of the doc's apartment.

Elijah watched Olivia through the monitor set up in the living room.

She'd bargained that morning for more medicine and supplies to help heal Gabriel. Had dutifully dressed his wounds, only to have a bigger mess on her hands later that evening.

"Why do you keep torturing him?" she'd asked Elijah earlier, oddly calm thanks to the first round of drugs she'd recently been given, and of course she couldn't know what DMH was about. It was neither to her benefit or detriment in terms of her survival . . . whether Dr. Strohm was of consequence to his organization remained to be seen.

"Why do you do what you do?" he answered her question in kind, avoiding answering.

"That's not the same thing at all."

"You're right. Your profession tends to give people false hope. Mine, not at all."

She'd looked stunned for a moment, then her eyes sparked fire, despite the drugs. But she didn't say anything more, had never spouted the usual *You won't get away with this* nonsense.

She knew better. But she was fighting. Not physically, no, she hadn't attempted any kind of escape or fight with his men. But she was emotionally fierce . . . the way her brow furrowed, even while she slept, as if she was constantly thinking on how to get through her confinement the best way she knew how.

She was hanging on to hope.

He could tell her that it was the worst choice to make, that hope was really for the weak and that there was so much more Olivia could do with her skills.

She intrigued him, the first woman to do so since Mariana. That alone made Elijah wary, almost had him allowing her to be absorbed into the skin trade and sold for a good price to whomever would take her once Gabriel and Skylar were eliminated.

She would make him a small fortune. But no, she would stay with him in the organization and he would utilize her profession. He could keep her on a tight leash. And he would personally escort her to the next location—her training ground before she would be allowed into one of the exclusive clinics, reserved for those patients who could pay a steep price for black market organs, and for those who donated theirs, by choice or by force.

Olivia Strohm would give them quite a bit of trouble, he was sure. And he would make sure he enjoyed it all.

CHAPTER
17

For a long moment, Cam stared at the scar that ran along Sky's side, his mind racing.

It was so fucking obvious—and something he'd never considered.

How could he hate the man who saved the woman he'd fallen for? And yet, he did. "I hate him, Sky. If he were here right now..."

His hands were fisted in front of them and he clenched them even more tightly. Until she laid her hands over them and said quietly, "I know, Cam."

"I hate talking about this with you. I hate that you know."

"Know what, that you have emotions?" Her hands remained on his, rubbing lightly. "I know those were supposed to stop existing when you became a soldier, but hey, it can be our secret."

He stared at her. "How the fuck are you taking this so calmly?"

"I'm not." She pulled her hands away. "But it's nothing I didn't know already. The thing is, Cam, you hating him means that you also hate a part of me."

He swallowed hard. "I couldn't hate you. I wanted to . . ."

"When you look at me, how are you not going to see him? How is that not going to come between us?"

He didn't have an answer.

"Can you let it go?"

How? How could he do that?

The only thing he could promise was that he'd do the right thing. "We'll find your father. We'll save him."

From there, it would be anyone's guess. "You know I could never have hurt you."

"I know you could've, from the second you found me," she countered. "You told me so yourself that first night. But if those men hadn't been after me . . ."

"I would've left you."

She flicked her eyes toward his, but didn't say anything.

When he spoke again, it was with a tightness in his throat. "Five months ago, your father gave you a kidney. Five months ago, your father freed me from service. Your illness saved my ass. If Gabriel had pushed me at that point, I would've snapped. Broken." So, in truth, he owed her everything. "I'll do whatever you need."

"Cam."

"I said I'd do what you need—I'll save your father. I owe you."

She blinked, but it wasn't nearly enough to hold back the tears. "The fact that you'd do this . . . that means—"

"Don't. All it means is that I haven't turned into a fucking monster." He paused, and then, "What's he like?"

It took her a second before she realized what he was asking. "You mean, my father?"

"Yeah."

"He's funny. And kind." She shifted as his gaze never wavered from hers. It was probably nothing he wanted to hear, but it was important to her that he know the truth. Her truth. "He could be cold and distant . . . usually after he'd been away for a while. It was like it would take him a while to get back to normal."

He nodded slowly. "Sometimes it does. It feels like everyone's moved on and you come back and it's different and you're different."

"So the distance, it wasn't anything I did?"

"What? No, not at all. There's nothing you could've done to make it better either. It just takes time."

"Is it always like that for you?"

"Pretty much every time. Sometimes worse than others." This, this talking about Gabriel, was a mistake. He didn't want to know that Gabriel brought donuts to his wife and daughter, read stories to Sky at night, normal at home, cold-blooded in the field.

Just like Cam himself.

What kind of fine line did Cam skate every day, every mission?

What would stop him from turning, the way Gabriel

had? Then again, Gabriel seemed to be the same way he'd always been—the duality hadn't changed at all.

And still, for his family, the man would do anything. *Anything.*

Cam would have to find his own peace the only way he knew how. The only peace he'd truly ever had was in Sky's arms, and how the hell could any of this end well?

It will just end, he told himself firmly.

"Did it help?" she asked. "Talking about my father. Did it help?"

He cleared his throat. "It didn't hurt."

Sky could clearly see the struggle Cam was having. The fact that he'd chosen to help her proved that he wasn't, and never could be, a monster.

Her instincts had been right the entire time. And still, moving forward, there was a great deal to go through before either of them could be at peace.

"How are Dylan and Riley going to feel about this? I can't imagine Riley is going to be happy either." She relaxed her stance a little, letting the blanket fall around her waist as she turned to face him.

"Riley's here. She'll have to be open to whatever the plan is. Dylan's going to be harder to convince, because he's seen firsthand how working for your father affected me," Cam told her, and she could see the strain on his face.

"I know what a big risk this is."

"I'm not doing it for Gabriel. I'm doing it for you. Because if we don't deal with this now, you'll never be safe."

"I might never be anyway, Cam. What matters is you."

"Yeah, well, right back at you." He shook his head. "What Dylan told you before, that your father might off himself before he lets himself be rescued . . . he's absolutely correct."

"I know that."

He continued. "We don't even know if he's still alive—you know that, right?"

"Yes. But I also know I couldn't live with myself if I didn't do something."

He didn't say anything more about it. She knew he was thinking about what happened after—about the possibility of things, like her being put into witness protection.

She didn't want to go there yet. Better to focus on the task at hand.

She thought Cam would go back out to Dylan and Riley, but instead he shifted so he leaned against the headboard, rubbed a spot between his eyes for a few seconds. "I don't understand . . . your father's always so careful. It's been over ten years and I'm just now getting intel on his undercover work with the OA. He's been with DMH for three months and he's made by Riley—someone who's not even in the organization?"

He moved his hands away and stared straight ahead. And then he brought his eyes back to her, looked like he wanted to say something else.

"What is it, Cam?" she asked, moved a little closer to him.

"I think I know." He swallowed hard. "The transplant is the key."

"How?"

"You said, in order for him to do that, he had to put himself literally on the line."

"Yeah, because he risked his life for me by giving me the kidney."

"There's more to being a donor than that. He had to prove he was related in order to consent. In order to speed up the process, he had to be himself."

Her mouth opened, in surprise, in understanding. "He used his real name to register—he had to."

"And that's how Riley found him. Before that, his name was impossible to find in any database. Trust me, I tried," he muttered, ran his fingers through his hair.

"So it's my fault."

"None of this is your fault, Sky. If anything, you saved me."

"What are you talking about?"

"If you hadn't been dying, needing your father, I wouldn't have been set free—I wouldn't have survived."

Even now, just talking about it, he felt broken. Like making it through this conversation could let it all rush back to him, fresh and raw. "Do you know how fucked up it is that I'm grateful to you for your illness?"

"I don't think of it like that. I'm just so sorry that you had to—" Her voice caught before she could finish.

"Don't. Don't you feel sorry for me. I couldn't stand that."

His voice held a dangerous edge, ran through her like a warning: *Don't get close, don't touch.*

Certainly, don't give away your heart.

Too late. She pushed his arms aside and climbed into his lap. Ignoring the warning growl of, "Not now," she traced the inside of his collarbone first with a finger and then with her mouth, tasting the warm skin.

Her breath stopped being slow and steady when her hands traveled down between their bodies. Her hand rested on the warm, soft cotton of his jeans, his arousal pushing against her palm.

"Can't help that you do that to me. All I have to do is look at you, think about you... hear your voice," he told her, and heat flooded her.

"Now we get down to what's real," she told him, and for a second, the urge for fight or flight clenched his chest.

"Sky—"

"Not because you owe me, or you're using me. But because you want to. Only if you want to." She paused for a moment and then asked, "Do you?"

"Yeah, I do."

"Then nothing else matters right now."

She was right. Living in the moment. Hell, he did it with his job all the time.

She curled up against him and he traced her scar with his finger. "I know how much I'm asking," she told him.

"Could you ever forgive me if I didn't help you?"

Could she? He was saving her, and that's what her father would want. He didn't owe her father anything. Gabriel had put Cam through hell for years.

"We need to do this, for both our sakes," she whispered. "And then..."

And then...

"This is your safe place," she said.

"Yeah, I thought it was. But walls don't make you safe."

"They will, for now." She ran her hands through his thick hair.

He pulled her close and he held her until he couldn't put off sharing his decision with Dylan and Riley any longer.

Dylan and Riley both looked like shit. Riley worse, thanks to the bruises that circled her neck and the ones on her cheekbone. Cam was pretty sure he looked almost as bad—couldn't remember the last time he'd shaved. His shoulder ached, but at least the fever had stopped.

Dylan was rubbing Riley's back, the two of them had their heads together and were talking, until Dylan looked up and saw Cam.

"Hey, how is she?" he asked as Riley turned toward Cam as well.

Cam shrugged.

"Zane called—no one's reported the doc missing yet," Dylan told him.

"Shit." Cam rubbed the back of his neck.

"What's wrong?"

They all turned to see Sky, standing in the doorway of the bedroom. Jesus, he was getting soft if he could let her sneak up on him like that—and by the looks on Dylan and Riley's faces, they felt the same way.

"It's about Olivia, isn't it?"

Dylan attempted to break the news gently. "I sent my brother to check on her. She's definitely been taken."

"She's hurt. Because of me." Her voice sounded hollow.

"None of this is your fault, Sky." Cam held her by the shoulders and did everything but shake her to get her to meet his eyes. "None of this. I keep telling you that. This world your father's gotten involved in, it's dark and it's sick and it's scary. It's not meant for the general public to see."

"Yes, I know the quote—something about rough men keeping us safe in our beds," she murmured softly, reached out to touch his cheek. For a second, they were the only ones in the room and Cam wondered if it would always be like that. If he'd always have the chance to feel that way.

"We need to get a plan together to find Gabriel." He waited for the fallout from Dylan and Riley, which came instantly.

"What the hell are you talking about?" Dylan demanded, and Riley went pale. Sky could clearly see the circle of bruises around her throat now—bright purple, as if they were very new.

"Gabriel Creighton's hurt every person in this room, and now we're going to save his ass? That's bullshit," Dylan continued.

Sky couldn't let that comment go. "Yes, my father's done things that I'm sure would make my stomach turn. But he's still my father, and he was there when I needed him. He's the reason I'm alive today. He made sure after my mom died that no one knew he had a kid. They'd hidden me from the beginning—different last name and all that. After she died, it was even more extreme. But I was glad, because I knew what could happen to me. Then, when it looked like I wasn't going to make it, he took months off work— he went through all the tests and spent two months recovering with me in a safe house in New York. So you can say what you want about him, think what you want, but he gave me life."

"What is she talking about?" Dylan asked Cam.

She'd wrapped herself back into the sweater she'd been wearing that first night, drawn it around her tightly as if it was her only means of protection and she answered Dylan instead of Cam. "My father gave me a kidney—that's how DMH knows about me." She watched as both Riley and Dylan connected the final pieces of the puzzle.

Riley spoke first. "That's why Gabriel let his guard down. Why I was able to track him so easily, when I'd never been able to before."

Sky shrugged. "He left me after two months—earlier than doctors wanted him to. But Olivia said he was in great shape and that he'd be okay if he took it easy. She had no idea what he did for a living—probably thought he worked behind a desk because we actually went to her office for visits, the only time we left the safe house. We didn't want her to be involved, or to get suspicious."

"He went back too soon. Left himself vulnerable. And I took advantage of that." Riley turned away and Sky reached out for her.

"He might've hurt your family, in ways I can't imagine. I can't defend what he's done in the line of duty—but I have to believe that's why he's done the things he has. Like Cam, I can't blame you for hating him, even wanting him dead, but you have to understand, he's still my family."

Riley nodded. "Even if we come up with a plan that might work, where does that leave you? You'll be completely at risk if we're taken."

Cam shot Riley a look after he heard Sky's surprise gasp at her words. Yeah, he'd known Sky hadn't thought the whole plan through—he hadn't wanted her to. Hadn't wanted her to worry.

"I'm going with you. I won't stay here while you put yourself in danger," Sky insisted.

"You can't come with us, Sky," he told her gently. "You're still recovering. And I'm not putting you at risk like that."

"I'm not staying behind, Cam. I barely trusted *you*. Who would you leave me with? The CIA? A bodyguard? I'm not doing that. So unless you're okay with leaving me alone in a room with a gun to protect myself..."

He wasn't. No fucking way. "Just give me a few minutes, okay? Let me get everyone on the same page."

She nodded. "I'll make us all something to eat."

When she crossed to the kitchen, Cam turned to Riley and Dylan. "You've got to keep the threat-level shit under control. She's fucking terrified and doing a damned good job of hiding it, okay?"

Riley nodded. "So we're taking her with us."

"We can bring her with us and then have Zane watch her," Dylan offered.

Cam's eyes narrowed. "He hits on anything that moves."

"He'll behave. It's perfect. I can't get him involved in any kind of kidnap/shoot-out mission when he's still on active duty—bad enough you are. But he won't let anything happen to Skylar. You know that."

Cam did. "Caleb doesn't know, does he?"

Dylan shook his head. "None of your team does. Figured that would make things easier when you went back to lead them."

"If I go back," Cam countered.

"If, when—as long as the decision's yours, that's all that matters." Dylan was already ringing his brother. Cursing at him too, which was pretty typical of all the conversations Cam had ever heard Dylan have with Zane, although he'd never met the man before. When Dylan hung up, he said, "Zane should be here within the hour. He's up for going with us to keep an eye on Sky."

"I'll bet he is," Cam muttered, and noticed Dylan had a serious look on his face. "What's wrong?"

"It's this doctor thing—it's freaked Zane out."

"Freaking Sky out too. DMH is really going whole hog for Gabriel's intel." Cam glanced into the kitchen, where Sky appeared to be lost in thought while making sandwiches. He turned back to Riley. "It's time to start telling me everything you know about DMH."

Riley nodded, grabbed Cam's laptop and began to type, pulling up maps of Minnesota. "This is where Bullet—Elijah Killoran—grew up. His family home is still there—it's under his mother's name, but she died years ago. But someone is still paying the taxes. DMH uses a lot of other safe houses, in the Midwest, mostly, and this would be a perfect place to bring people you don't want found. Tiny town, lots of space between houses. Sentimental value."

"You're counting on a terrorist being sentimental?" Cam asked, raised an eyebrow at her. Granted, he definitely believed in gut instincts, had traveled on them more times than he cared to count—safely, for the most part. But to put Riley's theory to the test with so much at stake...

"DMH wants to kill me, Cam. And I need to make sure that doesn't happen. I'm not happy about getting close to them, but I'll do what it takes. For Dylan. For Skylar," Riley told him.

"I know a lot about DMH," Cam said roughly. "Delta's been following their operations for years. Mainly, they work from a home base of Morocco. Sell their secrets and their services to terrorists and warlords. They've grown to a size where they've become impossible to control and hard to track down. They did that purposely, and it's certainly worked for them."

The good thing about DMH was that they traveled in relatively small numbers and rarely all gathered in the same place.

The bad thing about DMH was that they traveled in relatively small numbers and rarely all gathered in the same place.

No, they scattered to the wind, and catching them in the past had been like trying to grab a snowflake and keep it from disappearing in your fist. "We're going to have to do a smash and grab," Cam said. "We get in, take out who we can and grab Gabriel—and hopefully Olivia, if they're together. The DMH men won't know what the fuck hit them."

That, he was sure of.

CHAPTER
18

Get her dressed and ready."

Olivia struggled, but they shot her up again with some kind of narcotic. Happy juice. A low enough level that she could concentrate, but if they did it enough, she could easily become addicted. Which was probably their intention.

They'd been doing that, hourly. She hadn't seen Gabriel for a while, but any sense of time was slipping away, and she didn't dare ask about him. She was so damned tired—tied to a straight-backed chair, her arms bared for the shots.

She could've kicked so they'd miss, bust her vein, but she still had plenty for them to find. And so she stayed still and let the drug burn through her until the man with the goatee spoke again.

"You're going to work for us."

"I don't work for terrorists." She spat at him, jerked herself hard against the bonds.

"Ah, she's still feisty. We'll break that out of her."

Break that out of her. Oh, God, where were they taking her?

The panic must've shown, even through her drug-filled haze.

"Don't worry, Doc, you'll get to use your surgical skills a lot where you're going—you won't get rusty at all."

The plane had boarded on time. They'd caught the last flight out of New York for the foreseeable future—the two later ones had been canceled, as they'd hoped, due to weather on Minnesota's end, which would make things all the more interesting when they arrived.

The five of them traveled in first class, because it was easier—kept them near the exits and able to watch the passengers boarding. Once they'd landed in Bemidji, they'd driven several hours and secured their motel room outside Crookston. Cam left Zane and Sky behind while he and Dylan and Riley gathered the weapons they couldn't bring on the plane.

Now they rode out around the possible DMH house. It was just before dusk and Cam forced his thoughts away from Sky. She was as safe as he could get her, barring being with him.

It was time to make sure she stayed safe for good.

Cam didn't ever go into a situation cold when he could help it. Recon as a survival tool had been drilled into his head for a long time—and Dylan knew better than to argue.

Although he did. "If they make us..."

"They won't."

Dylan shook his head and muttered as he tapped the steering wheel. Riley remained silent in the back, save for her readying the various guns they'd gotten from a friend of an associate Dylan knew.

"It's up ahead—we're going past now," Dylan said, maintaining the same speed as they did, the road about a quarter of a mile away from the house, which was built on a large piece of land and set back far enough not to be bothered by traffic.

Not that this town would have much of that. The house was in one of the more desolate and isolated sections of the already-small-enough-to-be-off-the-map town.

Dylan had taken the rental plates off the SUV and replaced them with local ones he'd borrowed from the motel lot, and he and Cam were wired to each other—and to Zane back in the motel, in case they got into trouble.

Bringing Zane in would be the last resort. Cam would make sure it would not come to that.

"This is the closest house to Elijah's mother's place—two miles out," Dylan said, pulling down the long driveway to get a better view. At least the service road and the main road to this house had been plowed.

"Looks deserted," Cam confirmed when they pulled behind the old barn and got out to view Elijah's suspected house from this safe distance. "There's no way to do a distract and grab—we'll have to go in. There's a mile worth of these woods." He gestured to the left of the house as he studied the map on his GPS. "And an open field to the right. I'll do the rest of the recon on foot."

The plan was in motion.

The walk in the woods did Cam some good. Freezing cold, rough terrain, and his mind totally focused on the task ahead, he finally felt back in his element. Mission-ready.

He checked in with Dylan periodically while he moved as quietly as he could. The woods were dense, which helped, and he'd dressed in his cammies to blend. Carried a rifle too, because if noticed, he would pretend to be a lost hunter.

Finally, he was close enough to study the house without aid of binoculars. Three stories and small windows with bars visible, indicating a basement—pushing up through the snow-covered ground—most likely where they would be holding someone. He only hoped they'd brought both Gabriel and the doctor to the same location.

This was the closest known DMH location to New York—the easiest place to bring the doctor. And the most private of all the DMH houses Riley had given to them.

"Cam, you still with me?" Dylan's voice crackled in his ear.

He was just about to answer when he heard a scream. A woman's scream.

"What the fuck was that?" Zane demanded, breaking into the conversation from back at the motel, via headset. "Who's screaming?"

"Gotta be the doctor," Dylan said.

"Dammit." Cam swore under his breath as the screams got louder, more frantic. He needed to get a visual without breaking cover, so he dropped to his belly and commando-crawled the rest of the way to the clearing.

"Can you get a visual?" Dylan asked, and dammit, Cam got more of one than he'd wanted—saw two men strong-arming a woman who matched the picture Zane had brought from the doctor's apartment.

"It's her," he confirmed, heard Dylan curse softly.

She was still screaming when he lost sight of her. They took her behind the dilapidated barn behind the house. It took everything he had not to go after her, but he knew that was a death wish. He forced himself to sit still as he listened to her yells, until they were suddenly cut short and replaced by the sounds of a motor.

Moments later, he caught sight of a Cessna cruising across the clearing, readying for takeoff.

The screams had grown silent. "She's on the plane."

"Plane? There's no airport around here," Dylan said.

They didn't need one—just enough space for a landing strip, and there was plenty of flat surface around this place. He watched helplessly as the plane lifted off, knew there was no way to help the doctor right now. They were under-manned and didn't have the resources to take the plane down safely.

"She's gone for now," he said flatly. "We'll get intel on where they're taking her, and we'll find her. You and Riley head this way."

"We're coming to you now, Cam," Dylan told him.

Cam finished his assessment of the house, ruthlessly pushing the screams of the doctor from his mind, even as Zane continued to swear in his ear.

No cars were visible, although there was a two-car

garage with tinted windows. On the second floor of the house, he saw men passing by the window—two or three of them. None outside, as far as he could see.

Dylan and Riley came up behind him within fifteen minutes, weapons strapped on and at the ready.

"Should we try to take one of them alive?" Dylan asked.

Cam shook his head. "We'll take these men out and then go after the others once we've secured Gabriel—and Sky."

"We'll gas it, get the men to come out and pick them off," Dylan agreed. "Better than going in blind, since we don't have the house's floor plans."

Cam's nerves were on edge, his body primed and ready for a fight—for this fight.

No matter what else happened, he needed Creighton's cooperation. It was the only plan that could keep Sky safe. All her father had to do was agree with it.

Even in the dark, he could see how close Dylan kept to Riley. And he knew just how personal all this was for her, could practically hear the wheels in her mind turning.

But Dylan was cool and calm—this wasn't personal for him. This was all business, and both Cam and Riley needed to remember that, to get their minds focused. In the game.

It was time.

Last night in bed, Cam had asked her what she wanted to do when all of this was over. When she was a year out of surgery and given the okay to be less cautious.

Sky couldn't think of anything except being with him.

And now she was beginning to rethink what she'd asked of him, of all of them.

But she couldn't get the pictures out of her mind—of her father pushing her on a swing, sitting in the audience of her first dance recital…surprising her on her thirteenth birthday.

She pushed all those thoughts aside when Zane took on a sharp tone, but he wasn't speaking to her. No, he'd kept the headset on, connecting him to Cam and Dylan, but nothing had happened until now.

By the look on Zane's face, something finally had.

In seconds, she was up from the bed where she'd curled, attempting to watch mindless TV. "What's wrong?"

"They're okay," he said roughly; he had covered the mike before he spoke to her. "Cam, Dylan and Riley are fine."

"Someone's not." Her father?

He pushed the headset off slightly, and although his voice was angry, it wasn't directed at her. "There was a plane that took off from a field behind the house. Olivia was dragged on it."

"Wasn't there anything they could've done?"

Zane pressed his lips together and she saw in his eyes that, yes, there might've been something, but Cam and Dylan and Riley had to make a choice.

And she'd won, at Liv's expense. "This is my fault."

"It's not," Zane told her. "Look, there was no way to get to her—they were on foot. They would've been too vulnerable. And I know my brother—he won't stop looking for Dr. Strohm. I won't let him."

He stopped, as if not wanting to upset her, but she

could see *he* was visibly upset when he'd talked about Olivia.

"She's strong. Really strong," Sky said, trying to convince herself.

"Then she'll get through it. And so will you," Zane told her, and he pushed the headset back into place so he could help make sure of that.

CHAPTER
19

After she threw the canister of liquid gas through the window, Riley moved around to the back door and kicked it open with a booted foot, shattering the wood from its hinges.

"Nice job," she heard Dylan say from behind her, and they both tugged on the masks they'd brought to protect them from the gas. He gave her the signal and she stepped forward, into a house that seemed frozen by time, as if none of the decor had ever been updated.

Cam remained outside, watching the perimeter and waiting for their all-clear signal.

She could see right through the small living room into

the even smaller kitchen. "All clear," she called, even as the pounding of footsteps greeted them overhead.

They didn't have to go upstairs, as the men were headed quickly down the staircase toward them. Stumbling, actually, hands swiping their tearing eyes, hacking up smoke and acrid air from their lungs.

Riley didn't recognize either man. She lunged to take the first one down the stairs with a kick to the gut. He fell forward and rolled and she moved with him, allowing Dylan to grab the other man as he arrived at the foot of the stairs.

Her man was down, but not out, and when he lunged for her, she chopped the gun neatly out of his hand with the butt of hers and put two bullets into his chest. Fast and easy.

Why was all of this so easy?

Dylan had already taken down the man who'd been coming for him and was now looking around the house for clues to anything.

"Trap?" she asked, her voice sounding muffled through the mask.

"They weren't ready for us," he pointed out, and then headed up the stairs for a final sweep. She followed close behind, the two of them searching the three bedrooms easily. Two were empty.

The third had been turned into a makeshift surveillance room, with bridge tables and a coffeepot, a television and surveillance cameras for both the road and what appeared to be two basement cells.

One of them was empty. The only thing left behind was a pair of blue hospital scrubs that looked to have been cut.

Riley could see that they were streaked with blood. "The doctor."

"She was alive enough to yell for help. She's a tough one," Dylan said, but his tone was grim.

She followed his gaze to the second monitor—an identical cell, with a man standing by the door as if listening to something. To them. "Cam, get in here."

Cam was by their side in seconds.

"Is that him?" Dylan asked after he'd pulled his mask off. Riley did the same, pushing it to her forehead. She could still smell the chemicals from the gas, but its effects, short-lived to begin with, were long gone, thanks to the air whistling through the window the gas canister had broken.

"That's him. Cover me." Cam was down the stairs before either of them could respond.

It was only then that they heard the crunch of a car on the icy driveway, to the left of the house. Riley peered out the window and saw six men getting out of a truck.

"We've got to get the hell out of here," Dylan muttered.

"Or we stay and fight. Maybe get some intel." She pointed to the monitor showing Cam kicking a door in.

"It's not the time, Ri. But there will be one. I promise you that."

She nodded, and then blurted out, "I love you, Dylan. So much."

His eyes lit up. "You had to tell me that now, when there's a small army headed this way to try to kill us?"

"There didn't seem to be a better time."

He kissed her, then, "Love you, Ri. Now, let's get the hell out of here, so you can keep telling me that for a long time to come."

The minutes stretched by as Sky and Zane remained standing together, listening for any news on the mission to save her father.

Sky stood close enough to Zane to hear the sounds of gunshots crackle over the headset. She fought the urge to ask Zane what was happening, because she knew as much as he did at the moment. And he had to listen carefully, because if Cam needed anything, she was prepared to make sure Zane left her here with a gun and went to help them.

The moments ticked by slowly as more gunfire erupted. Zane was standing stock-still, as if measuring the sounds he heard through the headset.

The tension rolled off him in waves as the shooting came to a crescendo and then stopped suddenly, leaving a pit in her stomach.

"Dylan, do you read me? Over." Zane's voice was tight-sharp.

Seconds stretched into minutes, until finally she heard a voice. Zane nodded and turned to her. "They're all okay. Your father's alive. Cam got him out of the house."

"But it's not over yet, is it?" she asked.

"No. But they're close." He winced and held the headset away from his ears.

"More shots?"

He shook his head. "No, just some interference. Weird." He jiggled the switches on the machine that connected the devices and even she heard the feedback. The sound grew louder, more high-pitched, and she resisted the urge to cover her ears. Zane cursed and pulled the headset off. And then he suddenly went still.

And then he asked, "How did DMH track you?" his voice deadly serious.

"My BlackBerry. When it was turned on, they were able to find us. But Cam took the battery out; it hasn't been on for over twenty-four hours."

"Do you have it with you?"

She nodded, rifled through her bag and handed him the phone. He studied it for a second, and then he was prying it apart to look inside, at the guts of the small machine.

Suddenly, he put it down and picked his gun up from the table. He went to the window, moved the curtain aside—just barely—and then dropped it.

"Sky, grab your weapon. Put on your coat and boots—dress warmly. Grab your bag. Now."

She didn't ask questions, just did as she was told, as quickly as possible.

When Zane spoke again, her stomach plummeted. "DMH is close. They jammed the signals so I can't get Cam. I'll call but we've got to get out of this room before DMH arrives. If we can."

Also dressed warmly, he opened the door, and the wind assaulted them immediately. He held out his hand to her and she grabbed for it gratefully as they left the room.

Their room on the second floor came in handy. There were two staircases to the ground—and it wasn't a far jump if necessary.

But it was snowing and slippery and they didn't have a car. Still, they moved quickly down the stairs and through the snow, which was up to mid-calf on her once they reached the parking lot.

The boots she was wearing were high, which helped keep the snow from getting to her feet, but she didn't have a scarf, so the cold whipped her cheeks until they stung.

Zane pulled her close, whispered "They're here" against her ear before guiding her toward the back of the motel and into the thick woods beyond.

Gabriel had spent the last hour staring at the ceiling, using the tedious work of counting off minutes to hours to keep his mind off the fact that Olivia Strohm had been taken away from the house, to God knows where. He only knew he heard her screams, and then silence after a small plane took off.

He'd known she wouldn't fare well. He hadn't seen her for the last twenty hours. His torture had stopped during that time as well.

And then the entire tone of the house above him had changed. Fire from automatic weapons. Bodies falling to the ground. And then . . . silence.

Trouble was, with the concussion he was suffering from and the disorientation he was experiencing because of it, it was hard to tell if those changes were for the better. With an ear to the door and years of instinct backing him, he made a quick decision.

Escaping by himself would work. He'd been waiting to make sure they truly did not have Skylar, to see if Cameron Moore had kept his daughter safe. He'd suspected they hadn't gotten her, because they'd have immediately tried to break him with her.

It had been nearly seventy-two hours since Gabriel had heard his daughter's voice on the phone. Without Skylar's appearance at the house, he forced himself to think the best . . . while still planning for the worst.

And even though he knew what he should do—needed to do in order to ensure Sky's safety—he continued to wait, as though he'd somehow get a pardon from heaven.

Never going to happen. He pushed himself away from the door because he heard footsteps on the other side. Moved against the wall, hoping for the element of surprise, and when the door got kicked nearly off its hinges, he got a surprise of his own.

The man on the other side of the wall was Cameron Moore.

He hadn't seen him for ten years.

There was no emotion in Cameron's eyes, but a hand had been extended. And Gabriel was in no position to refuse it. "What now?"

"You have to die, Gabriel. You know that as well as I do."

CHAPTER
20

Gabriel looked like shit, beat to hell, but he was breathing and on his own two feet. Cam grit his teeth, handed the man a gun and headed back upstairs.

The sound of gunfire stopped him.

"How many men?" he asked Gabriel.

"At least ten at different times," he responded. "I think there's a bigger window in the other basement cell."

Gabriel began to backtrack to the other room. The door was open, and Cam caught sight of bloodied scrubs on the floor.

If Gabriel noticed them, he didn't give any indication—simply moved like a machine to break out the window, which didn't have any bars on it.

A tight squeeze, but both men managed. Riley and Dylan were handling the men who'd come back to the house—through his headset he heard Dylan bark that things were under control.

Still, the fact that there had only been a few men guarding Gabriel to begin with was odd. And they'd sent in maybe three others, at most.

He turned to Gabriel and grabbed him by his shirt. "What the hell makes you so valuable to them? And why haven't you tried to escape?"

Gabriel attempted to shrug him off, but Cam had age and noninjury on his side.

"We don't have time for this now, Cameron."

"We do—most definitely. Start talking—and just know that the only reason I'm saving your sorry ass is for your daughter."

Gabriel's face went pale. "It's true, then—she really is with you. Thank God. That's the reason I stayed in this hellhole."

"You were waiting here for her?"

"I was sure they'd get her. I knew they'd bring her close to me—I was waiting for that, praying you were keeping her safe . . . even though you owe me nothing."

All Cam said was, "I'm in love with her," as the upstairs windows blew out of the house.

"We're good—get the hell out of here," Dylan barked in his ear, and he dropped Gabriel's shirt and the two began a dead run toward the woods, where Cam had planned to meet up with Dylan and Riley.

When the two men got there unharmed, they crouched down behind a grouping of trees and waited. Gabriel's breathing was harsh, unnatural. Definitely had broken ribs along with his other, more obvious injuries, like the bruises on his face and neck. And Cam was sure those were just the beginning.

They'd tortured the shit out of him for information.

"What now?" Gabriel asked.

"We're waiting for my friends. They should be here."

"If they can get through DMH. I'd have expected better planning from you."

"You fucking bastard. I should break your neck right now." Cam spoke into the darkness, felt Gabriel go still next to him.

"You should," Gabriel said quietly. "It's the only option. You and I both know that. DMH will never stop looking for me."

Cam didn't say anything for a long moment, and then, "The only reason I won't is Sky. I'm doing this for her. Only for her."

Gabriel sat back on his heels, assessing him. "You want answers. You all want your goddamned answers, but none of you can handle it. I thought by now you'd understand."

"I do. I understand a lot of things."

"You think I've ruined your life. Would you rather be sitting in that prison cell?"

Cam knew he was being goaded, since Gabriel had been the one to put him there in the first place. Bastard. His hands curled into fists and it took all he had not to slam Gabriel against the nearest tree.

"Typical Cameron. Stoic till the end," Gabriel muttered.

At that, Cam did strike, ended up sitting on Gabriel's

chest, his hands at the man's throat. "You put me in that fucking cell. You killed my father."

"He was going to blow a major CIA sting."

"He gave up three years of his life to be a part of that sting. Let his marriage crumble. I want to know why you killed him."

"You don't, Cameron. Trust me. It's been kept from you for good reason."

"I can handle anything, Gabriel. I handled the fact that you left me in prison for two years."

"I was finishing the job. I couldn't very well free Howie's son from prison when I was still undercover." Gabriel gasped for breath, his hand around Cam's wrist. And even though Cam wasn't squeezing that hard, in the cold it was enough to cut the airflow by a third.

"Tell me why."

Gabriel laughed, a hollow, wheezing sound. "Your father got scared. Paranoid. He called in the FBI with an anonymous tip and they were waiting for you. But I surprised them, with several members of the OA in tow. There was nothing else I could do, Cameron. They would've blown my cover. And, as you know, even one agent's blown cover causes a lot of damage."

Collateral damage. That's what Cam and his father had been to Gabriel. And in that moment when Cam let his guard down, Gabriel took the advantage, rolling the younger man away and slamming him to the ground.

It was Cam's turn to have a hand across his throat. "Is that what you wanted to know? That you were a pawn to your father most of the time? That he tried his best but in the end he chose his job over you?"

"That's exactly what you've done your entire life."

"I've made no bones about that," Gabriel agreed. Cam brought an arm up and slammed the side of Gabriel's head. The grip on Cam's throat loosened and the two men were rolling in the snow, punching each other, their grunts and yells hidden under a blaze of gunfire that erupted from the house.

Cam managed to get on his feet. Gabriel did the same, stumbled toward him, although Cam kicked him back against the tree.

After another kick or two, Gabriel was down and Cam picked him up, shoved him against the trunk of a tree... and realized how easy it would be to end this. To shoot Gabriel, leave him in the snow, tell Sky he'd been too late to save him.

It would truly be over then. But when he looked in Gabriel's eyes, he saw the whole story, and he knew exactly why he wouldn't carry out that plan.

"You want me to kill you. To do your dirty work, because with you dead, DMH will leave her alone. But I won't have your death on my conscience, no matter how badly you want it." He let go of Gabriel. "You're a sad old man. You've got nothing. At the end of the day, you're left with your crimes and your conscience, and that's all."

Cam knew his hands were shaking from anger. He closed them into fists, turned away from Gabriel and thought about Sky.

That calmed him enough to make it through the rest of

the op. He was doing this for her. For himself. For their future—this was the first step to actually having one together.

After ten long minutes with silence between them, Dylan and Riley finally arrived, in a near-silent run through the trees. The gunfire had stopped abruptly just before that, and Cam had been torn between staying with Gabriel to make sure he followed through on the plan and going to help Dylan.

"You all right?" Cam asked, moving to check on his friend.

"Fine. We're both fine," Dylan assured him, his eyes cutting to Gabriel. "Another car just pulled in. Four men, from what we could see—all armed."

"Let's get this done fast before we attract the police," Cam said.

"Take this," Dylan instructed, handing Gabriel a pill. "It'll depress your breathing—and everything else—for five minutes, long enough for them to check you for a pulse, short enough that the oxygen deprivation won't hurt you long term."

Gabriel held the pill in one hand and stuffed the throwaway cell phone in his pants with the other as Dylan fitted a fake blood pack inside of his shirt. "Cam will shoot you in front of them. Hopefully, they don't give as much of a shit about us. From there, you're on your own." Dylan paused, and stared directly at Gabriel when he continued, "You know they'll take your body."

"I'll make it work," Gabriel said firmly.

"You have no choice. It's our only shot for DMH leaving Sky the hell alone from now on," Cam reminded him.

"You want this to be real," Gabriel said.

"You're damned straight I do. You strung me along for ten motherfucking years. Almost drove me crazy doing your dirty work."

"It was for the greater good." Gabriel didn't back down, just the way he didn't back down from anything and Cam knew that if need be, the man would put up a hell of a fight to save himself. But the only need, for all of them, was to make sure Sky never had to deal with anything like this again.

"I never told Bullet—Elijah—that we were involved in the death of his son. He'd never have stopped hunting you," Gabriel said. A parting gift, so to speak, and it was a small comfort.

Very small. In fact, it made Cam want to punch the man right in the face.

"Stick with the plan and shoot me instead," Gabriel said, as if he'd read Cam's mind.

"With pleasure," Cam bit out.

"You both ready?" Dylan asked.

"Ready," Gabriel said.

Cam nodded. "Ready."

With that, Gabriel took off first, faster than Cam would've thought possible, through the trees and into the clearing.

DMH wouldn't shoot to kill. They wanted Gabriel alive too badly. No, Cam would have to be the one to fire. And when Gabriel turned around to face him, Cam looked through the scope, first at the man's face and then he moved his shot down and fired.

Sky was as close as she possibly could be to Zane without actually being inside his coat. Once they'd gone around the back of the motel and gotten down to parking lot level, they'd remained in their position, and she was nowhere near as calm as he was as they watched the two men break into their room.

It was too dangerous to move. They were better off playing statue, as they'd barely made it away from the line of sight in time.

Except, without cover from the earlier storm, she felt like a sitting duck—like any minute, there would be a sniper's scope aimed directly at her.

"We're fine. Covered," Zane told her. "We'd have been spotted in a car."

And I can't run fast enough to make a good getaway.

Zane was kind enough not to blame her, but she knew that if she weren't with him, he'd be gone by now—or fighting. Of course, the only reason he was here at all was to protect her.

His weapon was drawn, at his side, and she took comfort in that, and the fact that she knew Zane could fight like hell—and would, under Cam's orders.

God, the cold cut through her sharply, the adrenaline coursing through her body doing little to abate the sting.

As still as she tried to hold, she was shivering so hard her entire body ached. It seemed like hours passed, when she was sure it was mere minutes, and that as soon as the men realized the person they were looking for wasn't in the adjoining rooms, they would come out and search the area.

And as soon as she had that thought, they emerged from the room. Looked around. Pointed at various places and then checked them thoroughly.

She sank against Zane, as if to become invisible, increasingly aware that it was his strong arm around her waist keeping her on her feet. Because below-frigid temperatures and fear did not make for a good combo in any scenario.

The men strode across the parking lot, heading in their general direction. One of their phones rang, echoing loudly in the quiet poststorm air.

Zane barely made a sound, but his words registered.
Move aside. Hide. I'll get them.

He would too. His fury at what happened to Olivia earlier was barely couched, his body was tense behind Sky's—and oh, God, *Liv.*

"Do you think they know about Liv?" she asked quietly.
"Maybe."

"Make them talk, Zane."

"You are my priority."

It pained him to do nothing about Liv—she felt it. Although doing nothing in this case included being prepared to keep her safe at all costs.

Her body sagged as the men began arguing loudly. And then, miraculously, they went back to their truck, got in and peeled out of the lot at top speed.

She released the breath she hadn't realized she'd been holding, a white puff of air forming in front of her face.

"Why would they suddenly leave like that?" she asked, her voice still low. "It doesn't make sense, unless . . ."

She stopped then. Felt the frigid air go straight through

to her bones in a way that made her think she'd never be warm again.

Unless the plan had worked. Unless they thought her father was dead.

Of course, he might really be so. It was part of the risk, one she knew he would take to save her life.

"I don't feel well, Zane," she heard herself whisper, and realized Zane was well ahead of her, had actually begun carrying her toward the parking lot, where he was trying different car doors as he walked.

Finally, one opened. He placed her into the passenger's seat, buckled her in, closed her door and raced around the to driver's side. He jumped in and yanked wires out from under the wheel, starting the car quickly.

He's stealing a car to take me to the hospital was her final thought before she passed out.

The police were coming.

Cam had the truck off-road, and when he heard the sirens, he pulled over for a few seconds, lights off, until they passed.

They would find chaos and blood, but little else. That didn't mean they wouldn't be looking.

Finally, when the two police cars zoomed by, Cam turned the lights on and headed back to the motel.

The last thing he'd witnessed at the scene was two members of DMH loading Gabriel's body into the back of an SUV.

His own survival—and Sky's—was on his head now.

Cam said a quick prayer that he would pull it off, and knew that, no matter what, this mission was far from over.

Dylan was talking to Zane, tapping the headset impatiently. "Dammit, we lost contact."

"When?" Cam asked as he sped up.

"Not sure. Last time I heard him was before all hell broke loose at the house. Maybe fifteen minutes ago." Dylan ripped the headset off, and suddenly everything else was forgotten. Cam's one and only concern was getting to Sky. And fast.

He slowed down as they entered the motel parking lot after a grim ten-minute ride.

"Door's open," Riley said as she pointed to the second floor. She was out the door before Cam stopped the car fully, her weapon drawn. Dylan and Cam were right behind her, with Cam overtaking her on the stairs.

The place had been trashed. But all their bags were there, and so was the listening equipment. And Sky's cell phone, ripped open.

"Shit." Cam grabbed it and studied the wires. After discovering the tracking bug in the battery, he hadn't delved further. "They've been tracking us the entire time."

Dylan's phone was ringing. He flipped it open quickly. "Hello?" He listened for a second and nodded before he said, "Zane got her out. They're on their way to the hospital."

"Why?"

"Sky fainted. Possible hypothermia."

Cam was out the door before Dylan could say another word. He wanted to drive like a maniac to the hospital, but he understood that they were in a stolen car, with weapons.

And so he kept close to the speed limit, telling himself that Sky would be fine, as if he could will it true.

When he slammed through the door of the ER, the first person he spotted was Zane. The man apologized his ass off, until Cam shut him up with, "You saved her fucking life."

"They won't let you see her," Zane continued. "I told them she was a transplant patient, and they immediately took her to isolation. She was awake. Said she was okay."

"Her meds—"

"I grabbed them when we left the room. It happened fast." Zane shook his head, still visibly upset.

Dylan joined them, put his hand on Zane's shoulder. "We made it through, that's what counts. Come on, we've got to go back to the motel and do some damage control."

"I'll stay—get some food from the cafeteria for you," Riley added, and Cam nodded gratefully. He wanted to be alone—needed to be, to decompress. To wait this out. And within ten minutes, a young doctor with the last name of Holister was introducing himself.

"Any family?" Dr. Holister asked, and Cam shook his head.

"Just me."

"You're her husband? Brother?"

"Neither."

"I'm sorry, but we're really only supposed to release information to family members."

"She's got no one else. Can you understand that? She just lost her father—you're going to have to report to me."

He didn't know if it was the growl in his voice or the

crazed look he no doubt had in his eyes, but the man in the white coat paled a little.

"I just got back from my tour," Cam lied, not wanting the doctor to call security. "She's all I have too—I plan on marrying her as soon as she's well."

That did it. Mentioning military status usually did, and although Cam never liked to pull that card, for Sky he would.

"I have a brother in Iraq. I understand," Dr. Holister said. "She's running a pretty high fever, but so far, she shows no signs of rejecting the kidney."

"I told her not to go running when she wasn't feeling well, but she didn't listen. She's stubborn. Strong." Cam gave the doc the cover story to keep him convinced of his and Sky's relationship, and to keep the cops and DMH from zeroing in, if necessary.

The doctor nodded and said, "You can see her in a little while—let us get her fever down first, okay?"

"Thank you."

During the last minute of their conversation, Cam's phone had started vibrating in his pocket.

When he looked down at it, he realized that his white lie to the doctor was about to become a reality. His CO was phoning home, beckoning Cam to the mothership, ASAP.

CHAPTER
21

This time, Gabriel had been prepared to die. Knew full well that Elijah could've ordered his men to shoot him again and again, or dismember him, or bury him before he could regain consciousness.

Instead, he woke with a start in the back of a moving SUV, heard talk of *disposing the body*, and knew he'd regained consciousness in time. He took shallow breaths, his ribs sore from where the fake rounds had hit. They'd done the job, and his plan was much different than the DMH one.

He'd been damned lucky that DMH hadn't put a bullet through his head for good measure.

Or maybe *luck* wasn't the right word. Time to get his

shit together, because, as Cam had said, Gabriel was on his own.

After this, he truly would be, and although now wasn't the time to get maudlin, the thought of not being able to throw off a cover, walk through the door of his house and simply be Skylar's father was unsettling, even heartbreaking. And yet, this sacrifice was worth it if it meant saving her.

He'd been fighting for the fine balance between real life and cover story for years, and failing. Now he'd have a clean slate, simply by rolling over and playing dead.

The consolation lay in the fact that Cameron Moore loved his daughter. But if Skylar loved Cameron as well, no doubt Cam would tell her what Gabriel had done to him.

And that, he'd never been prepared for.

He flexed his hands, shifted his legs quietly, making sure his muscles were functioning after the pill that had rendered him more than unconscious. It had basically depressed his breathing rate so severely that he'd appeared dead.

From the way the car shimmied, he could tell they were off road and already well into a deserted area. He heard their voices rise as they spoke over one another.

"Here. Right here's a good spot."

"No, go farther along, more remote. More coverage."

"Stop here—we can't waste any more time. The police are all over the fucking place."

The car finally stopped, and the men got out, still bitching. Perfect.

Gabriel readied himself, kept his eyes closed. Waited

until they'd pulled his body out of the car before he made his move. Opened his eyes and caught the first man directly in the throat with his elbow, knocking him backward. For the second man, who lunged, Gabriel grabbed him, pressed along the side of his neck until he passed out. He did the same with the first man, who had continued to gasp for air.

And then he stood over them for a few minutes, at a loss for the first time since entering the CIA.

This was all really over. Say good-bye to Gabriel Creighton.

And then he dragged both unconscious men back to the SUV, into their respective seats and sent the car over the edge of the cliff.

As he watched the SUV burst into flames down in the canyon below, he pulled out the cell phone he'd hidden inside his pants earlier and dialed a familiar number. His old handler, who owed him one last favor.

It was high time Gabriel collected.

Zane had been climbing the walls until his brother and Riley and Cam arrived at the hospital. Now he supposed they all were; three men and a woman, all used to helping people, now had their hands completely tied while waiting to hear word on Sky.

"She'll be fine, man. You got her out," Dylan continued to reassure him as they drove back to the motel.

"I shouldn't have let her stand out in the cold like that."

"She can survive the fever."

But if DMH's men hadn't been called off, thanks to

Gabriel's faked death . . . well, Zane didn't want to go there, and forced himself not to think about it.

Instead, he focused on charming the female manager of the motel into not calling the police. Or the owner. Paid for the damage to the room and the door, while Dylan collected their things, wiped the room clean of fingerprints and got rid of the weapons stashed in the back of the truck.

Zane didn't bother to ask what he did with them. He'd learned long ago that Dylan didn't like questions, and that most of the time Zane wouldn't necessarily like the answers.

Although lately, Dylan had . . . changed. The ruthlessness Zane had once seen behind his brother's eyes was gone, replaced by . . . something softer.

No doubt, Riley had a lot to do with that change.

Finally, on the drive back to the hospital, Zane allowed himself to broach the subject he knew would weigh heavily on his mind for a long time to come. The one he'd been avoiding. "Any idea where they took Olivia?"

Dylan shook his head warily. "No. Tracing the flight's been next to impossible, but we'll keep looking. Riley has some contacts overseas who are intimately acquainted with DMH—they might be able to tell us more."

Zane knew Riley would have to tread carefully. In the eyes of DMH, according to what Dylan had told him, she had a price on her head. "What the hell would they want with Olivia if they didn't have Skylar?" Zane asked.

Dylan looked reluctant to tell him, but Zane had left him no choice. "Right now, this is only speculation on my part. There's a need for transplant surgeons on the black market. They kidnap them, have them perform the surger-

ies for a couple of years—or less, depending on how fast
they burn out."

"Why would any doctor go along with that?" Zane demanded.

"They get them addicted to drugs—the doctors will do
anything after that," Dylan explained.

"Jesus." Zane ran a hand through his hair. "I want to
look for her."

"You're taking this so personally. Like you know her or
something."

Zane felt like he knew her, wanted to tell his brother
that every time he closed his eyes, in his mind he saw that
picture of her laughing.

Zane got the feeling Dr. Olivia Strohm didn't have the
opportunity, or the desire, to laugh very often. "It's just that
no one deserves what could happen to her."

Dylan watched him carefully. "I agree. But you've got to
get back to the teams."

Zane didn't say anything. As much as he attempted not
to think of his own past—his childhood—finding the
newspaper clipping in Olivia's apartment had been like a
knife to the gut. Brutal and surprising all at once. "She was
kidnapped before, when she was a kid."

Dylan swore under his breath, and in that second, Zane
knew his brother understood.

Neither of his brothers had ever really talked about why
Zane was adopted into their family, about how his parents
had found him for sale in Sierra Leone, and all the horrified
couple could think to do was buy him.

"Riley and I will find her. Trust me, we're not stopping
until DMH is destroyed," Dylan told him finally.

His brother's voice was steel, and Zane could only pray they wouldn't all be too late. Olivia Strohm was a survivor, but everyone had their breaking point.

Cam sat on an orange plastic chair, head in hands, numb. Waiting. When Dr. Holister tapped him lightly on the shoulder, he straightened and immediately realized how stiff he was. How drained.

The doctor sat next to Cam. "Skylar's okay. She needs a lot of rest and monitoring, but she's awake. Her fever's abating—body temp is nearly normal."

I should've just checked her in from the beginning.

"She's asking for you. Go see her."

He pushed himself up, his body sore as shit, and walked to Sky's room.

God, he hated seeing her lying in that bed, all the machines hooked to her. He knew she no doubt hated it too.

"Cam, I'm okay. My kidney's okay. I was just cold—and I'm a little sick as a result. That's all," she reassured him as he walked over to her. But her voice was strained and sounded sleepy. "Are you okay?"

He stood next to the bed and took her hand in his. "I'm fine."

"Dylan? Riley?"

"They're fine too."

"Zane blames himself . . . But he shouldn't. He saved me."

Cam nodded. She didn't say anything else, was waiting for him to tell her about Gabriel. "Everything went according to plan."

"The rest is up to him." Sky had been let in on the plan from the beginning. "I'm sure we'll hear something soon, one way or the other."

"The important thing is that DMH thinks he's dead. There's no good reason for them to come after you now. That's what counts." Cam heard the fierceness in his own voice, as if he was trying to convince himself as much as he was her. And really, Sky was of no use to DMH. Hadn't seen any of the men, and certainly didn't know any of Gabriel's intel. "You might not see him again, you know."

She nodded. Had almost counted on that, since it appeared to be the only way to untangle her from the mess of DMH. "I'm so sorry, Cam. I should never have put you through all of this."

"It's over. That part... it's all in the past." He paused. "Sky, they took Olivia. Dylan and Riley are going to look for her, but there was no way to stop them. We didn't have the manpower—"

She put a hand on his. "I know you did everything you could."

She hadn't been expecting any kind of warm, fuzzy reunion when and if Cam found her father. And still, she thought she could separate her father from the CIA agent. But after knowing what he'd done to Cam...

He'd told her one thing her father had done but she could see so many horrible stories lingering behind his eyes, things he could never—would never—tell her. Memories that could screw a man up for life... and still he'd somehow managed to fall in love with her.

She'd broken through. And she knew that's what mattered most.

But now it was Cam's turn to look worried. "I can't believe I'm saying this now, but I've got to go. Work."

She knew what that meant, knew that he couldn't tell her where he was going, or when he'd be back.

Her insides tightened. Him leaving her now—the timing couldn't be worse.

She was losing too much.

"I understand," was all she told him.

He caught her chin with a finger, forcing her to look him in the eye. "I'll be back for you, Sky."

She wanted desperately to believe that was true, didn't want to upset him with tears. All she could do was nod.

"Riley and Dylan, they'll get you back to the city. Or . . . you can stay at my house. I'd really like it if you stayed there. For lots of reasons. Because coming home to you . . ." He trailed off, his voice raw.

"You're leaving right now?"

"I'm due back at base in less than ten hours." He tucked a lock of hair behind her ear. "Can you do what I'm doing, Sky? Can we move forward and leave the past behind—really? Because if you'd asked me last week, I'd have said no. I've always wanted to be with someone, but it's something I never thought I could have."

"Me neither." She bit her bottom lip. "Cam, I'm never going to be out of danger, with the transplant, and I—"

He stopped her words with a kiss. When he pulled back, he told her, "I can handle that danger. Starting now, we live for today, not the what-ifs, okay?"

"I can't have children," she blurted out, as if she needed to tell him all the things that could possibly push him away and see if he'd run.

"So we won't have kids. Or we'll adopt. Doesn't fucking matter to me, Sky. The only thing that does is that you think I'm a good man, that you know it."

"I know it, Cam. I always have." She held back the tears until he left the room, and then she wasn't sure she would ever stop crying.

CHAPTER
22

For the first two weeks Cam was gone, Sky didn't get so much as a text from him. Not that she'd expected one, but she'd hoped.

Oh, she'd really hoped.

But it was back to business for her—she had no choice.

Two days after Cam left, the local papers near Crookston, Minnesota, reported a fiery crash off one of the steep roads. From the wreckage, they'd pulled three bodies. Two of the names Skylar hadn't recognized. The third body had been identified as her father's . . . or at least that's what was reported. She knew through Cam that the article had been part of the plan, that her father would call in help from his former CIA handler to make it happen.

Whether or not Gabriel Creighton was truly dead was something she probably would never know for sure. She never expected to hear from him again. His bank accounts were strangely emptied and she'd discovered that his apartment in Washington had been long sold.

She truly had no family now, and in order to keep surviving, she needed to keep writing, if for nothing else than to keep paying for her medical insurance.

The one thing that held her sanity together was that she'd decided to stay in Cam's house, not because she felt she needed the protection of his well-built fortress, but because it made her feel close to him.

She worked in his office, wore his far-too-big-for-her T-shirts and sweats most of the time. And she wrote—morning until night. Sometimes all through the night too.

She made the drive into her new doctor's office for her tests every other week. Kept a month's supply of meds with her and talked to Riley and Dylan daily to ease the loneliness. They visited weekly.

Today was a hospital-visit day. The air was crisp—spring was still a pipe dream, but the constant snowstorms had ceased. The snow still on the ground was nearly blinding, and she slid on her sunglasses as she walked out of the hospital, another good report under her belt.

Three more months and she'd be at a year since the transplant. That would nearly triple her chances of not rejecting the kidney, her doctors told her, and for once, she believed them.

When she got into her car and pulled out of the lot, she found herself thinking about Olivia, the way she always did after these trips. Still no word on her, even though she knew that Dylan and Riley were working hard to find her.

Sky knew she had to try to reconcile the fact that they might never find her, and as she took her hand off the gearshift to wipe the tears from her eyes, a hand closed on hers.

She gasped, then prepared to exit the car any way she had to. She would fight.

"Skylar, relax. It's only me."

Her father—his voice, his hand on her shoulder. "Keep driving to the end of the road. There's a turnoff for a campground. Pull over there."

Her breath still coming fast, heart hammering in her chest, she followed his directions, trying hard to recover from the initial shock.

She turned and saw him sitting up in the backseat of Cam's car, looking no different than he had last time she'd seen him. Whatever injuries he'd sustained, he'd healed. "You're okay."

"So are you," he said. "That's what counts."

She wanted to climb into the backseat with him. To hug him. To hear him tell her that everything would be all right. But, for the first time in her life, she knew he wouldn't be telling the truth.

"I know how torn you are, how angry," her father began. "Cameron told me about the two of you. He said he loves you."

"He does."

"And you feel the same."

"I do." She twined her fingers together nervously. "Tell

me what happened with Mom. Did it happen the way you always said it did?"

The look in her father's eyes was one she'd seen the afternoon her mother had been killed. Haunted. "DMH killed her. They found out she was an agent who'd infiltrated their organization and they killed her. She never saw it coming."

She pushed back the tears, managed to choke out, "I hate your job, this life you and Mom chose. I hate it and I love you at the same time."

"When you love someone, you're vulnerable. Always. And that's the scary part," he agreed quietly. "But everything's a risk, Skylar. You know that—you always have."

She didn't know what to say, and then he continued, "I want you to come with me."

"What are you talking about?"

"I have a safe place for us both."

"Cam and Riley—people you hurt for years—they were willing to help you because of me," Sky said fiercely. "I'm not walking away, especially from Cam."

"He put your life in danger."

"And he was also there to save it. You yourself say that life is all about balance. A good deed balances a bad one, right?"

"Not in this case." Gabriel's teeth were gritted so tightly, it looked as though his jaw was made of stone. Maybe parts of him were, because Sky couldn't understand how someone could go through so much and still function at such a high level without cracking.

In all these years, her father had never cracked. Not in

front of her, at least, and somehow she couldn't picture him doing it at all. "Did you kill Cam's father?"

Gabriel looked his daughter square in the eye. "Yes."

She flinched as if she hadn't expected that answer. "Did he try to hurt you first?"

"He'd outlived his usefulness. Gone over the edge. Became addicted to the biker lifestyle, and the drugs. He wasn't the first man to get turned around on an undercover assignment. But Howie wasn't the one who set Cameron up. I simply took advantage of a bad situation."

"You've ruined a lot of lives."

"Cameron has his life," he countered. "And anything I asked him to do was for the greater good."

"You can keep telling yourself that, but I don't think even you'll ever believe it." She fell silent, because what else was there to say about that? "What are you doing now? Are you still after DMH?"

"As badly as I want to be, I'm giving up that fight. There are other people who will fight them now. My continuing would put you back in danger."

"What will you do?"

"Don't worry about me, Sky—there's plenty of work for someone like me. And eventually, I'll come back." Gabriel motioned behind him. "I don't need witness protection— I already know how to disappear. But you shouldn't have to. And I never should have asked you to join me." With that, he opened the door and slid out. "One day, Skylar, I'll make you proud of me again."

"One day," she whispered, and realized she was speaking only to herself.

Cam was going out of his fucking mind pacing the first floor of his house, waiting for Sky to return.

She's at the doctor, Cam. Calm down, Dylan had told him.

But she'd forgotten her phone, which Cam now held in his hand. Was practically holding his breath too.

And when he finally saw his truck coming up the long driveway, he exhaled and went to meet her in the garage.

She didn't notice him at first, was busy pulling her bag out of the truck, but when she got halfway to the door, she looked up and saw him. And dropped everything in order to run to him.

He buried his face in her hair, held her as close as he possibly could while still letting her breathe. And then he was kissing her, hard and demanding, and she was kissing him back with the same fervor.

God, he never wanted to let her go. Wouldn't. He carried her inside the house and put her down in front of him and simply stared at her for a second. And then remembered he was angry.

"Where the hell were you?" he demanded. "You should've been back hours ago."

"I'm sorry. I was driving around for a while."

"What's wrong? Did something happen at the doctor's?"

"No, that's all fine—my health is perfectly fine. I was with my father," she admitted. "He was waiting for me in the car when I came out of the hospital. And I had to talk to him, to finish things."

He nodded, because he understood. "And did you?"

"He wanted me to go with him. He said he's not going after DMH anymore. He told me ... things I didn't want to know. About your father, what he'd done. And he said he'd told you."

"He did."

"I know why you hate him so much." Her voice sounded pained, and he touched her cheek, managed a small smile for her before he said, "No, not anymore. Like you said, Gabriel's a part of you—and if I hated him, then I'd always hate a part of you."

"He knows why I refused to go with him, knows it was because I want to be with you."

Her voice—its strength couched in soft tones—stripped away any defenses he had left. If he was honest with himself, that had happened nearly immediately, when he'd walked into that vacation house ... and stripped them down and lay with her. Taken her.

Claimed her.

She was his. "I'm always going to make sure you're safe."

"I've been fine."

"I know that. Dylan and Riley keep me up-to-date."

"They watch me?" She shook her head. "I should've known. I thought they were just being helpful because you were gone."

"Well, there's that too. They like you, you know. It hasn't exactly been a hardship."

"You really think I need to be looked after still?"

"I wasn't taking any chances. I'd have done it myself if I could have, but I had commitments to honor first. I've done my last mission for Delta, though. It's time for a fresh start."

She frowned a little. "You're not going to give up helping people, are you? You're really good at it, you know."

"I won't be stopping that, no. But for a while, I'd just like to *be*." When he'd looked in the mirror to shave that morning, he'd been startled at the difference, how much more at peace he looked than the man who'd showed up at Sky's door that first night.

"I can understand that," she told him softly, let him envelope her in his arms for a moment before pulling back to look at him.

"Besides, I have a bigger job now." He slid his hands in hers. "Keeping you healthy and safe."

"What if that takes a long time?"

"It could take forever. And I'll be right next to you."

She nodded, tears in her eyes, and he knew that the feeling of contentment that surrounded him would be more than enough for him, would be what he'd been searching for all this time.

He was finally home.

If you loved LIE WITH ME,
don't miss the next book in Stephanie's
red hot Shadow Force series

PROMISES
IN THE
DARK

Coming December 2010

Read on for a sneak peek . . .

PROLOGUE

The past is never dead.
It's not even past.
William Faulkner

Freetown, Sierra Leone

*O*hmohs... Ohmohs?
How much?

The incessant calls echoed in his ear, a mix of Krio and English he wouldn't soon forget as he ran through the crowded marketplace along the narrow streets by the harbor. He'd long ago grown immune to the noise, the dust, the bodies that passed too close. Learned how to be invisible so he could steal food, clothes and whatever else he needed to survive in the busy place. Even pickpocketed the occasional tourist.

To blend in, he'd covered his head so the blond hair wouldn't make him stand out more. Rubbed his face with a fine dust and kept his eyes averted, because there was nothing he could do about the blue color, which got more intense as his skin tanned under the hot sun.

He would not get stolen or sold again.

He remembered the last town he and his parents had traveled to. The soldiers had come in one night, and if he concentrated hard enough, he could still hear his mother's voice, begging, *Don't hurt my son.*

He hated that that was the only thing he could recall of her now, the rest overshadowed by the horror he'd seen.

And they *had* hurt him, dragged him away from his parents and put a cloth in his mouth that made him sleep.

When he'd woken up, he was with a new family.

Udat wan ehn uswan yu want?

Which one do you want?

He'd lasted for a day before he escaped, even though there was no one to go back to. He'd found a deserted alley to sleep in for a few nights, until some other boys found him. Some American, some African.

All had the same story. And so those friends he'd made became his family. Together they stayed free, and he lost track of the long days that stretched into even longer nights.

There were five boys altogether, the oldest being twelve.

He was eleven, but felt so much older. He ached in a way he shouldn't, because he knew too much.

The oldest boy taught him, kept them all moving from place to place. Recently, they'd crashed in an abandoned warehouse that seemed promising for longer than a few nights. Plenty of spots to hide.

There were rumors of a place close by that helped kids, but the oldest boy warned that it would happen again if he told his story.

No one wants to help us.

He didn't feel well, hadn't wanted to go hunting through the stalls for something to eat, but the rest of the group was counting on him. His stomach burned, tight from hunger. He'd never get used to that, the gnawing feeling that he would never be full or comfortable again.

Even after he ate, he felt sick.

That didn't stop him from grabbing bread filled with fish and rice. The tourists haggled, the locals smiled and the music pounded in his ears.

Today was easy—the market was packed and the small

fight that had broken out helped him. He moved past the chaos toward his escape route.

"Boy." A man clapped a hand on his shoulder and spoke loudly. "You shouldn't be alone."

The feeling closed in on him again—he was too small, too weak. Suffocating under the disguise. He opened his mouth to say, *I'm with my mother,* to point to some unsuspecting woman who would not claim him, but nothing came out.

Instead, he jerked away from the man, who no doubt had seen him steal one of the day's prizes, and ran down the alley. No one followed, and he considered it a victory, stuffed some of the bread into his mouth and chewed, the roiling in his stomach abating for the moment.

He would go back to the warehouse and share the rest.

But as he slowed to a walk, a bag went over his head, blocking both light and air. He struggled, but the body against his was bigger and stronger.

Later, he would learn not to struggle, that going limp was actually a better move. That a swift skull to the attacker's chin with the element of surprise was damned effective.

But then he'd known next to nothing . . . except for the fact that no one would ever get the best of him again.

When he opened his eyes, he was in a drug-filled haze. It might've been minutes later, or hours, or days—and he knew it didn't matter anyway.

A man and a woman stood over him. They looked concerned, but he had to get away from them.

Panic turned to terror, even as the man held him to stop him from shaking and the woman spoke of home and brothers. School, play and *nothing bad will ever happen again under our watch.*

This time, he didn't have the strength not to believe them.

CHAPTER
1

Seventeen years later, Kambia, Sierra Leone

This was the place—the small house with the light purple facade that looked like every other tin-roofed pastel-colored one that lined the wide dirt road; the market that ran nearly down the center, allowing a small area for cars to lumber through, and teemed with people, none of who seemed to notice or care that it was hotter than hell at 0800. Music blared from one of the opened windows, an incessant fixture, as if it covered the violence and misery and fear and lightened the worry.

Maybe it worked. This area was more prosperous than most, and the feeling of hope remained here. Or maybe that was his own projection.

From out of his pocket, he took the picture—worn from carrying it around for the better part of six months—and shoved it at the African man who waited at the door.

The man stared at it, frowned, then nodded. "Yes. I've seen her."

"Where? Show me."

"She is there." The man pointed to a spot on the equally worn map that was held out to him, then took the money—American dollars—pressed into his opened palm. "You are military? Soldier?"

"Just a tourist. Here for the scenery."

The man furrowed his brow, not believing a word of that. "You are not the first one to look for this woman today."

But I'll be the first one who gets her, Zane promised himself. It was the third town he'd visited in less than twenty-four hours. He'd done this one on foot because the last driver refused to come this far out into the bush. But he'd known he would hit pay dirt here.

The man stepped back into the shadows after drawing a crude map of the exact location Zane needed, even as the children who'd been eyeing him from afar ran past when they thought he wasn't looking and then circled around to approach him.

One of them didn't turn away when Zane eyed him. The brave one, who'd lost his fear years earlier.

Zane recognized the look, chin jutted with bravado—real or faked, it didn't matter, it was an *I'm not scared of you* attitude.

"Money?" he asked in English as he held out his palm, defying Zane to say no.

Zane dug into his pocket, pulled out some crumpled bills and watched the kid's eyes widen as he handed them over. Then he turned and walked away.

Stick with those you can save, because you sure as hell can't save them all.

He stood taller than most here, looked over the crowds as the smell of cooked fish and rice floated through the warm air, as women and men tried to sell him everything from carvings to homemade falafel. Even weapons were fair game, with those vendors whispering to him from dark corners as he strode past in search of any kind of goddamned vehicle to take him farther in-country.

He'd have to pay in order not to have a driver, but he

didn't need the added burden of another person. And when he found an old Land Rover, he bargained with the owner until he was able to drive away alone, kicking up dust behind him, his roll of money a lot smaller.

But he had cans of gasoline and the engine was decent. With the windows rolled down and his weapons hidden under a false third seat, an added bonus, he was prepared for various checkpoints and other assorted fun times in this country.

He should check in with his brother Dylan; would when he got farther along. Right now, there was nothing to report other than he was closer to his goal.

They'd been *closer* to the doctor for months now. Frustrating as hell, and Zane wasn't about to jinx it.

When Dylan told him about the new intel on Olivia, Zane had taken leave and insisted on going to Africa. Didn't give a fuck that Dylan and Riley couldn't join him immediately.

He wouldn't waste a day waiting for backup. Not in this case.

If Dr. Olivia Strohm had truly spent the last three months successfully evading DMH—an extremist group with terrorism ties and business all over Africa ranging from skin trade to black market weapons—rescuing her was something he could damned well do on his own.

We'll meet you in seventy-two hours, Dylan had promised. *That should give you plenty of time.*

He would meet his brother at the port in Freetown. A place he'd never thought he'd go to again.

In his time with the military, he'd traveled to many cities along the western edge of Africa, in the Ivory Coast and Liberia and elsewhere. Somehow, Freetown was always avoided, because it was a major port—too crowded for stealth.

PROMISES IN THE DARK

The crowds had been the thing that saved him once. Now the thought of going back made his blood run cold. The Kambia District was close enough, the market smaller than he'd remembered and far more dangerous than he could've known when he was merely a boy.

Thank God for small miracles.

His life had been built on small and not so small miracles, from his adoption to his live-for-the-moment lifestyle, which had worked really damned well for him. For Zane, time off had always equaled trouble—he liked to keep busy, keep moving, and when he was on leave, his brother—the spy for hire—could always find him something to do. Black ops, gray ops, it didn't matter, had been on as many missions with both the SEALs and his brother in an unofficial capacity. But this was by far the most important one he'd ever done.

The party facade he'd built up like brick walls around his past crumpled down last year with no warning, and he'd barely had time to roll out of the way and avoid the fallout.

Most of it anyway.

Maybe if he found Olivia, things would go back to normal. *His* normal. So he took the leave because his brother promised they were close to finding her. And then, *finally*, after three months of dead fucking ends, they had a bead on Dr. Olivia Strohm.

Which would've been great if it hadn't been a possible death report.

"A clinic was bombed in Morocco. No patients died, but DMH staff did," Dylan informed him. *"The papers said it was a suspected illegal clinic. There was no note, no one ever claimed responsibility for the bombing."*

"That's strange." Groups who did shit like that always wanted to take responsibility. It was what they did—they

wanted the notoriety, making a name for themselves was a huge part of their deal.

Then again, no group would be stupid enough to go after DMH in that capacity. No, most wanted to work with them.

"Rumors were that the clinic was involved in black market organ trafficking," Dylan said. "All the staff was identified, all except one. A female."

Zane shook his head hard, as if Dylan was right in front of him as opposed to across the phone line—and the continent.

Zane. That's what Mom and Dad named him in the hotel. Dad was a huge Zane Grey fan. Wanted his new son to have a fresh start. "Olivia didn't deserve what she got."

"Most of the good ones don't."

But then, just last month, reports started trickling in that DMH had been offering a reward for the capture of a woman. That she'd been spotted in different African villages and towns. Some called her a healer, and some a killer, but they all agreed on one thing—she was American, and danger surrounded her.

Now he planned on following that lead, no matter where it led him.

Some people might consider this place hell, but Olivia Strohm knew it wasn't. No, Kambia was far from it, and since she'd been to hell on earth twice already, she considered herself something of an expert.

It was nearly dark, but the heat wasn't retreating. Wouldn't.

She wrapped the rag around her hair and rubbed another cloth over her neck. She took a long drink of water because her body demanded it, even though she'd long grown used to ignoring most of her body's needs in exchange for freedom. She had work to do, and that super-seded anything else.

She hadn't needed much money here. No, with her services, she'd been able to barter for the more important staples, like food and clothes and places to stay. This house was hidden behind two others, abandoned long ago. But the women she'd met had hustled her back there and helped her settle in without question.

Later that first night, they came back. Shy. With questions, with medical problems, some she could help with and some she couldn't. There was a clinic twenty miles away that she could refer some of them to. For women like Dahia, who'd lost her child to typhoid two months earlier, Olivia had to be the one to tell her, after an exam, that more children were impossible, just as the midwife had after the child's complicated birth.

Sometimes, she felt as if she did more harm than good, but Dahia brought her cassava and bread later as a thank you.

For the last two days, there had been ripples of gossip in the small village that a pregnant woman was looking for help and running from an important man, who'd followed, intent on taking her back.

Olivia had run too, and she'd learned that no man was that important.

In the past months, she'd killed several men—on purpose—and in the aftermath struggled with her conscience. Wondered if she could even function back in the real world, and decided no.

She was safer here. Alone, with no real ties. And even though the local women insisted that she shouldn't get involved with the pregnant woman heading her way, that the men who ran the human trafficking ring would take her away and lock her up—or worse—she didn't listen. Told them her home would give shelter to whoever needed it.

She'd survived so much already, she would not let the threat of a random stranger take her down or destroy her will.

Outside the small, three-roomed house, she heard a rustle in the bushes. It could be an animal ... or it could be a woman, too frightened to come inside.

She'd left a candle burning outside—a signal, Ama once told her. Ama, the angel who'd helped her for months after she'd escaped and taught her some of the ways to survive in this harsh place.

Ama, who had not deserved what had happened to her.

The lump rose in her throat, but she pushed it down ruthlessly. *No, not now.*

She grabbed a heavy iron skillet for protection before she stepped outside onto the creaky porch and stared out, but was unable to see anything but shadows.

"Come, come," she said, her voice low and urgent in the dark. She repeated herself in Krio as well, *Kam naya,* to encourage the woman to come forward.

You can't save them all. But you can help some.

Those words from her first year of residency rang in her ears more often than she'd like to admit.

And so she waited, impatiently shifting from one foot to the other, fighting not to let her nerves get the better of her. But it wasn't a woman who came forward. No, it was the outline of a man. She saw the fatigues and the guns and thought it might be one of the soldiers who would stop by and try to close her makeshift office down.

She would have to pay—or close up and move. Or possibly fight for her life.

She tightened her hand around the cold handle of the skillet held behind her back and waited for the bark of an order.

But this man stepped into the light with his hands in view, free of weapons. Blond. Blue-eyed. Face of an angel and the devil mixed, and the throb in her belly overrode the sudden, sharp fear.

She was being rescued. And that was the worst thing that could happen to her now.

"Dr. Strohm? Olivia?" The voice was deep and dark, washed over her like a sudden rain.

He knew her. But she'd never seen him before in her life—she would've remembered. "What do you want?"

He came closer, through the tangle of bushes and up the small red dust path to the house she'd taken over. She'd moved in, swept it out and cleaned it as best she could. It didn't matter what it looked like. It was temporary.

Everything about her life now was temporary.

She held the skillet hidden behind her back. "Who are you?"

"I'm Zane Scott. A friend of Skylar's."

Sklyar. Her former patient. Her friend. One of the reasons she was in this mess to begin with, and yet, she felt no malice toward the woman. Only the hot stab of fear at being found. "What are you doing here?"

"I'm here to help you."

There was a calm in his voice that nearly mesmerized her. He'd gotten close now, was in front of her and had extended his hand toward her. When she glanced down, she saw that she was actually holding out her free hand as well.

She pushed it down by her side again.

"Has anyone else come here tonight?" he asked.

"No, you're the only one." Her voice came out more softly than she'd intended. Fear, she told herself. Nothing to do with the contact with someone who might be from her not so distant past.

The wind rustled the bushes again, and when Zane

turned to check that no one was behind him, she struck, surprised him with a blow to the side of his head.

He sank to the ground with a heavy thump and her heart beat wildly, because she had no plan. There was nowhere for her to go tonight. No, she'd have to wait until morning to leave, to escape this seemingly well-meaning man.

Which meant she'd have to keep him with her.

Zane Scott was tall—over six-foot-three—and heavy with muscle, although he wasn't overly broad when he'd stood in front of her. No, he was just right.

It took all her strength to get him inside the door and close it behind them. She stood, panting, and realized that she'd only been here for three weeks.

How had she been found?

Trouble comes in pairs, Ama used to say. A warning for Olivia that just because one bad thing had happened, she was not to let her guard down against the possibility of more.

That was rare. Even her sleep was broken and uneasy. Dreams replaced by nightmares. If she could physically do so, she'd stay awake all night, every night. As it was, the few hours cost her. Her hands shook and her focus was off.

Good thing the medicine she practiced here was battle-field, because oftentimes, it wasn't pretty.

Zane was wearing green jungle-print camouflage. Military. He appeared to be alone, but he wasn't the only one who knew where she was—he could have reinforcements that would come to help him.

Has anyone else come here tonight? She rifled through his pockets, bypassing the weapons, until she pulled out a roll of money. A further search yielded nothing—no dog tags, nothing that would identify him as military beyond his

clothing and weapons, nothing that told her anything—
until she checked the pocket by his thigh.

A note from Skylar. *Zane is one of the good guys. Trust
him,* she'd written, and for all Olivia knew, it was written
under duress. But it was written on Skylar's personal sta-
tionary, and she recognized the signature since Sky had personally signed all of her books for Olivia.

Behind the note was a photograph—well worn and
instantly recognizable. It was from her apartment back
home in New York.

It was a picture of her and her mom, taken in Central
Park. She'd been laughing. If she turned the picture over,
she'd see the handwritten note.

He really was here looking for her. And something in
addition to Skylar's letter told her that he wasn't DMH.
No, those men would not talk to her the way he had. They
would just take her, the way they had before.

Zane stirred, and she froze. But he only came to for a
second, just long enough to open his eyes and stare at her.

He murmured, "Beautiful," and passed out again.

The only mirror she'd seen in the past months was a
small piece that had remained in the frame, long after the
rest of the oval mirror was shattered.

She wondered if maybe she'd hit him harder than she
thought. Because beautiful was not how she felt. Ragged,
but not beautiful.

She no longer resembled this picture...couldn't recognize herself no matter how hard she stared.

No matter how hard she tried, she couldn't remember
the last time she'd laughed. Not since DMH had kidnapped her from the parking lot of the hospital in New
York.

Escape from the extremist group had been easier than

she'd thought, and to this day she still questioned whether her conscience had been destroyed along with that clinic.

She didn't feel sorry for the staff that died. Illegal black market organ transplants were a lucrative field and the doctors working there had to know what they were involved in. The patients knew it—they were paying through the nose; but she bet they had no idea that some people were being killed for their organs and others had them taken out against their will.

Maybe those who paid the high price for their new organ wouldn't care. Faced with death, their survival instinct went into overdrive, pushing them to risk everything, even jail, to save their lives or the lives of their loved ones.

Olivia had done her share of survival well enough to understand their reasoning.

And she had names of doctors—in both the States and Europe—who were part of DMH's illegal operation. Which meant she was valuable to DMH, and the only way they would leave her alone was when she was dead.

She slid the stiff rope around her rescuer's wrists, tying them awkwardly behind his back, and then went to work on his ankles. She took his weapons and placed them out of his reach. Stared at the guns and the knife and remembered how she'd had one of each when she'd left the clinic, how they'd stayed by her side while she lay on the floor of Ama's house and gotten the drugs DMH had been feeding her out of her system.

The withdrawal had been the worst. Olivia could still feel the bile rise just thinking about the hours and days that blended as she writhed in pain on the floor. Sweating. Shaking. Alternately praying for death and wanting to get strong enough to take revenge on DMH.

Bastards.